EYE for an EYE
EAR for an EAR . . .

A pall of silence descended on the table. To call a gambler a cheat was an open invitation to a gunfight. Yet the men in the game knew Holliday had given his word not to kill anyone in Dodge City. A gentleman's oath, taken to avoid embarrassing Wyatt Earp.

"You're a lucky fellow," Holliday said. "Under normal circumstances, you would be a dead man. Tonight, I choose not to kill you."

"What a load of crap!" Keifer snarled. "I think you turned yellow."

"Back off," Ben Thompson said. "Turn around and walk away or I'll shoot your ear off."

"I'm not talkin' to you," Keifer said. "Just mind your own business."

Thompson pulled his gun and fired. The slug clipped Keifer's left earlobe in a spray of blood. "You sonovabitch!" he yelled, clutching his ear. "You shot me!"

Keifer backed away, blood dripping from his ear. He turned and hurried toward the door. Holliday chuckled softly.

"Ben, you are a marksman of some distinction. Thank you for coming to my aid."

"Why, hell, I saved his life. You would've killed the bastard."

"Yes," Holliday said quietly. "I would have indeed."

DODGE CITY

MATT BRAUN

St. Martin's Paperbacks

This is a work of fiction. Names, characters, places, and incidents either are the product of the author's imagination or are used fictitiously, and any resemblance to actual persons, living or dead, business establishments, business entities, events, or locales is entirely coincidental.

DODGE CITY

Copyright © 2006 by Winchester Productions, Ltd.

ISBN: 0-312-93816-0
EAN: 80312-93816-1

Printed in the United States of America

St. Martin's Paperbacks edition / May 2006

St. Martin's Paperbacks are published by St. Martin's Press, 175 Fifth Avenue, New York, NY 10010.

10 9 8 7 6 5 4 3 2 1

To
Darren and Lucinda
Constant for all seasons

DODGE
CITY

ONE

The courtroom was crowded. Everyone in Dodge City treated criminal trials as a form of entertainment, theater with a lively cast of actors. Today the spectators were there to see a horse thief who was legend.

Dutch Henry Borne stole horses on a mythical scale. He allegedly operated out of No Man's Land, a sanctuary for rogues beyond the reach of the law. His gang of brigands was believed to have stolen over a thousand horses just in the last year. He had no equal on the western plains.

The problem for the prosecution was to prove it. Dutch Henry, despite his vaunted reputation, had never actually been caught stealing horses. Nor had he been charged until now, much less convicted of a crime most cattlemen considered a hanging offense. He was a will-o'-the-wisp, evading the law and eluding capture with maddening ease. Today was the first time he'd ever been brought to trial.

The spectator benches were packed, the walls lined with people standing at the back of the room. Nick Klaine, editor of the *Dodge City Times,* was seated in the first pew behind the prosecution table. His counterpart Dan Frost of the *Ford County Globe*, was on the opposite side of the aisle, behind the defense table. Fireworks were expected, for the opposing lawyers were bitter political rivals. Dutch Henry was the catalyst for the best show in town.

Mike Sutton, the county attorney, was seated at the prosecution table. He was a man of slight stature, scarcely five feet six, with a neatly trimmed mustache. His slim build and short frame belied a formidable legal mind combined with overweening ambition. A northerner by birth, he was a rabid Republican.

Across the aisle was Harry Gryden, counsel for the defense. Tall and dapper, with a mane of wavy hair and a full mustache, he was attired in a vested suit. His clients included horse thieves, murderers, and whorehouse madams, and among the criminal element he was the lawyer of choice. A southerner to the core, he was a die-hard Democrat.

The adversarial relationship between Sutton and Gryden was one of long standing. The date on the court docket was January 24, 1878, and they had been battling matters of law for several years. Sutton saw the future of Dodge City as a sober and settled community, governed by sober citizens. Gryden liked to think of it as the Bibulous Babylon of the Frontier, a town where sin and sinners led the parade. The men detested each other with stubborn pride.

The crowd murmured as a door opened near the defense table. Bat Masterson, the sheriff of Ford County, escorted Dutch Henry Borne into the courtroom. Masterson unlocked the manacles from Borne's wrists, his expression stolid, and assumed a watchful position by the wall. Borne seated himself in an empty chair beside Gryden.

"Bat's a little edgy," Borne said with an amused smile. "Figures I'll try to escape again."

"Dutch, you've no need to escape," Gryden said confidently. "You will be a free man by this afternoon."

"You sound mighty sure of yourself."

"I am indeed."

"*All rise!*"

The bailiff's voice brought the crowd to their feet. A door opened at the left rear of the courtroom and Judge Jeremiah Strang mounted the steps to the bench. The Ninth District Court of Western Kansas was his domain, and he ruled it with casual wit and an iron fist. He peered down at Sutton and Gryden.

"Are you gentlemen prepared to proceed?"

Sutton nodded. "The prosecution is ready, Your Honor."

"The defense as well," Gryden added. "In fact, never more ready, Judge."

Strang stared at him a moment, then motioned to the bailiff. "Bring in the jury."

Twelve men filed through a door at the rear of the courtroom. All of yesterday had been devoted to jury selection, and Gryden had demonstrated a talent for weeding out potential jurors who posed a threat to his client. He disqualified ranchers by provoking admissions of bias against horse thieves in general and Dutch Henry in particular.

Farmers and workingmen, who seldom experienced livestock theft, were strenuously opposed by Sutton. After both sides had exhausted their preemptive challenges, Gryden was the clear winner. The jury was composed of seven farmers and five townsmen.

Judge Strang offered the jurors a benign smile, waiting

until they were settled in their chairs. Then he nodded to the prosecutor. "Call your first witness, Mr. Sutton."

Carl Benson was called and sworn in by the bailiff. A rancher, with a large spread fifteen miles southwest of Dodge City, Benson was a burly man in high-topped boots. Sutton approached the witness stand and quickly took him through the preliminaries. The lawyer established that Benson's outfit, with a thousand head of cattle, was located on Elm Creek.

"Now then," Sutton said, "I direct your attention to November 21 last year. Would you tell the court what happened?"

"Horse thieves raided us," Benson replied dourly. "Sneaked in late at night when ever'body was asleep. Got off with nearabouts thirty head."

Sutton led him through the events of the following day. Benson and his cowhands had tracked the gang west along the Cimarron River and overtaken them late in the afternoon. A gunfight ensued, resulting in the wounding and capture of one of the gang members. The others fled into the wilds of Indian Territory.

"The man you captured," Sutton prompted. "Did he make a statement?"

"Shore did," Benson said with a sly smile. "Told us him and his bunch worked for Dutch Henry Borne."

"Did he say where they were headquartered?"

"Yessir, he claimed they operated out of No Man's Land. Said there was four gangs workin' outta there. All of them run by Dutch Henry."

"What did you do then?"

"Why, I rode straightaway here to town. Saw Sheriff Masterson and swore out a warrant for Dutch Henry."

"No further questions," Sutton said. "Your witness, Mr. Gryden."

Harry Gryden walked to the jury box. He turned to Benson with a bemused expression. "This desperado you captured, what was his name?"

"Roy Suggs, leastways that's what he said."

"And why isn't Mr. Suggs here to speak for himself?"

"'Cause he's dead," Benson announced. "We was ridin' back to the ranch, and I guess he was wounded worse'n we figgered. Fell off his horse and broke his neck."

"Actually"—Gryden looked at the jurors with a knowing smile—"Mr. Suggs fell off his horse and broke his neck when you hanged him, isn't that true?"

"No, by golly, that ain't true! Happened just like I said."

"So we have only your word for the alleged confession of Mr. Suggs. Correct?"

"I reckon my men could vouch for what was said. They heard it clear as me."

"But where are they?" Gryden feigned a close inspection of the courtroom. "Oh, of course, the prosecution declined to subpoena them as witnesses. Is that because they would testify that you hanged Roy Suggs?"

Benson flushed with anger. "I done told you how it was."

"So we have neither Roy Suggs nor your men to corroborate your story. We have only the word of a man who resorts to lynch law."

"Objection!" Sutton exclaimed. "Counsel is badgering the witness."

"No, Mr. Sutton, _I_ object." Gryden walked away, shaking his head. "You've brought a perjurer to the stand in an effort to railroad my client. Your tactics insult the good men of the jury."

"Enough, Mr. Gryden," Judge Strang ordered. "I will not tolerate such remarks in my court."

"No offense intended, Your Honor."

Bat Masterson was next called to the stand. Under Sutton's questioning, Masterson testified that he had arrested Dutch Henry Borne, who was in the Alhambra Saloon and had been taken without incident. Then, on the night of December 4, Borne had escaped from the county jail.

Sutton glanced at the jury. "Hardly the act of an innocent man," he said. "Tell us, Sheriff, how did the prisoner manage to escape?"

"Picked the lock on his cell door," Masterson said sheepishly. "The deputy on night guard was asleep, and Borne slipped out. We didn't know it till the next morning."

"How did you effect his recapture?"

"I put out an alert of his escape on the telegraph. A couple weeks later I got a wire from the sheriff in Trinidad, Colorado. He'd taken Borne into custody."

"And you brought him back yourself?"

"Yessir, I did, on New Year's Day."

Sutton considered a moment. "What do you know of Mr. Borne's horse theft ring?"

Masterson explained that No Man's Land was an expanse of wilderness bordered by Kansas, Texas, Indian Territory, and New Mexico Territory. Every stripe of outlaw found sanctuary there, and even U.S. Marshals dared not venture into the isolated stronghold. The horses stolen by Borne's gang, once the brands were altered, were sold far away from home ground. Kansas horses in Texas and New Mexico horses in Colorado. It was all but foolproof.

Gryden could have objected on any number of grounds. But he remained silent and allowed Sutton to plow along with conjecture and hearsay. Finally, on cross-examination, Gryden walked forward, thumbs hooked in his vest. He looked at Masterson with a puzzled frown.

"Sheriff, do I understand correctly, you've been to No Man's Land?"

"You understand wrong," Masterson said. "Lawmen who go there don't come back. I'm not that dumb."

"So you haven't seen this 'foolproof' operation for yourself?"

"No, not personally."

"Then how do you know it exists?"

"Everybody knows."

"How do they know?"

"There's no secrets about Dutch Henry and his gang. Word gets around."

Gryden turned to the bench. "Your Honor, I move to strike Sheriff Masterson's testimony. Hearsay and blatant speculation are not admissible."

"Nonsense," Sutton countered. "The sheriff's testimony is based on common knowledge. The court, in its discretion, may accept as fact the common knowledge of the public at large."

Gryden laughed. "Your law books must be different than mine. Good try, but no cigar, Mr. Prosecutor."

Judge Strang ordered the jury to disregard all testimony regarding the defendant and No Man's Land. Strang then directed the court stenographer to expunge such testimony from the record. Sutton was fuming, but he had no further witnesses; he grudgingly rested the case for the state. Gryden called only one witness to the stand.

Dutch Henry Borne looked anything but an outlaw. He was ruggedly handsome, with a sweeping mustache, attired in a dark, conservative suit. Gryden, playing to the jury, brought out testimony as to the defendant's sterling background. Borne was the son of industrious German emigrants who had settled in Pennsylvania. As a young man, he had come West seeking opportunity; after a stint as a buffalo hunter, he had served as a scout under George Armstrong Custer, when the 7th Cavalry was posted in Kansas. Borne's current occupation was that of a mustanger, a man who captured wild horses and broke them to saddle. He sold livestock wherever he found a market.

"I ask you now," Gryden said point-blank. "Are you a horse thief?"

"No, I am not," Borne said earnestly, looking straight at the jury. "Wild horses are my trade, not stolen horses."

"Nothing more nor less than an honest tradesman. Hardly the Rob Roy of the plains the prosecution would have us believe."

"Your Honor!" Sutton protested. "Is counsel asking a question or making a closing argument? And who the devil is Rob Roy?"

"A Scottish rogue of ancient times," Gryden said patiently. "Made famous in Sir Walter Scott's novel. Pure fiction, Mr. Sutton, as is your case here today."

The jury was out less than thirty minutes. When they returned, the jury foreman announced the verdict of "not guilty" in a loud voice. The crowd, thoroughly entertained, applauded when Judge Strang ordered the defendant released from custody. Dutch Henry Borne shook Gryden's hand with a firm grip.

"Thanks, counselor," he said, smiling broadly. "You pulled the rabbit out of the hat."

"Don't get caught again," Gryden warned him. "I doubt the same defense would work a second time."

"Dodge City's seen the last of me. I think I'll stick close to No Man's Land."

"I'd say that's a wise decision, Dutch."

Mike Sutton caught Gryden on his way out of the courtroom. The prosecutor's features were wreathed in a dark scowl.

"Gryden, I deplore your tactics," he said. "But I have to give credit where credit is due. You suckered me with your ruse about Rob Roy."

"More than you know, Mr. Sutton."

"What are you driving at?"

"Sir Walter Scott wrote a novel, but it wasn't all fiction. He based it on historical fact."

"Are you saying Rob Roy was real—an actual outlaw?"

"True, blue, and large as life."

"Just like Dutch Henry. . . ."

Gryden grinned. "Exactly."

TWO

The sky was overcast, a brisk winter wind whipping down from the north. Outside the courthouse, Gryden turned up the collar of his overcoat and crossed the street. He walked along Second Avenue toward the center of town.

Dodge City bordered the Arkansas River. The Santa Fe Railroad tracks, which bisected the town east to west, were north of a bridge spanning the river. The business district was spread along a broad plaza opposite the tracks.

Gryden turned the corner onto Front Street. Down at one end of the plaza were two blocks of business establishments, including the Long Branch Saloon, the *Ford County Globe,* and the Dodge House Hotel. Up the other way were another two blocks of storefronts and buildings, housing concerns such as Wright's General Store, the Granger's State Bank, and the *Dodge City Times.* Farther north, beyond the plaza, was the residential district.

Fort Dodge, the nearest army post, was situated five miles east along the Arkansas. Until 1872, with the arrival of the railroad, Dodge City had been a windswept collection of log structures devoted to the buffalo trade. But now, hammered together with bustling industry, it had sprung, virtually overnight, into the rawest boomtown on the Western Plains. Civic boosters, never short on hyperbole, had dubbed it the Queen of Cowtowns.

The fabled Chisholm Trail was all but abandoned. Cowtowns that had flourished over the past decade—Abilene, Ellsworth, Newton, and Wichita—were now civilized and settled, the domain of farmers. The new Western Trail, which began deep in southern Texas, wound its way northward to the Red River. From there, it meandered through the wilderness of Indian Territory, crossing into Kansas above the Cimarron. The trail ended on a vast stretch of bottomland along the banks of the Arkansas, directly across the river from the Queen of Cowtowns. Texas cattlemen bragged there wasn't a fence between Red River and Dodge City.

Gryden had moved to Dodge City in 1875. Originally from Virginia, he had served as a cavalry officer in the Confederate army during the Civil War. After the war, he finished his education and was admitted to the bar in 1868. Upon departing from Virginia, he'd left behind a failed marriage, which had produced divorce rather than children, and headed west seeking a fresh start. At the time, Dodge City was in transition from a shipping point for buffalo hides to a cowtown and he'd sensed opportunity. He opened his law practice just as the economic boom got under way.

The riotous atmosphere of a cowtown appealed to Gryden. A man of southern charm, not yet thirty-five and still adventurous by nature, he was drawn to the nightlife of the town's sporting district. His law practice soon revolved around the sporting crowd, the people he mingled with on a social level, gamblers, saloonkeepers, and others of shady reputation. He was a cynic with a sense of humor, whose wit found a ready target in those who took an elitist attitude toward the common folk. He detested nothing quite so much as do-gooders who cloaked their arrogance in political altruism.

The Dodge House was at the corner of Front Street and Railroad Avenue. A three-story frame structure, it was the finest hotel in town, located near the train station. Gryden was a permanent resident, preferring the amenities offered by a hotel to the burdens of maintaining a home. Deacon Cox, the owner of the Dodge House, was a fellow Democrat and shared Gryden's distaste for the Republicans who largely controlled Ford County. Cox was talking with the desk clerk as Gryden came through the door.

"Well, Harry," Cox said pleasantly. "How'd it go in court?"

"We routed them," Gryden said. "Dutch Henry was exonerated and Sutton's got egg on his face. Wait till you read what Dan writes in the *Globe*."

The town's newspapers were openly adversarial. Nicholas Klaine's *Dodge City Times* supported Sutton and the Republicans, and Dan Frost of the *Ford County Globe* was aligned with the Democrats. Frost was certain to write a scathing critique of Sutton's defeat in court.

Cox practically danced with glee. "By God, Harry, you're aces high! Wish I'd been there to see it."

"Deacon, it was worth the price of admission. Chalk up one for our side."

Gryden waved and mounted the stairs. The hotel had only two suites, one of which he leased on a yearly basis. A few moments later he rounded the stairwell on the third

floor and walked to his quarters at the front of the hall. A
faded Persian carpet covered the sitting-room floor, and
grouped before the fireplace were several chairs and a
chesterfield divan. The bedroom was appointed in the
Victorian style, with an armoire, a fancy chest of drawers,
and a standing washbasin. A series of curtained windows
overlooked the plaza.

"I'm in here, sugar."

Gryden doffed his coat and hat and followed the voice
to the bedroom. Belle London stood before the mirror on
the armoire, inspecting the fit of her taffeta gown. She
was a woman of bustling vitality, smallish and compact,
with a dazzling figure. Her features were animated, with
larkspur eyes and a sensual mouth, and her hair hung long
and golden. There was a mischievous verve about her,
something impudent and puckish. She turned from the
mirror.

"You don't have to tell me," she said with a quick
smile. "I can see it all over your face. You won, didn't
you?"

Gryden laughed. "You might say I beat his pants off.
Sutton won't recover anytime soon."

"Aren't you the clever devil!" She threw her arms
around his neck and kissed him full on the mouth. "I'm so
proud of you it gives me goose bumps."

"Well then, that's the best reward of all."

"You'll get the best reward of all later tonight."

"Belle, you're a wicked woman.

"Would you have me any other way?"

"I like you just the way you are."

They had been lovers for almost a year. Belle was the
star attraction at the Comique Variety Theater, the top

nightspot in town. She spent her evenings prancing about the stage, where she belted out songs in a husky alto and bewitched the crowd with her sultry good looks. The combination made her the toast of the South Side sporting district and every man's fantasy. Yet she was one man's woman, his only woman. And he was her man.

Sometimes, particularly when they made love, she wondered if marriage was in the cards. They were an item of gossip all over town, and their affair seemed to her more than simple lust. He was educated, a man of some sophistication, but it was obvious he preferred the sporting crowd to the uptown crowd. She was taken by his mix of quiet tenderness and sardonic wit, and he relished her earthy wisdom and racy sense of humor.

She thought she might quit the stage if he ever popped the question. Then again, she wasn't sure she loved him more than the applause. The crowds were like an opiate, and yet she wasn't concerned one way or the other. She was content to wait until he asked.

"Omigosh!" she said, suddenly glancing out the window. "We'd better get supper, sugar. It's almost dark."

Gryden smiled. "I have a strong hunch they'd hold the curtain for you."

"Well, even so, tonight's not the night."

Their evenings were by now all but ritual. They had an early supper in the hotel dining room and then he put her in a carriage for the theater. As the star of the show, she refused to walk three blocks in the dark and cross the tracks to the South Side. Her deal with the Comique included a carriage every evening from the livery stable. A lady, she often said, should always go in style.

At the door, she turned and again kissed him with

warmth. "You're the sweetest man on the face of the earth. I'm so proud to be your girl."

"Not half as proud as me."

"You mean it?"

Gryden nodded. "Cross my heart."

A light snowfall blanketed the town with a dusting of powdery white. The air was crisp and sharp, and the plaza was dark except for the three uptown saloons. There were few people on the street.

Gryden emerged in a spill of light from the Long Branch Saloon. He was an inveterate gambler, with some degree of skill at the games of faro and poker. His evenings were usually spent at one of the town's gaming dives, where he was considered a regular at the tables. When he was winning, he might play until two or three in the morning. Poker was sometimes more profitable than the legal profession.

Tonight was not one of his better nights. The cards had gone against him and he was almost fifty dollars down. His fee from the Dutch Henry Borne trial was three hundred, and he might easily have played longer. But luck was a capricious thing, and some nights a man was wiser to quit rather than chase bad cards. Gryden decided the better play was to catch Belle's show at the Comique. He knew it would make her happy.

A swirl of snowflakes peppered his face as he crossed the railroad tracks. The sporting district, which spread for several blocks along the river, was known simply as the South Side. The main thoroughfare was Second Avenue, and wedged together on both sides of the street were saloons and dance halls, variety theaters and gambling parlors. Farther on, closer to the river, were nearly a dozen whorehouses.

Vice in all its variations was restricted to the South Side. There, during trailing season, cowhands were allowed a no-holds-barred pursuit of drunkenness and depravity, gunplay excepted. But at the railroad tracks, locally dubbed the Deadline, all rowdiness ceased. The lawmen of Dodge City, with a no-nonsense attitude toward troublemakers, rigidly enforced the ordinance. Anyone who attempted to hurrah the town north of the tracks was guaranteed a night in jail.

Gryden thought it a highly sensible arrangement. The wages of sin on one side of the tracks and the fruits of commerce on the other. The neutral ribbon of steel in between served as a visible, and clearly effective, dividing line. The ordinance containing drunken soldiers, Texan cowhands, and other ruffians to the sporting district seemed to work uncommonly well for all concerned. On the north side of the Deadline, the townspeople went about their business in relative peace.

The Comique was a combination saloon and gaming parlor, with a spacious theater separated by a wall at the rear. Belle was the headliner, and variety acts were imported from around the country, some from as far away as New York. The crowd tonight was comprised of railroad workers, townsmen, and soldiers from Fort Dodge. Even in the midst of a snowy winter, there was rarely an empty seat in the house.

Lloyd Franklin, owner of the Comique, greeted Gryden as he entered the theater. Gryden was always assured of a reserved table down front, positioned directly before center stage. Franklin got Gryden seated, snapping his fingers at a waiter, who quickly produced a bottle of bourbon and a shot glass. Gryden settled back to enjoy the show.

A dwarf on roller skates whizzed around the stage. Dressed in a clown costume, his face was painted white with crimson cheeks and a bulbous red nose. He leaped into the air and performed a flying head-over-heels somersault, landing smoothly on his skates. Then he executed a dizzying pirouette, spinning round and round, his tiny arms flung overhead, his clown's face gleeful in a peg-toothed grin. The audience applauded wildly as he skated backward offstage on one foot.

The curtain rose a moment later to reveal Belle at center stage. Her gaze went past the footlights, spotting Gryden at the reserved table, and she blew him a kiss. The crowd roared with delight and Gryden toasted her with his shot glass raised high. The orchestra struck up a catchy tune as Belle waltzed about the stage, her breasts jiggling over the top of a peekaboo gown. Her husky alto voice lofted out across the hall.

"Oh, don't you remember sweet Betsy from Pike,
Crossed the great mountains with her lover Ike,
With two yoke of oxen, a large yellow dog,
A tall Shanghai rooster, and one spotted hog!"

THREE

Saturday was the busiest day of the week. Farmers and ranchers from the surrounding countryside came into town to conduct business and order supplies. Front Street was crowded with wagons, and the hitch racks were lined with horses.

Gryden moved along the boardwalk shortly before eight that morning. He'd played poker until two, winning several large pots, and he had managed only four hours' sleep. His head was pounding, his eyes were bloodshot, and he wished he'd stayed in bed. He cursed his weakness for cards.

The date was February 2, the first Saturday in the month. On another day he might well have slept through, but the first of the month, particularly Saturday, was always a busy time. So he'd dragged himself out of bed, knowing there would be a steady stream of clients through the office. He hoped no one required sage legal advice.

The law offices of Gryden & Jones were in a storefront between Zimmerman's Mercantile and the Long Branch Saloon. When Gryden came through the door, his secretary, Velma Oxnard, looked up from her desk. A spinster, she was a plain dumpling of a woman, her hair pulled severely away from her face in a tight chignon. She gave him a measured inspection.

"Aren't you a sight," she said with a rabbity sniff. "Have you just come from a card game?"

"Good morning to you, too, Velma." Gryden removed his hat and overcoat and hooked them on a coatrack. "Appearances notwithstanding, I am in tip-top form. Alert as an eagle."

"You certainly could have fooled me."

A wood-burning stove hummed in the center of the reception room. Gryden accepted a cup offered by Velma, gingerly tested the handle of a coffeepot on top the stove, and poured his cup full. He took a long swig and felt faintly restored as the coffee spread through his system. He thought caffeine might just get him through the day.

Col. Thomas Jones appeared in the doorway of his office. "Late night, Harry?" he said indulgently. "You look a bit the worse for wear."

"We have consensus," Gryden said. "Velma is of the same opinion."

"Well, it's true!" Velma huffed. "You burn the candle at both ends."

"Exactly so," Jones agreed with a chuckle. "Harry never does anything by half measures. All or nothing, that's the ticket."

Gryden and Jones had been partners for two years. Jones, coincidentally, was also from Virginia and a graduate of the University of Virginia. He had served in the Confederate Army as a regimental commander, and the honorary title of "Colonel" followed him into civilian life. He was twelve years Gryden's senior, an erudite man of dignity and old-world manners.

Following the Civil War, Jones migrated west to outdistance the Reconstruction Era occupation imposed on the South. He settled in Spearville, east of Dodge City, but his law practice all too often required his presence at the Ninth District court. In Gryden he found a kindred spirit, and finally, in 1876, they became partners and he moved to Dodge City. His interests were in civil law, and Gryden, more flamboyant by nature, was drawn to criminal matters. They made a good team.

Gryden reveled in defending murderers, horse thieves, bunco artists, and robbers. His reputation for sensational trials drew attention to their firm and lured clients to the office. At any given time, the bulk of their caseload were upright townspeople and hardworking homesteaders who were involved in civil actions and disputed land claims. The routine matters, what Gryden considered the drudgery of law, gave them a comfortable income. The criminal cases, apart from headlines, were looked upon as found money.

Gryden refilled his coffee cup. "I almost hate to ask. What's on the calendar today?"

"Bread and butter," Velma said, consulting her appointment book. "Mr. Ortmann is coming in to discuss the land suit against his neighbor. And George Kellogg wants to get his will written."

"A will?" Gryden groaned.

"Yes," Velma said smugly, "and that's just this morning. There are five appointments this afternoon."

"Wonderful," Gryden said. "Nothing like a day devoted to the mundane."

Jones chortled. "Dutch Henry Borne doesn't walk through the door every day. The mundane pays the bills."

"Upstanding citizens are your department, Tom. I prefer consorting with criminals."

Gryden hardly meant it as a jest. Dodge City was steeped in a rich history of mayhem and violence. By 1874, its reputation as the Sodom and Gomorrah of the plains was firmly established. That year over a million buffalo hides were shipped east by local merchants on the Santa Fe Railroad. The buffalo hunters celebrated their good fortune by setting a new record for bloodletting. Twenty-eight men were planted in the Boot Hill graveyard outside town.

In 1876, with the slaughter of the great buffalo herds complete, the hide business was replaced by the cattle trade. The town's notoriety for violence nonetheless thrived as Texas longhorns were trailed to the bottomlands across the river. The volatile mix of gunmen, cardsharps, and drunken cowboys brought on a round of killings to rival the buffalo hunters'. Horse thieves, cattle rustlers, and bank robbers added to the death toll across the plains of Ford County. A criminal lawyer never lacked for clients.

Jones followed Gryden into his office and waited until the younger man had seated himself behind a desk littered with legal documents. His expression was pensive.

"I ran into Mike Sutton on the street this morning. He's still steaming about your shenanigans at Dutch Henry's trial."

"I'm delighted to hear it," Gryden said derisively. "I'd gladly tie a knot in his tail, if he had one."

Jones wagged his head. "There's no need to antagonize him unnecessarily. Men of differing political views can still behave in a civil manner."

"Tom, you are too much the gentleman for the likes of Sutton. Duplicity and guile are his stock-in-trade."

"I have no misconceptions about his character. I'm simply saying it's sometimes imprudent to poke a bear with a stick."

"A scoundrel deserves poking from time to time."

Gryden's remark was the offshoot of bitter experience. Dodge City was a mecca for Texas trailhands intent on drinking, gambling, and whoring. During cattle season, some fifteen hundred cowboys roamed the South Side and the sporting crowd profited by well over a million dollars. Ordinances passed by the town council levied stiff taxes on prostitution and gambling, and the city treasury was largely fueled by vice. The prosperity generated by the cattle trade was, in Gryden's view, the backbone of the economy. His feelings were tempered as well by his strong bond with the sporting crowd.

Sutton and his reform faction, known locally as the "Gang," were of a different view. Over the past two years a wave of German emigrants had settled throughout Ford County, purchasing right-of-way grants from the Santa Fe as well as claiming farmland under the Homestead Act. Dodge City and the county were quickly affected by the civilizing influence of respectable women whose lives centered on churches and schools. North of the railroad tracks, where brothels and coarse behavior were not permitted, the town was in large degree a family community. There was little tolerance for Texas cattlemen and their rowdy cowhands.

The merchants of Dodge City, for the most part, supported Sutton and his Gang. Farmers were a steady source of income and far more reliable than saloons and gaming dives. As well, the merchants profited from the distribution of trade goods off-loaded at the Santa Fe docks. Every year 5 million pounds of assorted goods were hauled by freighters to outlying towns in western Kansas and army posts in Indian Territory. The farmers, the merchants, and the respectable people of town enabled Sutton and the Republicans to control the government of Ford County.

Col. Thomas Jones, a former Confederate and a fellow Democrat, shared Gryden's political views. Yet now, standing in the younger man's office, he was reminded that Gryden was rarely an advocate of compromise. Jones shrugged, one eyebrow raised.

"Sutton may be a scoundrel," he conceded, "but a little tactfulness goes a long way. Why make such a display of your contempt?"

"Why not?" Gryden said lightly. "Sutton knows what I think of him. Pretending otherwise won't change anything."

"Perception often counts more than reality where voters are concerned. You might win support for our cause by *appearing* less combative."

"I'm no diplomat, Tom. I won't masquerade as something I'm not."

"Well, think about it," Jones said with no real conviction. "Who knows, you might change your mind."

"Not where Mike Sutton is concerned."

Jones again wagged his head, laughing softly as he turned out of the room. Gryden understood the logic of his partner's reasoning but wasn't persuaded by the argu-

ment. He recalled something he'd once read, something
to the effect that a man who was true to himself could not
be false to any man. His recollection was that the line was
from one of Shakespeare's plays, and that reaffirmed his
stance toward Sutton. Advice from Shakespeare was advice well taken.

At noon, having written a client's last will and testament, Gryden left the office for his midday meal. He
walked next door to the Long Branch Saloon, where two
bits bought a man a beer and a sandwich. From a tray at
the end of the bar he slapped together slices of beef and
cheese between thick slabs of rye slathered with mustard.
The bartender brought him a cool schooner of draft beer.

The owner of the Long Branch was Chalk Beeson.
One of the town's original settlers, he was also the former
sheriff of Ford County and the founder of the Dodge City
Brass Band. A staunch Democrat, Beeson was outspoken
in his opposition of Sutton and the reformers. He stopped
at the bar as Gryden took a long sip of beer.

"How's things, Harry?"

"Another day, another dollar," Gryden said, wiping
foam from his mustache. "Drafting wills and such ought
to pay better."

Beeson nodded. "All that paperwork gets a little dull,
does it?"

"Chalk, I'd much rather be in court. A lawyer needs a
jury to get the juices flowing."

"All those scalawags you defend probably wouldn't
agree. They'd sooner never see a jury."

Gryden took a bite of his sandwich. He munched a
moment, then smiled. "What they'd sooner never see is

the inside of a prison. Lucky for them, juries usually buy what I say."

"Harry, you're a corker, damned if you're not."

Beeson wandered off to greet other customers. The saloon was busy during the noon hour, even though play at the gaming tables was unusually slow. Luke Short, who was Beeson's partner in the gambling operation, was seated behind a faro layout. There was no action at Short's table, and after a glance at the other tables, all nearly empty, he got to his feet. He crossed the room to the bar.

"Harry, I can't make a nickel for everybody stuffing their faces. How about a few hands of faro?"

"I regret to say I can't be spared from the office. Maybe I'll try my luck tonight."

Gryden and Short were old friends. Originally from Texas, Short had bought a share in the Long Branch two years ago, just as Dodge City boomed as a cowtown. A professional gambler, he was known for an honest deal at mining camps and railheads all across the West. He was always cordial, never raised his voice, and was never to be antagonized. He was reputed to have killed five men in gunfights.

"Talkin' about luck," he said now, "heard about the game at the Comique last night. Somebody told me you won big."

"Luke, I couldn't be beat," Gryden said with a wide grin. "One of those nights when the cards fall your way. I came out very well."

"Yeah, there's nothing like it when the lady's sittin' on your shoulder. I always say, when the streak's running strong, don't get off it. You ought to drop by tonight."

"The question is, will my luck carry over from poker to faro?"

"Cards are cards," Short said. "When you're hot, the game doesn't matter."

"All right, I'll see you this evening."

"Good, I'll save a seat with your name on it."

Short nodded, smiling, and walked back to his table. Gryden thought he'd been conned into a game and studied on it as he finished his sandwich. Gamblers like Short were always eager to take on a man fresh off a big win, simply because he had a bankroll. But as he drained his beer stein, Gryden decided it didn't matter. A night of faro would be a godsend after a long day in the office.

Even if he lost.

FOUR

Gryden's first client that afternoon was Otto Schmidt, a farmer. Velma escorted him into the office and he took a chair in front of the desk. His hands were large and knobby, the hands of a man who performed hard labor.

"Mr. Schmidt," Gryden said. "How can I help you?"

"I going to be buying more land soon now. I think I need a lawyer."

Schmidt was a German emigrant, one of the first settlers in western Kansas. He owned a section of land some ten miles outside town, along the Santa Fe tracks. He stared across the desk with a sober expression.

"Pardon my curiosity," Gryden said. "There are lawyers who specialize in land transactions. Why have you come to me?"

Schmidt grunted. "Everybody say you're the smartest lawyer in town. Who else I come to?"

Gryden was of two minds about farmers. For the most part, they bought the bill of goods peddled by Sutton and his political cronies. They were united in opposition to Texas cattlemen trailing herds through southern Kansas and voted a straight Republican ticket. From a moral standpoint, they also advocated closing the South Side, banning saloons and gaming parlors and, most of all, the whorehouses. Yet farmers were solid citizens, quick to pay their debts, and often in need of legal advice. A lawyer couldn't afford not to do business with farmers.

"Very well," Gryden said. "How much land do you propose to purchase?"

"Mebbe two, three thousand acres," Schmidt told him in a firm voice. "I do good on my farm, save my money. Time to get bigger."

"Well, Mr. Schmidt, you're talking about a lot of land. Are you that well off?"

"*Ja,* don't you worry. I got the money."

"And who would you buy the land from?"

"Santa Fe," Schmidt said. "That's why I come to hire a smart lawyer. Railroad men all thieves."

Gryden thought it an understatement. Railroading in America was a study in graft and political skulduggery. As an inducement to build west, railroads were awarded government land grants that encompassed millions upon millions of acres of public domain. These grants were in the form of alternate sections (640 acres) along the railroad right-of-way, from ten to fifty miles in depth. Senators and congressmen were corrupted with stock and outright payoffs and quickly became the tools of the robber barons. America, in wholesale lots, was sold to the railroads.

The Santa Fe produced an illustrated guidebook extolling a Garden of Eden known by the name of Kansas. The guidebook, along with circulars and a series of advertisements, was translated into German, Dutch, Swedish, French, Danish, and Russian. Afterward a campaign reverberated across all of Europe, depicting farmland ripe with thick black topsoil never touched by a plow. The stuff of dreams, the sales pitch offered a new start in a bountiful land, where opportunity beckoned and the rich earth yielded abundance beyond man's comprehension. A migration of people from the Old World boarded the boats for America.

Otto Schmidt was of the Mennonite faith. Unlike most Germans, who were avowed Lutherans, the Mennonites were subjected to intolerance and persecution by both the church and the state. Their gentle ways were peculiar and offensive to other Germans, and their eyes turned toward America, where Mennonite colonies had already settled in Pennsylvania and Illinois. They sought refuge from tyranny and oppression, and the Santa Fe advertisements brought about one of the world's great displacements of humanity. Some four thousand German Mennonites embarked on a pilgrimage to the plains of Kansas.

Yet life on the plains was hardly the utopia depicted in railroad brocures. Winters were harsh and unrelenting, and summers were blistering hot, with never enough rain. Of all the settlers who came west, whether American or European, the Mennonites were the hardiest and most industrious of the lot. They brought with them red Turkey wheat, which flourished on arid plains, and they planted vast groves of mulberry, wild olive, and apricot. Their farms dotted the prairie along the Santa Fe right-of-way, surrounded by orchards and great fields of wheat. For them, Kansas was indeed the Promised Land.

Gryden, like everyone else in Dodge City, was familiar with the prosperity of the Mennonites. As he looked across the desk now, it occurred to him that Otto Schmidt was perhaps more prosperous than his brethren. "I share your opinion of the Santa Fe," Gryden said. "How do you wish me to represent your interests?"

Schmidt leaned forward. "Do you know this Santa Fe man, Leonard Parker?"

"Yes, Parker's the General Superintendent for the western district."

"I want you to deal with him for me."

"Are you talking about negotiating a land sale?"

"*Ja*," Schmidt said. "My farm, it's on railroad right-of-way. Sections behind me go on south for ten miles. I want to buy mebbe five sections."

Gryden did a quick calculation. "That's something over three thousand acres. How much are you willing to pay?"

"Dollar the acre."

"I assume you know unworked land is selling for three dollars an acre."

Schmidt smiled craftily. "That's why I hire me a smart lawyer."

"Not that smart," Gryden said. "Parker will never let it go for a dollar an acre."

"So you haggle with him, make him think he win. Mebbe dollar fifty the acre."

"You sound like you could negotiate it yourself."

"Parker look at me and see old German begging for deal. He never come down."

"To negotiate for you, I have to know where to stop. What's your top offer?"

"Two dollar," Schmidt said. "Won't go no higher."

Gryden looked at him. "Do you have seven thousand dollars readily available? Can you pay in cash?"

"Save every penny from farm and brought money from old country. *Ja,* I pay cash."

"As to my fee, it will be four hundred dollars, half in advance. That includes filing all the legal papers."

Schmidt pulled a wad of bills from his pocket. He wet his thumb and counted out two hundred dollars. "There," he said, nodding emphatically. "You my lawyer now?"

"Yes, Mr. Schmidt, I am now your lawyer."

After Schmidt left, Gryden placed the greenbacks in his desk drawer. He reviewed the discussion in his head and decided that Schmidt was far shrewder than he appeared. Perhaps, he told himself, he should have charged a higher fee.

Velma stepped through the door. "Mr. Jack Driskill is here to see you. He doesn't have an appointment."

"Jack Driskill the rancher?"

"The very one."

"Did he say what it's about?"

"Only that he wants to talk with you."

"Life's just a basketful of surprises. All right, Velma, show him in."

Jack Driskill was a large, rangy man with weathered features and a soup-strainer mustache. He wore a battered mackinaw and a dusty Stetson and he offered an ore-crusher handshake. He took a chair in front of the desk.

"Has something changed?" Gryden asked. "I thought you favored Mike Sutton in legal matters."

"Still do," Driskill informed him. "But you're the one that gets Dutch Henry and such rascals turned loose. Figured we ought to talk."

"About Dutch Henry?"

"Him and all the other thieves stealin' stock. I'm here as head of the Association."

Driskill owned the largest cattle spread in Ford County. His ranch was along the banks of the Cimarron, some sixty miles southwest of Dodge City. A leader in introducing Hereford shorthorn cattle to the state, he was the president of the Western Kansas Stockgrowers Association. He was also a Republican and a major supporter of Sutton's political Gang. Driskill detested Democrats almost as much as he hated Texas longhorns.

"Well now," Gryden said, still at a loss. "How can I be of assistance?"

"Want to talk some business," Driskill replied. "The Association holds a board meeting the first Saturday of every month. We just voted to hire you as our legal counsel."

"Did you?"

"For a fact."

Gryden was dumbfounded. "I have to say I'm more than a little astounded. Why would the Association hire a Democrat?"

"I already told you," Driskill said. "You keep gettin' these thieving bastards acquitted when they should be hung. We aim to take you out of action."

"Take me out of action—how?"

"You wouldn't defend no more of the sonsabitches. You'd be on our payroll, instead."

"When you say 'sonsabitches,'" Gryden inquired, "who do you mean exactly?"

"Horse thieves and cattle rustlers," Driskill said. "Anybody that steals livestock."

"Mike Sutton has always acted as legal counsel for the Association. How would he feel if you retain me?"

"Why, he'd be tickled pink. I talked to Mike before I put the idea to the Association board members. Way he figures, without you in the courtroom, he'll get some of these bastards convicted."

"Yes, I just imagine he would."

"So you're agreeable?"

Gryden was silent a moment. "Mr. Driskill, you have to understand that criminal law represents a large part of my practice. I defend accused lawbreakers on a regular basis."

"And get 'em off, too," Driskill said sourly. "Look here, we're not talkin' murderers and robbers and such. We're just talkin' livestock thieves."

"Nonetheless, that eliminates a great number of men from my client list. I would require a very substantial retainer—and a contract."

"How much?"

"Ten thousand dollars a year."

"Jesus Christ!" Driskill squawked. "That's highway robbery!"

"Not from my standpoint," Gryden said. "I enjoy defending the sonsabitches of the world, and I especially enjoy whipping Mike Sutton in court. The fee is not negotiable."

"You're sayin' take it or leave it."

"I believe I am."

Driskill gowered across the desk. He mentally weighed the fee against the value of horses and cattle stolen every year from Association members. Even more, he weighed the deterrent effect of livestock thieves at last being sentenced to prison. Finally, with a heavy sigh, he bobbed his head in a curt nod.

"Write your contract," he said gruffly. "When it's ready, I'll sign it."

"I should have it ready early next week."

"Just so's we understand things, as of today, you're through defendin' rustlers and such. Agreed?"

"Agreed."

Driskill stalked from the office without offering a handshake. Gryden tilted back in his chair, almost saddened by the lost opportunities to thrash Sutton in court. But then, on second thought, he decided ten thousand a year was a handsome consolation prize. He walked through the reception room to his partner's office. Jones looked up from drafting a legal brief.

"Good thing you're sitting down," Gryden said. "I just made a deal with the devil."

"Indeed?" Jones said. "Which devil might that be?"

"Jack Driskill."

Gryden recounted the details of his conversation with Driskill and the yearly retainer. At the mention of ten thousand dollars, Jones abruptly sat forward, his mouth ovaled in amazement. He blinked, shook his head.

"Driskill was right," he said. "It is highway robbery."

"I don't work cheap," Gryden said drily. "Particularly when I'm hired to represent law-abiding Republicans."

"You'd really rather represent the thieves, wouldn't you?"

"Tom, against my better principles, I succumbed to temptation. I couldn't resist the money."

"And you're sorry for it."

"Life's about to be a lot less fun."

Gryden wondered if Belle would feel he'd sold out. He wondered the same thing himself.

FIVE

The evening westbound train pulled away from the depot. The sky was clear, sprinkled with stars, and cinders from the smokestack swirled like fireflies in golden flight. The train chuffed off into the night.

Gryden and Belle emerged from the Dodge House. Belle was wrapped in a snug shawl and Gryden wore his topcoat. A phaeton carriage, with an enclosed cab, waited at curbside to take her to the Comique. As Gryden opened the coach door, she turned and brushed his cheek with a kiss. Her breath was frosty in the chill night air.

"Will I see you later?"

"You certainly will," Gryden said. "I'll be there for the last show."

"Oh?" she said in a teasing lilt. "And what if you're still winning?"

"I'd have to be very lucky to beat Luke Short at faro. In any case, win or lose, look for me at the theater."

Gryden always made it a point to be there on Saturday night. During the trailing season, when the Texans were in town, the South Side ran wide open seven days a week. But during the winter, when business was slower, the sporting district was closed on Sunday. Gryden and Belle thought of it as their special day, the day they were never apart.

"Well, anyway," she said, stepping into the coach, "I hope you bust the bank, sugar. I'll keep my fingers crossed."

"Then I won't have to take along my rabbit's foot. You're all the luck I need."

"I'm all the luck you can handle."

She laughed as the carriage trundled off down the street. Gryden smiled to himself, watching after her a moment, then moved along the boardwalk. For all his talk about Luke Short, Gryden was actually feeling lucky tonight. The deal he had negotiated that afternoon with the Stockgrowers Association made him the highest-paid lawyer in Dodge City. Even Belle agreed he'd made the right decision.

Apart from the saloons on Front Street, the plaza was quiet. By late afternoon on Saturday, the farmers and their families had begun the long trek back home. Gryden passed the Alhambra Saloon, which was owned by Dog Kelley, the mayor of Dodge City and one of Sutton's political Gang. Farther on, he crossed First Avenue and halfway up the block turned into the Long Branch. He felt ready to try his luck.

The saloon was crowded. The bar was lined with townsmen, soldiers, and ranch owners who often spent Saturday night in town. Opposite the bar were three faro tables, a twenty-one layout, and a chuck-a-luck table with a birdcage dice box. At the rear of the room, ranged along the wall, were three poker tables lit by overhead lamps. Waiters worked the floor in white aprons, balancing trays as they scurried from table to table. Gamblers were served fresh drinks hardly before they emptied their glasses.

Luke Short was dealing a hand of faro. There were three men at his table: a rancher, a grizzled master sergeant from Fort Dodge, and a teller who worked at the First National Bank. The cattleman was Seth Mabry, one of the larger ranchers in Ford County and a longtime board member of the Stockgrowers Association. Short looked up as Gryden approached the table.

"Well, Harry," he said amiably. "Told you I'd save you a seat. Glad you made it."

"Gentlemen." Gryden nodded to the other players. "Is Luke dealing winners tonight?"

"Off and on," Seth Mabry said. "So far, I'm a sight more off than on."

The master sergeant and the bank teller grunted agreement. Gryden dug a sheaf of bills from his pocket and placed a hundred dollars on the table. "Time for the worm to turn," he said, grinning. "Luke, you're luck's just run out."

"Get a hunch, bet a bunch," Short said, exchanging chips for cash. "Always did like a man who thinks he can't be beat."

Mabry glanced across at Gryden. "Talked to Leonard Parker this afternoon. He says you've signed on with the Association."

"Yes, I have," Gryden acknowledged. "Although it won't be half as much fun as defending horse thieves."

"Maybe without you around we'll see the skunks put behind bars."

"Mr. Mabry, I'd venture to say you're exactly right."

Short rapped the table. "Place your bets, gents."

Gryden studied the layout a moment. The baize spread was arranged with printed duplicates of cards, deuce through ace of spades. The other players hesitated, watching intently as he placed a ten-dollar chip on the queen. Then, one by one, with chips of differing amounts, they placed their wagers on the queen as well. Short smoothly slipped a card from the dealer's box, a nine. The second card out was a queen.

"Goddamn!" Mabry crowed. "You broke his run. Queen wins!"

Short smiled, as though joining in the laugh, and paid off the bets. He was small and wiry, with the quick hands of a professional, and he wasn't in the least concerned. He knew that the odds, which already favored the house, were merely increased when players all bet on the same card. He thought the Long Branch was in for a good night.

Everyone watched as Short moved an ivory counter to the queen on an abacus-like device, known as the casekeeper. Positioned to one side of the table, the casekeeper indicated the cards already dealt and allowed bettors to figure percentages on cards remaining in the deck. Gryden stared at the casekeeper a moment and then placed a chip on the ace. The other players followed along.

Faro, even more than poker, was governed by the luck of the draw. An old and highly structured game, it had originated a century before in France. The name derived from the king of hearts, which bore the image of an Egyptian pharaoh on the back of the card. All betting was against the house, known in Western parlance as "bucking the tiger."

The cloth layout depicted deuce through ace. Only the

value of the card counted; the suit, though displayed, was not relevant to the bet. After being shuffled, the cards were placed in the dealing box and then drawn in pairs, shown faceup. Before the turn of each pair, players placed bets on one or more cards of their choice. The first card out of the box was a losing bet, and the second was a winner. All bets were canceled if there were no wagers on either card.

By watching the casekeeper, players could bet win or lose on the layout. To wager on a losing card, they "coppered" their bet by placing a copper token on their chips. A daring player, convinced that luck was on his side, often bet win and lose on the same turn. He was, in a very real sense, bucking the tiger.

Short flopped a jack, then an ace. Gryden laughed out loud and the other players pounded him on the back. After they'd collected their winnings, Gryden scrutinized the casekeeper at length. Some inner voice told him to press it to the limit, and he bet twenty on the queen to lose and an equal amount on the six to win. Mabry paused, considering a moment, then coppered the queen and played the six to win. The master sergeant and the bank teller wagered only the six.

The first card out of the box was a queen, a winner for Gryden and Mabry. The second card was a six, a winner for all four players. Gryden shook his head, grinning, with the look of a magician who had just pulled a dove from beneath a silk scarf. The other players whooped, staring incredulously at the layout, as if they couldn't credit their good fortune. Short paid off the bets with a wry smile.

"Winners all around," he announced, "Harry, I'd say it's your night to howl. Where's your lucky charm?"

"Don't need one," Gryden said jovially. "I was born under a lucky star. Fortune smiles on my every endeavor."

"Goddang right!" the old master sergeant agreed. "You pick 'em and we'll bet 'em."

Short suddenly glanced past them. His eyes narrowed and the expression on his face abruptly went tense. Gryden caught the startled look and turned in his chair, scanning the room. He saw Tom O'Haran just inside the door, his gaze fixed on the bar. O'Haran held a pistol in his hand.

Gryden instantly grasped the problem. Deputy U.S. Marshal Hiram McCarty was standing with a group of men at the bar. Two weeks ago McCarty had arrested O'Haran for stealing a mule from the livestock pens at Fort Dodge. O'Haran was something of a dimwit, so slow mentally he was jokingly referred to as the "village idiot." Without thought to the army brand on the mule, he'd attempted to sell it to a Dodge City livestock dealer. He was arrested the same day.

O'Haran sometimes worked as a swamper at South Side saloons, mopping floors and emptying spittoons. Ham Bell, who owned the Lone Star, generally gave him more work than other saloonkeepers. When O'Haran was arrested and placed in the county jail, Bell took pity on him and made bond with the court. Aside from the usual jibes, no one gave it much thought, for O'Haran was an unlikely criminal, quiet and backward, not known for violence. He was currently out on bail, awaiting trial.

Luke Short suddenly yelled, *"McCarty, behind you!"*

The lawman turned from the bar to find O'Haran only a few steps away. "Why, Tom," he said in a calm voice. "What're you doing with a gun?"

"Come to kill you," O'Haran said without inflection. "You done made a fool outta me."

"Now you know that's not so, Tom. It was my job to arrest you."

The room was frozen in a silent tableau. Everyone stared at the two men, wondering if McCarty could talk his way out of a deadly situation. A wild look surfaced in O'Haran's eyes.

"Folks are makin' fun of me," he said hoarsely. "Callin' me a dummy, all 'cause of you."

"Well, we'll just shut 'em up," McCarty assured him. "You're no dummy and I'll tell 'em so myself."

"Won't do no good and you know it won't. Come to kill you and that's what I'm gonna do."

McCarty shook his head sadly. He started forward, hand outstretched. "C'mon now, Tom, you don't want to make more trouble for yourself. Give me that gun and we'll just—"

O'Haran extended his pistol and fired. The slug struck McCarty in the chest and a bright starburst spread over his shirt. He staggered backward into the bar, a surprised look on his face, and his legs buckled at the knees. He dropped dead on the floor.

The report of the gunshot reverberated through the room. Then, too quick to credit, Luke Short slipped from the crowd and thunked O'Haran over the head with the barrel of a Colt Peacemaker. O'Haran slumped forward, dropping his pistol, and toppled to the floor. He was out cold.

A moment later City Marshal Ed Masterson rushed through the door. He looked at the two men on the floor and then at Short, who still held the drawn Colt. "Luke, put that gun away," Masterson ordered. "What the hell's happened here?"

"O'Haran shot McCarty," Short said, holstering his pistol. "McCarty tried to talk him out of it, but it didn't work. He fired point-blank."

One of the men at the bar checked McCarty's neck for a pulse and solemnly wagged his head. Gryden walked forward, the faro game forgotten in the aftermath of the killing. He watched as Masterson stooped down and collected O'Haran's pistol off the floor. O'Haran groaned, blinking his eyes, and levered himself to a sitting position. He looked around the room with a dazed expression.

"You goddamn idjit," Masterson said, jerking him erect by the scruff of his neck. "You're under arrest for murder."

"Didn't murder nobody," O'Haran mumbled. "Just killed him, that's all."

Bat Masterson hurried through the door. Gryden was reminded again of the physical similarity between the Masterson brothers. They were both of medium height and muscular build, with square features and dark hair. They were peas from the same pod.

As sheriff, Bat immediately took charge. Murder was a capital offense, and Ed agreed that the prisoner should be lodged in the county jail. Watching them, Gryden was reminded as well that Ed was city marshal by virtue of Mike Sutton's political machinations within the town council. The law and the lawmen, he reflected, danced to whatever tune Sutton played.

Chalk Beeson volunteered to have the dead man's body transported to the undertaker's parlor. Bat and Ed Masterson took O'Haran by the arms and started him toward the door. O'Haran dug in his heels and looked over his shoulder at Gryden. He appeared somehow more lucid than before and afraid.

"Mr. Gryden," he said in a scratchy voice, "Ham Bell always says you're the smartest lawyer in town. Will you take me on?"

The crowd looked at Gryden as if he'd been asked a profound question. He hesitated a moment, then nodded to O'Haran. "All right, Tom, consider me your attorney."

"What's the matter with you?" Bat Masterson demanded. "He just killed a peace officer."

"Well, Sheriff, someone has to defend him."

"The crazy bastard doesn't even have a job. You won't get paid a nickel."

"Then I'll do it pro bono."

"What the hell's pro bono?"

Gryden smiled. "For free."

SIX

The dining room was furnished with a heavy oak table covered with a hand-stitched linen tablecloth. An oval mirror hung over a massive sideboard with elaborate carving and onyx drawer knobs. The room was lit by an ornate candelabra suspended from the ceiling.

Florence Sutton whisked in from the kitchen with a steaming platter of pork chops. She was an attractive woman, in her late twenties, with a stemlike waist and a rounded figure. After surveying the table, she turned to the mirror, patting her upswept hair and smoothing the bodice of her dress. She moved to the doorway.

"Sweetheart," she called out pleasantly. "Dinner's ready."

"Oh, good, I'm starving."

Sutton rose from an easy chair in the parlor. He walked to the dining room, waited until she seated herself at one end of the table, and then took a chair opposite her. The table was laden with bowls of mashed potatoes, boiled onions, and winter squash and a loaf of fresh-baked bread. Sutton unfolded his napkin, looking at the dishes with the relish of a man who appreciates hearty meals. He began loading his plate.

"All my favorites," he said. "You'll make a fat man of me yet."

"Small chance of that," she said, smiling. "You work so hard you burn it off in no time."

"Well, to quote some ancient sage, food fuels the engine."

"Did they have engines in ancient times?"

"Perhaps it was a modern sage."

"Or something you invented yourself."

"My dear, you've caught me out again."

The banter was that of man and wife who were also best friends. They had met and married three years ago, when she'd spent the summer visiting a cousin living in Dodge City. For a wedding present Sutton had built her a two-story Victorian home with a commanding view of the town. The house was located on Gospel Ridge, a residential area at the north end of First Avenue. They moved in upon returning from their honeymoon in Saint Louis.

Sutton considered their home a symbol of his station in life. Originally from New York, the son of immigrants, he'd served in the Union Army during the late war. After being mustered out in Missouri, he studied law between jobs and was admitted to the bar in 1872. Like many rootless men, he was attracted by boomtown rumors on the western plains, and he moved to Dodge City the spring of 1874. His law practice flourished as he made political alliances, and he'd been elected county attorney the fall of 1876. He often thought it was a far cry from the poverty of a New York slum.

Florence was no less proud of their position in the community. Her husband was a civic leader, eminently successful as a lawyer, and politically the most astute

man in Ford County. As his wife, she basked in the lime-
light, and she had only one regret with their marriage.
Over the years she hadn't become pregnant, and she'd
consulted with her doctor any number of times. Unable to
have children, Florence had become instead a dynamo
devoted to social causes involving the church and the prohibition of alcoholic spirits. She placed any form of
liquor, including beer, in the category of demon rum.

"How was your day?" she asked, always interested in
her husband's affairs. "I want to hear every last detail."

Sutton paused, a bite of pork chop speared on his fork.
A broad smile spread over his face. "I hatched a dandy lit-
tle scheme with Leon Parker and his rancher friends.
We've hamstrung Harry Gryden."

"Oh, my goodness! How did you manage that?"

"The Stockgrowers Association retained Gryden as its
legal counsel."

"Does that mean you are no longer on retainer?"

"Yes, but you haven't heard the best part."

"Then tell me!"

"Gryden will be prohibited from defending cattle
rustlers and horse thieves. His criminal practice will be
severely limited."

"Oh, how marvelous." Her eyes danced with excitement. "And that means he won't obstruct you in court so
much."

"Exactly." Sutton popped the bite of pork chop into his
mouth. "Harry Gryden will see far fewer headlines in the
newspaper."

"You are a sly one, Mr. Sutton. I adore it!"

"I'm rather pleased with it myself."

The political animosity between Sutton and Gryden reflected their personal differences as to acceptable moral standards for the community. Dodge City was still dependent on the Texas cattle trade, and Sutton's vision was one of an economy centered on farmers, the railroad, and local commerce. Old attitudes were at odds with a progressive view of the future.

The Sodom and Gomorrah image was, in Sutton's mind, a deterrent to progress. He felt the reputation as Queen of Cowtowns—with gamblers, prostitutes, and drunken cowboys—was a liability the town could no longer afford. Instead, he fervently envisioned Dodge City as the home of storekeepers and laborers, businessmen and professionals, a settled family community. Agriculture, to his way of thinking, was the economic foundation of Ford County.

The population of the township was now approaching two thousand. Common laborers and clerks were paid a respectable wage of seven dollars a week, and carpenters and railroad workers earned even more. Married couples with children under fourteen represented almost 50 percent of the population, and in Sutton's opinion the town needed schools rather than saloons. Virtue and values were preferable to the deplorable practice of settling disputes with guns.

Sutton saw the law as the armor of a civilized community. Even more, he believed the courts and the judicial system were the arena where personal quarrels should be resolved. The anarchy of the buffalo hunters was long gone, and the frontier code of violence seemed to him an anachronism that had outlived its day. Law and order, the basic rules of human conduct, were the very spine of economic stability and social progress. He never understood why Harry Gryden, an educated man and a formidable lawyer, sided with the sporting crowd.

The quandary of it occupied Sutton's thoughts as Florence served a chocolate cake for dessert. He took a large bite, savoring the taste, and nodded approval. She watched him, awaiting a compliment, and quickly became aware that his mind was elsewhere. She gave him a wounded look.

"Mercy sakes, your favorite dessert and not a word. Where are you off to?"

"No, no, it's delicious," Sutton hastily assured her. "I was just woolgathering about Gryden."

"Oh?" she said, picking at her cake. "What about him?"

"I've known him all these years and he's still an enigma. Why would he choose to consort with the South Side crowd?"

"Because he has the morals of a scruffy tomcat. I absolutely loathe the man!"

"Many people share the feeling," Sutton said. "But his disreputable behavior doesn't alter his professional standing. He's a brilliant lawyer."

"Honestly, Mike," she admonished. "Are you defending him?"

"Far be it from me to endorse Harry Gryden. I'm simply saying you can never underestimate him."

"Yes, but he's such a libertine. Gambling, drinking— living with *that* woman."

Sutton finished his cake. "You're perfectly right in calling him a tomcat. And if you think about it, that merely adds to the enigma. A man of commendable ethics with no personal morals." He paused, wiping his mouth with his napkin. "I'm not philosopher enough to unravel that riddle."

"Well, who cares?" she said with a pretty smile. "You're the county attorney and he's just another lawyer. Doesn't that say it all?"

"Yes, my dear, I suppose it does."

Sutton was serving a two-year term as county attorney. He received a comfortable salary plus a bonus of 5 percent of all monetary awards he won favoring the county. Ford County encompassed fully one-third of the landmass of Kansas, and his jurisdiction extended as far west as the Colorado line, over a hundred miles from Dodge City. And in his free time he was still entitled to pursue his private practice. All in all, a very lucrative arrangement.

By state law, the attorney general of Kansas could not approve any request of the county commissioners unless it was submitted through the office of the county attorney. The statute effectively gave Sutton legal and budgetary control over the commissioners, as well as the sheriff, the mayor, the town council, and other city agencies. In the opinion of many, including his own, Sutton was the most powerful man in Ford County. As local politicos termed it, the Kingfish.

So his wife's offhand remark, though true, still rang hollow. He was, in a very real sense, the lord of all he surveyed, and he certainly had no reason to envy Harry Gryden. Yet he did, and it ate at him, for he despised the man he envied. Which made the enigma all the more maddening when he thought on it too long.

Florence began clearing the table. She prided herself on not having household servants, much like a martyr seeking a cross. Sutton returned to the parlor, where tongues of flame flicked from logs burning brightly in the fireplace. After settling into his easy chair, he took a half-smoked cigar from an ashtray and lit it with a kitchen match. He went back to a story he'd been reading in the newspaper before supper.

The *Dodge City Times* carried a front-page article about small towns in northwest Ford County. The Homestead Act, passed into law by Congress, enabled settlers to claim a quarter section (160 acres) of public land. The influx of settlers had resulted in the growth of backcountry villages such as Dighton, Leoti, and Russell Springs. The article noted that the settlers, by and large migrants from northern states, were for the most part loyal Republicans. Their votes, the article concluded, might very well carry the November elections for county offices.

Sutton's term as county attorney expired at the end of the year. He fully intended to win a second term, and he was a great believer in planning well ahead. He thought it might be wise to schedule trips to outlying towns and organize campaign workers at the local level. November was only nine months away, and a politician was always wise to form alliances far in advance. He subscribed to the motto that sooner was better than later where elections were concerned. People voted for the man who went out of his way to earn their trust.

Florence came in as Sutton finished reading the article. She took a seat on the sofa, collecting her knitting needles and yarn from the cushion. Her fingers began working the needles in rapid clicks.

"I forgot to tell you," she said. "I received a letter today from Albert Griffin."

Sutton folded his newspaper. "Anything new to report?"

"Yes. He's quite enthused. He believes he's making progress with the legislature. He thinks a bill could be introduced in the fall session."

"Well now, that would be news."

Albert Griffin was president of the Kansas Temperance Union. The state Prohibitionist Party, with the Temperance Union in the vanguard, sought to ban the sale or possession of intoxicating liquors. Griffin was editor of the *Nationalist,* a newspaper devoted almost exclusively to the evils of demon rum. He spent most of his time in Topeka, the state capital, badgering legislators.

Dodge City was the western outpost for the prohibition movement, and Florence was a loyal soldier, ever girded for battle. Albert Griffin had appointed her the local delegate of the Temperance Union, and she in turn had cobbled together a coalition of the town's clergymen and women parishioners from their congregations. Her appointment as the local delegate had been based principally on the fact that her husband was the political leader of Ford County. She looked up now from her knitting.

"Perhaps you could have a word with Bob Wright. Mr. Griffin will need his support if a bill is to be introduced."

"Very well, my dear," Sutton said. "I'll have a word with him first thing tomorrow."

Once a drinker himself, Sutton had become a teetotaler following their marriage. Beneath her genteel manner, Florence was a strong-willed woman, and she had insisted he abandon alcoholic spirits. Yet, however much a convert, Sutton walked a fine line where the politics of liquor were concerned. Not all Republicans agreed that whiskey should be banned, and he faced an election in November.

Bob Wright, owner of Wright's General Store, was Ford County's representative in the state legislature. He and Sutton were in accord that a ban on alcohol would sound the death knell on vice and lawlessness in the South Side. Sutton would honor his wife's wishes and speak with Wright regarding the push to introduce legislation in the fall session. But he reminded himself now that there was something to be said for discretion and secrecy. In politics, voters were sometimes best kept in the dark.

A hard knock sounded at the door. Sutton exchanged a glance with Florence, then rose from his chair and crossed the parlor. He opened the door to find Bat Masterson on the porch.

"Well, Bat," Sutton said, surprised. "Come in out of the cold."

Masterson stepped into the parlor. "Evenin', Mrs. Sutton," he said, doffing his hat. "Sorry to bust in on you so late."

"Not at all," Sutton told him. "Is something wrong?"

"'Fraid I'm here with bad news. U.S. Marshal McCarty was killed about an hour ago. Tom O'Haran shot him in the Long Branch Saloon. Nothin' but cold-blooded murder."

"Good Lord," Sutton said, stunned. "Hiram McCarty was a fine man and an excellent peace officer. Do you have O'Haran in custody?"

"Got him locked in jail," Masterson said. "Harry Gryden's already agreed to defend him."

"How did Gryden get involved so quickly?"

"When the shooting happened, Gryden was in the Long Branch. O'Haran asked him to be his lawyer."

"I assume you have witnesses to the shooting."

"There's enough to get O'Haran hung three times over. Ought to be an easy conviction."

"Bat, I appreciate you coming by. Would you do me a favor and alert Judge Strang? I'd like to hold the arraignment tomorrow afternoon."

"I'll drop by his house and tell him now."

After Masterson was gone, Sutton turned back into the parlor. He walked to his easy chair and sat down, staring into the fire. His expression was sepulchral.

"A good man killed and Gryden is Johnny-on-the-spot. Just my luck."

"Your very good luck," Florence said with a firm nod. "You will humble him in court this time."

"What makes you think so?"

"Oh, call it woman's intuition. I just have a feeling."

"My dear, I hope you're right."

"I am."

Sutton pictured it in his mind, and despite himself, he smiled. Harry Gryden humbled in court was a sight no one had ever seen. Something long overdue.

And richly deserved.

SEVEN

The Ford County Courthouse was located at the corner of Second Avenue and Chestnut Street. The building was an imposing two-story edifice, constructed of milled native stone, housing county officials and the district court. The jail was in the basement, dark and dank, with thick limestone walls.

The trial of Thomas O'Haran got under way on March 18. Arraigned on February 3, the accused man had been denied bail and confined to his cell twenty-four hours a day. He slept there, his meals were served on a tray, and the jailer emptied O'Haran's chamber pot every morning. He hadn't had a bath in six weeks.

Editorials appeared in the newspapers almost on a daily basis. The language was inflammatory, reviewing the killing in gory detail, and openly demanded the death penalty. Nick Klaine of the *Dodge City Times* branded the accused a "savage, cold-blooded murderer without a spark of humanity." Dan Frost of the *Ford County Globe* labeled O'Haran a "bloodthirsty maniac who deserves a fast trial and a quick hanging."

The temper of the public echoed the editorials. In death, Deputy U.S. Marshal McCarty was remembered as a God-fearing man and a courageous lawman, and the townspeople were outraged by his murder. Sheriff Masterson, wary of trouble, assigned Undersheriff Joe Bohannon to secure the courtroom and protect the defendant. Deputies were posted at the door and behind the railing that separated the spectator seating from the court arena. One deputy, armed with a shotgun, was assigned the sole mission of protecting Thomas O'Haran.

A murder trial pitting Mike Sutton against Harry Gryden drew an overflow crowd. The spectator benches in the courtroom were packed, and in the hallway outside a line of people hoping for a seat stretched to the courthouse steps. Gryden and Sutton were at their respective tables, and Miles Mix, the deputy with a shotgun, stood directly behind Gryden. A door opened near the defense table, and several women gasped as Sheriff Masterson led O'Haran into the courtroom.

Gryden had refused to allow the prisoner to be made more presentable. O'Haran was filthy, his clothes so soiled the stench pervaded the courtroom. His hair was matted, his face dark with stubble, and his eyes darted about like a wild thing brought from captivity. He looked crazed, almost maniacal, which was exactly the way Gryden wanted him to look. Masterson unlocked the manacles from his wrists and guided him into a chair beside Gryden. O'Haran's hands jittered as he rubbed his wrists.

"All rise!"

The bailiff's crisp shout brought everyone to their feet. Judge Jeremiah Strang came through the door from his chambers and proceeded to the bench. As he took his chair, glancing down at the disheveled prisoner, the bailiff motioned the crowd to be seated. A moment of stark silence descended on the spectators as Strang stared out over the courtroom. His voice, when he spoke, was sharp and commanding.

"Let us understand one another. I will have no unruly behavior or outbursts in the course of this trial. Anyone who causes a problem will be removed from the courtroom, possibly even arrested. Do not try my patience."

The crowd stared back at him in another moment of rapt silence. He finally looked down at the opposing attorneys. "Do you gentlemen have any business for the court before we move to jury selection?"

"Yes, Your Honor." Gryden got to his feet. "I petition the court for a change of venue. My client simply cannot receive a fair trial in Ford County."

"Be more specific, Mr. Gryden."

"Judge, every man, woman, and child in Ford County has been exposed to the scurrilous attacks made on my client in the newspapers. Any potential juror has been tainted beyond redemption."

"Mr. Sutton?" Strang inquired.

Sutton rose from his chair. "Counsel for the defense has too little faith in the citizens of Ford County. There are twelve men good and true who will do their duty— honorably and without bias."

"I agree," Strang said. "Your petition is denied, Mr. Gryden. Anything else?"

"There is, Your Honor," Gryden replied. "I request a continuance of at least one month. The request is based on the treatment my client has received at the hands of the sheriff's department. He is not mentally prepared to stand trial at this time."

"Are you saying he has been ill-treated, Mr. Gryden?"

"Why, you have only to look at him, Judge."

Judge Strang leaned forward, peering down from the bench. The spectators craned their necks for a look, and even the deputy sheriffs turned to stare. O'Haran fidgeted in his chair, uncomfortable with the sudden attention. Gryden went on in a ringing voice, loud with indignation.

"Your Honor, as you can clearly see, Mr. O'Haran might well have been incarcerated in the Black Hole of Calcutta. Only the thumbscrews and hot irons of the Inquisition could have affected his mental state for the worse. In the interest of justice, I ask the court for a continuance."

"Very eloquent, Mr. Gryden," Strang said with a frosty smile. "Your client appears to need a bath, but your petition is denied. We will proceed with jury selection."

A jury panel of thirty-six men was brought into the courtroom, twelve at a time. Their number was comprised of townspeople, railroad workers, farmers, and cattlemen. The balance of the morning was devoted to Sutton and Gryden sparring to seat jurors sympathetic to their views. All of the panel members were familiar with details of the shooting, and to a man they supported the death penalty. By late morning, six townsmen, five farmers, and one rancher were selected.

Judge Strang adjourned court for the noon hour. At one o'clock, with the jurors seated, court was convened and opening arguments were presented. Sutton outlined at some length the state's case, calling the offense a "heinous act of premeditated murder," and urged the jurors to render not just a verdict of guilt but a sentence of death. Gryden, standing before the jury box, told the panel he would prove to their satisfaction that his client was innocent by reason of insanity. His remarks were brief, delivered without histrionics, and straight to the point. He told them he would prove the defendant was "crazy as a loon."

The first witness called by the state was Dr. Thadius McCabe, the county coroner. He testified that he had performed an autopsy on the deceased the morning after the shooting. McCabe went on to say that the cause of death was a gunshot to the heart and offered his opinion that death was instantaneous. Upon completion of testimony, Gryden waived the opportunity for cross-examination. He said, in an aside to Sutton, that there was never any question as to the cause of death.

Chalk Beeson, owner of the Long Branch Saloon, was then called to the stand. Under Sutton's prompting, Beeson related how he'd seen the affair from beginning to end and that the deceased had been killed with no chance to defend himself. Walt Prentice, bartender at the Long Branch, was the next witness. He testified that he was behind the bar, within arm's reach of Marshal McCarty, when the fatal shot was fired. Prentice further stated that the defendant, upon entering the saloon, had announced his intention to kill McCarty. Sutton passed the witness to Gryden.

"Mr. Prentice, I want you to think back," Gryden said, approaching the stand. "Did the defendant say why he meant to kill Marshal McCarty?"

"Yessir," Prentice said. "Clear as day."

"And the reason was . . . ?"

"He said he'd been made a fool of."

"In what way?"

"Because the marshal arrested him for stealin' an army mule."

"How did that make him a fool?"

"Why, he tried to sell the mule right here in Dodge."

"Too near to home, is that it?"

Prentice snorted. "Everybody in town thought it was dumb as dirt. Couldn't be no more of a fool."

"Objection!" Sutton called out. "Goes beyond the scope of direct testimony, Your Honor."

Gryden walked away. "I have no further questions."

Luke Short was called to the stand. After taking the oath, he testified to the shooting itself and went on to say he'd whacked O'Haran over the head with his pistol. Gryden declined cross-examination, and Sutton then called City Marshal Ed Masterson. The lawman related arriving at the Long Branch to find McCarty dead and O'Haran unconscious on the floor. Masterson ended by saying he had arrested O'Haran on a charge of murder. Sutton resumed his seat.

Gryden moved forward. "Marshal, would you tell the court what you called Mr. O'Haran when you arrested him?"

"Don't recollect," Masterson said. "That's been a while ago."

"Let me refresh your memory. You called him—and I quote—'you goddamn idjit.' Isn't that correct?"

"Yeah, that sounds about right."

"What does the word 'idjit' mean, Marshal?"

"Just another way of saying 'idiot.'"

"And for as long as anyone remembers, people have referred to Mr. O'Haran as the 'village idiot.' Why is that, Marshal?"

"Objection," Sutton protested. "Immaterial and irrelevant."

"On the contrary," Gryden said. "It goes to the marrow of the defense's case."

Judge Strang nodded. "You may answer the question, Marshal."

"Well . . ." Masterson hesitiated. "Folks call him the village idiot 'cause he's stupid. Don't know when to come in outta the rain."

"Not right in the head?"

"Yeah, I suppose you could say that."

"I believe you just have, Marshal."

Sutton appeared on the verge of redirect examination. He rose from his chair, then looked at the jury and shook his head, as if it were all nonsense. He turned to the bench.

"I see no reason to rebut a clever play on words. The state rests its case, Your Honor."

Gryden opened for the defense with Dr. Benjamin Milton. A portly man with gray hair and a studious manner, the physician was widely respected in Dodge City. Gryden first established that Milton was accredited by the Kansas Medical Board to diagnose people for mental competence. He then put into the record that Milton had evaluated O'Haran during the defendant's incarceration in the county jail. The jurors were now listening intently.

"Tell us, Dr. Milton," Gryden said. "Can Thomas O'Haran read or write? Spell his name? Do his numbers?"

"No, he lacks the mental capacity for such things."

"Does he know it's wrong to steal?"

"Yes and no," Milton responded. "As a child, he was taught the Bible by his mother. But mentally, he has no comprehension of 'thou shall not steal.' "

"What about 'thou shall not kill'?"

"The same thought applies. He may remember his mother taught him it was wrong. But in a moment of rage, he cannot distinguish right from wrong."

"In your opinion, was he sane when he fired that gun?"

"No, he was not in possession of his faculties."

"As you've testified, you are licensed by the state to certify people deranged and commit them to the Kansas Insane Asylum. What is your diagnosis of Thomas O'Haran?"

Milton shrugged. "By any medical standard, he should be committed to an institution. He is certifiably insane."

Gryden let the thought hang a moment, then walked back to the defense table. Sutton approached for cross-examination.

"I have only a few questions, Dr. Milton. O'Haran was arrested on January 20 for stealing a mule and he killed Marshal McCarty on February 2. Why did it take him two weeks to go insane?"

"Lunacy manifests itself in strange ways," Milton said. "In this instance, the day-by-day pressure became so unbearable that he finally snapped."

"At the time he pulled the trigger, did he know it was a hanging offense to murder Marshal McCarty?"

"Yes, in his own muddled way he understands the consequences of his actions. He simply hasn't the capacity to reconcile the consequences with his rage."

"So then, regardless of his mental deficiencies, he understood the law with respect to killing another man. Isn't that true?"

"Only in a general sense," Milton said. "Insofar as his mental state is concerned, he was helpless in the face of his rage."

"Yet your testimony is that he understood the law, understood the offense of murder. Correct?"

"Perhaps in a fuzzy—"

"Yes or no, if you please!"

Dr. Milton reluctantly nodded. "Yes."

Sutton turned away. "Nothing further of this witness."

Gryden got to his feet. He paused for dramatic effect, his features confident. "Call Thomas O'Haran."

O'Haran appeared confused. The bailiff assisted him across the room, patiently led him through taking the oath, and got him seated. Gryden walked to the stand, his tone quietly gentle.

"Tom, why did you kill Marshal McCarty?"

"'Cause he made a fool of me."

"Yes, but wasn't it wrong to kill him?"

"Nope." O'Haran looked off with a blank stare. "He shouldn't've got me mad."

Gryden bowed his head. "Have you ever killed anyone before?"

"Nobody ever made me mad."

"What about the people who were calling you a fool and a half-wit? Didn't you get mad at them?"

"Ain't their fault," O'Haran mumbled. "The marshal put it in their heads."

"When did this mad spell come over you?"

"Dunno as I could say. Just recollect walkin' into the Long Branch."

"Today, right now . . ." Gryden hesitated for emphasis. "Do you feel it was wrong to kill Marshal McCarty?"

"The one was wrong was him," O'Haran said. "He's just dead, and it's all over for him. Everybody's still callin' me a fool."

"Your witness, Mr. Sutton."

Sutton's voice was crisp, demanding. "The Bible tells us it is wrong to kill, Mr. O'Haran. You know it's wrong, don't you?"

"David slew Goliath," O'Haran muttered. "Samson slew the Philistines with the jawbone of a ass. Wasn't nothin' wrong with that."

"You are hardly David or Samson, Mr. O'Haran. You knew you were wrong the instant you pulled the trigger— *didn't you*?"

"Nope, he made me mad and I killed him. Wasn't no more to it."

"But you thought about it beforehand," Sutton persisted. "You thought about it, and you planned it, and then you did it. Isn't that the way it happened?"

"Mebbe. Guess it could've happened that way. I don't rightly recollect."

"All the same, you're sure of one thing, Mr. O'Haran. You're sure you were justified in killing Marshal McCarty. Aren't you?"

"Damn bet'cha," O'Haran said, nodding to himself. "Nothin' worse'n being made a fool of."

"No further questions," Sutton said, smiling at the jury. "I rather believe that does it."

Gryden rose for a last question. "Tom, I want you to think hard and answer me honestly. Did you ever *once* feel it was wrong to kill Marshal McCarty? Just once?"

"Nope," O'Haran said. "Was him that wronged me. Glad I did it."

Sutton was convinced he'd won a conviction. In closing argument, he derided the notion that O'Haran was now or ever had been insane. He told the jurors that the accused, out of his own mouth, had convicted himself. Gryden was equally convinced he'd won an acquittal. His closing argument went to the testimony of Dr. Milton and, even more, the testimony of the defendant. He pressed the jurors to consider the words of a man so deranged that the act of killing seemed normal, completely rational, no more serious than swatting a fly. The only reasonable place for the insane, Gryden declared, was the insane asylum.

The jury was out ten minutes. When they filed back into the courtroom, Gryden saw by their solemn look that there was no compassion for a lunatic; their sole concern was retribution. The jury foreman, a hardscrabble farmer, rose when the judge asked for the verdict. The unanimous finding was guilty of murder in the first degree, with a recommendation of the death penalty. The courtroom went still when Judge Strang ordered the defendant to rise.

"Thomas O'Haran, you have been convicted of murder with premeditation, and I hereby sentence you to death by hanging. I further order that said sentence be carried out at nine o'clock the morning of May 1, 1878, in Leavenworth State Penitentiary. May God have mercy on your soul."

Gryden began forming an appeal even as the sentence was pronounced. Then, in the next instant, he knew the court of appeals would be less merciful than God. Thomas O'Haran, insane or not, was on his way to the gallows.

And long after he was dead, he would still be known as the village idiot.

EIGHT

Sutton left the house shortly before eight the next morning. Florence kissed him soundly at the door, having fed him a breakfast worthy of Caesar. She was thrilled by his victory, all but dancing for joy.

The house on Gospel Ridge was four blocks from the office. Sutton walked west on Spruce Street, his mood jaunty and a spring in his step. He was invigorated by the bracing air, a clear sky, and golden sunlight washing across the plains. He thought he'd never felt more alive.

At the corner of Spruce and Second Avenue, he turned downtown. The courthouse was two blocks farther on and several lawyers were outside on the walkway, waiting for court to convene. They stopped him, lavish with praise on the O'Haran conviction, and wrung his hand with great zest. He walked away with the sense that he'd somehow grown taller.

The offices of Sutton & Colborn were on the second floor of Wright's General Store, at the corner of Front Street and Second Avenue. An outside stairway led to the upper floor, and a freight wagon was backed into the loading dock at the rear of the store. Bob Wright stood watching as a clerk checked the manifest of goods being unloaded from the wagon. He spotted Sutton and hurried down the steps at the end of the dock.

"Congratulations, Mike!" he said heartily. "You're the talk of the town."

"Thank you, Bob," Sutton said. "Modesty aside, I'm feeling pretty high myself."

"And well you should, my friend."

Robert Wright was one of the original settlers of Dodge City. In the spring of 1873 he'd opened a trading post for buffalo hunters, and shipped two hundred thousand hides before the onset of winter. Over the years, as the town grew and prospered, his firm became the contractor for supplies to Fort Dodge and army posts throughout Indian Territory. He was widely acknowledged as the wealthiest man in town.

Wright was also a lifelong Republican. At forty-two, he had served as councilman and mayor of Dodge City and currently represented Ford County in the state legislature. He and Sutton were political allies as well as close friends, and despite his wealth and influence, he deferred to Sutton in political matters. The younger man's cunning and guile seemed to him the attributes necessary to lead the fractious members of the Gang. He was content with Sutton as the Kingfish of Ford County.

"Mike, you've done well," he said now. "Marshal McCarty had many friends hereabouts, and they're downright jubilant you've sent his killer to the gallows. Come the November elections, that'll pay big dividends."

Sutton grinned. "I couldn't be happier with the way things turned out. Justice has its own rewards."

"Not the least of which is grateful voters. You don't need me to tell you, it's a damn good thing you won."

"How could I have lost, Bob? I had an airtight case."

"Nothing's airtight where Harry Gryden's concerned. I heard he made a strong case for O'Haran being a nitwit."

"Well, he is a nitwit, he's just not insane. The jurors saw through that right away."

"Good thing for us," Wright allowed. "Like they say, heroes ride and goats walk. We'll ride this one all the way to the elections."

"Bob, you're reading my mind. Hanging the right man definitely translates into ballots."

Sutton waved as he went up the stairway. The offices of the law firm occupied the entire second floor, with an anteroom, a library filled with law books, and spacious quarters for the two partners. Ted Nance, their secretary and law clerk, was seated at his desk in the anteroom. He looked up as Sutton came through the door.

"Hail the victor!" he said with an ebullient smile. "Have you seen the morning newspaper?"

"Why, something worth reading?"

"Let's just say you're the man of the hour."

Nance handed him a copy of the *Dodge City Times*. Sutton scanned an article on yesterday's trial that occupied most of the front page. After recounting the conviction and the death sentence, the article went on to say that the county prosecutor had "crowned himself in glory." The story praised the sheriff as well, calling Bat Masterson "the nemesis of lawbreakers." Then, lauding City Marshal Ed Masterson, the article dubbed Sutton and the Masterson brothers as the "catch 'em and convict 'em trio." Harry Gryden was mentioned only in the context of a "buffoonish" defense effort.

"The power of the press," Sutton said, folding the newspaper. "Nick Klaine has a knack for turning a phrase. I particularly like the allusion to 'catch 'em and convict 'em.'"

Fred Colborn came out of his office. "Has a nice ring to it," he said. "You should make it your campaign slogan in November."

"Fred, you might have something there. Voters are partial to a prosecutor who gets convictions."

"Not to mention the death sentence for a murderer. People subscribe to an 'eye for an eye' brand of justice."

Colborn was a stout man, almost bald at thirty-three, with florid features and a walrus mustache. Two years ago, shortly after moving to Dodge City, he had gone into partnership with Sutton. Originally from Ohio, Colborn had served during the war with an infantry company and distinguished himself by earning a battlefield commission. Following the end of hostilities, he read law under an established attorney and was admitted to the bar in 1869. Seven years later, in quest of greater opportunity, he'd moved to the latest boomtown on the western plains. He brought with him a wife and four children and a zealot's commitment to the law.

Sutton liked him for his feisty disposition. Colborn was a scrapper in the courtroom, never hesitant to trade barbs with opposing counsel, and noted for his stinging ripostes. He was also a pragmatic Republican who believed there was no substitute for winning and followed the code that the end justifies the means. Sutton, always the wheeler-dealer, persuaded the mayor and the town council to appoint Colborn to the post of city attorney. His powers at the local level, in both civil and criminal actions, were similar to those of Sutton's at the county level. Between them, they controlled the legal machinery for all of Ford County, and there was never any question as to who gave the orders. Colborn followed wherever Sutton led.

"Mr. Sutton . . ." Ted Nauce hesitated, fumbling for words. "I mean, if it's not telling tales out of school, could I ask you something? I'd never repeat it to anyone."

Sutton nodded. "What is it, Ted?"

"I was just wondering about O'Haran. Is he a simpleton, or is he really nuts?"

"Does it matter?"

"I guess that's what I'm asking."

"Suppose he'd murdered your father, Ted. On the one hand he night be a half-wit, and on the other he might be a lunatic. What sentence would you impose?"

"Yessir, you're right," Nance said with sudden comprehension. "Doesn't matter one way or the other. He deserves to hang."

"And twice over!" Colborn added hotly. "He murdered a lawman."

Sutton walked to his office, still carrying the newspaper. Overlooking Front Street, the room was furnished with padded armchairs and a tall desk chair crafted in lush morocco leather. The walls were lined with framed diplomas and civic awards, and at the far end of the office, centered between windows with a view of the plaza, was a massive walnut desk waxed to a high sheen. The room seemed somehow appropriate for the Kingfish of Ford County.

Colborn followed him in and took one of the armchairs. Sutton seated himself and spread the newspaper on top of the desk. He stared at the article a long moment, his expression abstracted. He arched an eyebrow.

"The reference to Gryden is amusing, but it isn't accurate. Gryden is far from a buffoon."

"After that defense he put on?" Colborn said. "Seems to me he deserves a little ridicule."

"Never underestimate your opponent, Fred."

Sutton pulled a cigar from his inside coat pocket. He nipped the end with a penknife, struck a match, and lit up in a haze of blue smoke. He motioned with the cigar.

"Downstairs, I ran into Bob Wright. He was full of talk about how the O'Haran conviction will carry the elections in November. I come into the office and, in so many words, you expressed much the same thought."

"Am I missing something here, Mike? You sound concerned."

"November is a long way off, almost eight months. And Harry Gryden will run against me for county attorney."

Colborn looked perplexed. "I haven't heard anything about Gryden running. How would you know that?"

"Simple deduction." Sutton tapped the ash off his cigar. "Gryden is the most prominent Democrat in the county, and he's a very capable lawyer. Who else would they nominate?"

"Gryden is the proverbial loose cannon. I doubt he'd seek the nomination."

"You couldn't be more wrong, Fred. Not only does he dislike my politics, he holds me in the utmost contempt. Perhaps he doesn't know it yet, but he will be the Democratic candidate."

"You just lost me," Colborn said. "Why wouldn't he know it yet?"

"Harry isn't a schemer," Sutton replied. "Life for him is an improvisation, one day at a time. But the Democrats will bring him around, long before November."

"And am I hearing this right—you're worried?"

"Voters have a short memory. In a race for county attorney, a candidate is only as good as his last case. Anything can happen between now and November."

"Yes, that's true," Colborn said. "But you took Gryden out of the mix with the Stockgrowers' Association. His criminal practice has been severely restricted."

"Not severely enough," Sutton countered. "Assault, robbery, and murder occur all too frequently. After all, this is Dodge City."

"What about a move to get Gryden disbarred?"

"On what grounds?"

"We could drum up some charges. Even if it didn't work, it would damage his reputation."

Sutton considered a moment, the cigar wedged in the corner of his mouth. "No, I think not," he finally said. "Falsified charges could easily become a two-edged sword. I won't be accused of playing dirty politics."

"I suppose you're right." Colborn suddenly leaned across the desk, tapped the newspaper. "How about what you said earlier, when you read this article? The power of the press."

"What about it?"

"Nick Klaine hates Gryden the way the devil hates holy water. He'd be happy to write a series of unflattering articles. Something on the order of an exposé."

"An exposé." Sutton spoke the word as though testing its merits. "What improprieties do you have in mind?"

"Well, let's see," Colborn said with a hard grin. "How about living out-of-wedlock with Belle London? Or consorting with cardsharps, and whoremasters, and South Side riffraff? A man's known by the company he keeps."

"You're talking about character assassination."

"All's fair in love and war, Mike. And I'd say politics qualifies as warfare. Wouldn't you?"

Sutton was reminded again that his partner lacked certain scruples. Yet in the same instant, he reminded himself that the future of Dodge City was at stake. Even more, some aspect of economic stability, and a decent life for the town's citizens. Harry Gryden, he reflected, was not the man to lead them into the future. He nodded to Colborn.

"I like the way you think, Fred. You have a gift for subterfuge."

"So you'll talk with Klaine?"

"Yes, although it will require discretion. Nick will have to be convinced that it was *his* idea. A suggestion here, a nudge there. Nothing overt."

"You'll pull it off," Colborn said confidently. "Discretion is your strong suit."

"Some senator in ancient Rome once said, 'I have often regretted my speech, but never my silence.' We'll let Nick sling the mud in his newspaper."

"And there's plenty of mud to sling!"

Sutton puffed a wad of smoke at the ceiling. He thought politics, even in a noble cause, was sometimes a tawdry business. And in the course of things, character assassination had its place.

No man was more deserving than Harry Gryden.

NINE

A bright ball of fire was lodged directly overhead. The snow was long since melted off, and on the last Sunday in March the plains were baked hard as flint. Cottony clouds scudded across an azure sky on a warm southerly breeze.

There were five horses in the race. Three were owned by cattlemen, the fourth by an army officer, and the last by a whorehouse madam. The course was a quarter mile, laid out on a stretch of prairie flat as a billiard table. The favorite in the match was a sorrel mare, staked by the madam and ridden by a wiry stable boy. Everyone had a bet down.

On Sunday afternoons, weather permitting, the races were held on a treeless plain east of town. The proper citizens of Dodge City rarely attended, but the South Side was always well represented. Oddly enough, the officers from Fort Dodge saw nothing unseemly in associating with the sporting crowd so long as it involved horses. The races invariably drew three or four hundred spectators.

Fully half the residents of the South Side owned horses. Gamblers, saloonkeepers, and bordello madams kept horses stabled for no other purpose than the races.

Cowboys and ranchers, whose mounts were descended from ancient mustang herds, found their stock was particularly suited to quarter-mile heats. The army officers were partial to thoroughbreds, or the offshoots of blooded stock, and preferred to wager on longer races. A typical Sunday brought seventy or more horses to the track.

Luke Short and Ham Bell were the unofficial bookmakers. They set the odds, based on their knowledge of the horses, and covered bets from the throng of spectators. For the most part the bets were under fifty dollars, but Short and Bell readily accepted anything up to a thousand. There were also wagers among members of the crowd and between owners of horses, side bets that were often for substantial amounts. On any given Sunday, thousands of dollars were at stake on every race.

The course across the grassy prairie was lined with people on both sides. Some were seated in buckboards or carriages, others were mounted on horseback, and a number walked the mile or so from town. The mix always included soiled doves from the brothels and showgirls from the variety theaters, accompanied by their beaus for a festive outing. Everyone came dressed to the nines, for it was the social occasion of the week among the sporting crowd.

The driver of a landau carriage near the finish line kept his team on tight rein. Gryden and Belle occupied the rear seat of the carriage, and across from them were Jim "Dog" Kelley and his longtime companion, Dora Hand. Kelley was the mayor of Dodge City, one of Sutton's chief cronies, and Gryden had agreed to the joint outing only because Belle and Dora were close friends. Dora was also a singer, the star of the Lady Gay Variety Theater, directly across the street from the Comique. Yet instead of being jealous, the two women had become best friends and confidantes. They shared secrets sometimes never revealed to their men.

The finish line consisted of two poles planted in ground some thirty yards apart, with bright streamers fluttering at the top. Luke Short was stationed near the finish, taking bets from spectators, while Ham Bell worked the crowd at the starting line. Short kept track of the wagers with a pad and a stub pencil.

"Luke!" Gryden called out. "I'd like to get a bet down."

Short walked over to the carriage. "Always happy to oblige folks rolling in money. What's your pleasure?"

"How about Sally's horse?" Gryden asked, referring to the madam's mare. "What odds are you giving?"

"Even money on the favorite."

"And Captain Womack's horse? The roan gelding?"

"Five to three."

"Put me down for fifty dollars."

"That's decent odds," Kelley interjected. "I'll take a hundred myself."

Dog Kelley's nickname stemmed from his pastime of greyhound coursing. He kept a string of ten dogs in a kennel tended by a worker at the livery stable. Army officers and several cattlemen also bred dogs, and greyhound meets were popular during the summer months. The matches were held on open prairie, with the hounds chasing jackrabbits and the owners following the action on horseback. Kelley was particularly known as a high roller when betting on his dogs.

"I'll make a bet, too," Belle said, opening her purse.

"Something tells me Sally's mare will win, and even money seems very fair. Twenty dollars, if you please, Mr. Short."

"Yes, ma'am," Short said, jotting in his notepad. "You likely picked yourself a winner."

"And me, too!" Dora said with a dimpled smile. "Ladies have to stick together."

Kelley frowned. "C'mon now, you don't have to use your own money. I'll bet for you."

"No, thank you, honeybun," Dora said pertly. "Belle and I know what we're doing. Don't we, Belle?"

"We certainly do," Belle agreed. "As Mr. Short said, we've picked the winner."

"We'll show you boys a thing or two about horses!" Dora added with a wink.

Dora Hand was an attractive young woman with a lush figure. She was billed as "Queen of the Fairy Lovelies" at the Lady Gay and, like Belle, put on a show of popular ballads and sprightly dance numbers. A veteran of the stage, she had played at variety theaters in New Orleans, Memphis, and other Southern towns before securing a headliner engagement in Dodge City. She was in her second season at the Lady Gay.

Dog Kelley, among other men, had courted her with unrelenting attention and lavish gifts. But unlike other men, Kelley was owner of the Alhambra Saloon, mayor of the town, and clearly considered money no object. His generosity eventually won her affection, and much to the consternation of the uptown prudes, she became his paramour. He was one of Dodge's original settlers, and his small house was south of the tracks, opposite the east end of the plaza. She'd moved in shortly before Christmas last year. Neither of them ever spoke of marriage.

"Oh, *look*!" Belle jumped from her seat. "They're almost ready."

The five horses were roughly lined up on the distant prairie. Ham Bell, who also acted as the official starter, raised his pistol in the air and fired. The riders were bent low in the saddle, jabbing with their spurs, and the horses burst from a standing start to a headlong gallop. The whorehouse madam's sorrel mare immediately took the lead, running neck and neck with Captain Womack's roan gelding. The horses covered the quarter-mile course with blinding speed, the crowd roaring and leaping about on the sidelines. The sorrel mare crossed the finish line half a length ahead of the gelding.

"We won!" Dora squealed. "We won!"

Belle hugged her, and Gryden and Kelley exchanged a look of mild disgust. The horses slowed a furlong farther on and the riders brought them about in a prancing walk. At either end of the course, the crowd broke and began milling around Short and Ham Bell. Sally Maxwell, the madam with the speedy mare, jubilantly bounced up and down in her carriage, surrounded by a bevy of her girls. Money began exchanging hands as winners laughed and losers groaned.

"Well, boys?" Belle said with an impish smile. "Aren't you sorry you didn't bet on the mare?"

"Not for even money," Gryden said indulgently. "Win big or lose big, that's my motto."

"And you lost," Dora gibed happily. "Maybe Belle and I should treat you boys to supper tonight."

"Don't rub it in," Kelley said glumly. "That mare only won by a nose."

Dora laughed. "I hate to say it, sweetie, but you're a big fibber. Isn't he, Belle?"

"Definitely," Belle said slyly. "Almost as big as Harry."

Bat and Ed Masterson threaded their way through the crowd. As sheriff and city marshal, they felt obligated to attend the Sunday races and maintain order. Sore losers were sometimes a problem, and anyone who tried to welch on a bet invariably brought on a fight. Bat, with Ed at his side, stopped by the carriage.

"Mr. Mayor," Bat said, nodding to Kelley. "Winning a bundle?"

"Not today," Kelley informed him. "Sally's mare just cost me a hundred."

"Well, maybe you'll win the next one."

"I generally win more than I lose. I've got no complaints."

Masterson glanced across at Gryden. "Saw that article about you in the *Times*. Didn't know you're such a sport."

The article had appeared in yesterday's *Dodge City Times*. A subtle piece, the article lauded Gryden as the most prominent criminal defense attorney in Ford County. But then, as though providing background material, the story went on to review Gryden's habitual play at the gaming tables and identify his many friends and associates among the sporting crowd. The impression left was that of an attorney with an unsavory reputation.

Gryden understand that Masterson, ever the good Republican, was now trying to needle him. He waved it off. "Sheriff, you shouldn't believe everything you read in the paper. Nick Klaine wouldn't know a fact if he stumbled across one."

Masterson managed a tight smile. "You callin' him a liar?"

"Not exactly," Gryden said. "I believe he's more of a propagandist."

"You lawyers always throw me with your two-dollar words. What's a propagandist?"

"Someone who twists innuendo to look like the truth."

Masterson nodded as though he understood. He tipped his hat to the women, glanced again at Kelley, and then led his brother off into the crowd. There was a moment of uncomfortable silence until Kelley cleared his throat. He turned to Gryden.

"That's a pretty serious charge. You called Nick Klaine everything but a liar."

"Dog, let's not pretend," Gryden said. "Klaine is the dummy and Mike Sutton is the ventriloquist. Everything in the article was straight out of Sutton's mouth."

"Hold on now," Kelley grated. "Sounds like you're callin' Sutton a liar."

Gryden, much to his own surprise, had always liked Dog Kelley. Although a Republican and a central member of Sutton's Gang, Kelley was straightforward and never given to duplicity. He was simply too gullible for his own good, an unwitting stooge. Gryden tried to soften his tone.

"There's no love lost between Sutton and myself. Let's just write it off as a personal matter."

Kelley rubbed his jaw. "All the same, you think he'd lie about you?"

"Yes, I do."

"Why would he do a thing like that?"

"Dog, if I knew, I'd tell you. I'm in the dark myself."

"Well, hell, Harry, it's not right callin' a man a liar when you don't even know why. Have you ever asked him about it?"

"I wouldn't trust Mike Sutton to tell me the truth."

"Boys, boys," Belle scolded. "We came here to have a good time. Let's not spoil it with politics."

"Belle's right," Dora added with a pouty little smile. "It's Sunday, and we're supposed to be enjoying ourselves. It isn't fair!"

"Now, honey, don't get yourself upset," Kelley said in a mollifying voice. "Harry and me didn't mean nothing by it. Did we, Harry?"

Gryden grinned. "Idle talk, ladies, nothing more."

The next race was a match race. Captain Gunther, a cavalry officer from Fort Dodge, offered to match his thoroughbred stallion against any horse, at a distance of a half mile. Carl Richter, whose ranch was south of town, accepted the challenge, trotting out a long-legged stallion he'd traded off the Cherokees, in Indian Territory. The stakes were set between Gunther and Richter, with agreement that the finish line would be moved across the prairie to a half mile. Luke Short and Ham Bell got busy working the crowd for bets.

Gryden and Kelley liked the look of the Indian horse, called Cherokee. Belle and Dora, after whispered consultation, bet on the army stallion, Steeldust. The horses were brought to the starting line, their riders mounted, and the crowd fell silent. Steeldust was a barrel-chested animal, all sinew and muscle, standing sixteen hands high and well over a thousand pounds in weight. A blood bay, with a black tail and mane, his hide glistened in the sun like polished redwood. Cherokee was tall and powerful, a rangy chesnut stallion, fiery-eyed and nostrils flared wide. He pawed the earth as if he spurned it and longed to fly.

Ham Bell fired his pistol into the air. The riders, digging hard with their spurs, exhorted their horses with loud shouts and surged across the starting line. Steeldust jumped to an early lead, clods of dirt flung from his hooves, with Cherokee scarcely a length behind. The crowd raised their voices in rollicking cries, fists pumping wildly, as the stallions pounded over the prairie. The race was even most of the way, the riders slashing with their quirts, first one horse, then the other pulling slightly ahead. A few yards from the finish line, Steeldust put on an explosive burst of speed and took it by a nose. The crowd shouted themselves hoarse.

"Oh, my God!" Dora screamed. "We won, Belle! We won again!"

Belle threw her arms around Gryden and kissed him so hard his teeth hurt. Kelley slumped back in the carriage seat, his features downcast, tossing his hands in the air. He looked at Gryden.

"Harry, we can't win for losing."

"No, Dog," Gryden said. "We're the big winners today."

"How do you figure that?"

"We've got the happiest fillies at the race."

"You know . . ." Kelley glanced at the women as they laughed gaily, their faces flushed with excitement. "Way things look, it might just be our lucky night."

Gryden smiled. "I'd bet the bank on it."

TEN

Belle looked like a small girl lost in sweet dreams. She lay curled on her side, her eyes closed, her hair fanned across the pillow in golden locks. Her expression was one of vestal innocence.

Gryden finished knotting his tie, watching her in the armoire mirror. He took pains not to wake her, for he thought the girl beneath the woman was never more apparent than in gentle repose. With a last look he slipped into his suit jacket and left the bedroom. He pegged his hat off the hall tree as he went out the door.

The morning was pleasantly sunny, a bank of cumulus clouds distant on the horizon. Outside the hotel, Gryden moved along the boardwalk as merchants opened their doors for business. A block downstreet, as he passed the *Ford County Globe,* he saw Dan Frost through the front window. Frost hurried to the door, motioning him inside.

"'Morning, Harry," Frost said. "Have you got a minute?"

"I can always spare a minute, Dan."

Gryden stepped into the office. Frost, like most frontier newsmen, ran a bootstrap operation. There was a battered desk up front, littered with foolscap, and at the rear an oily press stained dark with ink. The printer, his hands black, was swigging a mug of coffee.

Frost was a skeletal man, all knobs and joints, his clothes hanging loose from his slender frame. He pulled Gryden away from the window. "We need to put our heads together," he said in a conspiratorial voice. "That shabby article the *Times* ran on you can't go unanswered. The whole purpose was to smear your reputation."

"You're right as rain," Gryden said. "Sunday afternoon at the races, I told Dog Kelley it was Sutton's handiwork. He got Nick Klaine to do a hatchet job."

"The *Times* is nothing but a sleazy rag and Klaine's the biggest whore in Ford County. He'd sooner print a pack of lies than an iota of truth."

Frost was impervious to the irony of the insult. The Republicans charged him with partisan bias and labeled the *Globe* as an insidious organ for the Democrats. He went on with hardly a pause for breath.

"I say we retaliate with a piece on Sutton. Paint him upside down and inside out with a tar brush."

"Easier said than done," Gryden observed. "So far as I know, Sutton doesn't have any vices. He's a deacon in the church, he doesn't chase women, and he wouldn't play cards with Saint Peter. What would you say about him?"

Frost smirked. "I'd dub him 'Little Caesar.'"

"What does that mean?"

"Well, he's only slightly taller than a midget and he thinks he's the Julius Caesar of Dodge City. So we'll anoint him with the title—Little Caesar."

Gryden shook his head with amusement. "Dan, I have to say, you're a cruel man."

"Why the hell not?" Frost said, waving his arms. "After what they did to you, it's tit for tat."

"Nothing would crucify him more than ridicule."

"You like the idea, then?"

"Yeah, it's a real pip." Gryden checked his pocket watch. "I'm due in court and I have to stop by the office first. When will you run the article?"

"I'll start writing it today."

Frost walked him to the door. Gryden hurried along the street, quietly laughing to himself at the thought of Little Caesar. He told himself that Sutton would, at the very least, have a roaring conniption fit. A couple minutes later Gryden turned into the office.

Velma Oxnard was at her desk. "I was wondering where you were."

"Everything in the nick of time, Velma. Do you have those papers?"

"Just what you asked for," she said, offering a leather portfolio case. "A copy of the suit filing and the financial statements."

"Very funny," Gryden said. "I wouldn't have thought to call it a financial statement."

Thomas Jones stepped out of his office. "What's on tap for today, Harry?"

"The landmark case of the century. *Mix versus Hoover.*"

"Yes, of course, the vanishing water pump."

"Civil litigation at its lowest ebb.

"But as Velma says—"

"Bread and butter," Velma said.

"I know," Gryden grumped. "It pays the bills."

"Absolutely tragic," Jones said with a wry smile. "A criminal lawyer with no criminals to defend."

"So meanwhile, it's my turn in the barrel."

"Perhaps you shouldn't have accepted the retainer from the Stockgrowers Association."

"Tom, it's one of the great mistakes of my life. I'd much rather be defending a horse thief than litigating personal squabbles."

"But with no horse thieves—?"

"I'm stuck with the water pump."

Gryden tucked the portfolio under his arm. He waved, hurrying through the door, and turned toward the center of town. The date was March 26, scarcely a week since he'd lost the O'Haran murder trial. A petition had been filed with the state appellate court, but it seemed foreordained that Gryden's client would hang. He felt somehow diminished by his involvement in a niggling civil suit.

The municipal court was housed in a frame building across the street from the courthouse. Every township in Ford County had a municipal court, and the city judges were elected for a term of two years. The jurisdiction of the court included minor civil and criminal suits, preliminary hearings prior to impanelling a grand jury, and formal inquests involving death by suspicious or violent means. The judges were compensated with fees based on court costs and fines levied.

In Dodge City, as in other townships, the municipal court was a mirror image of the community. The presiding judge was charged with regulating every form of vice governed by town ordinance and state law. Destructive acts, such as disturbing the peace and malicious mischief, were considered greater offenses than prostitution or gambling. Bordellos and gaming dives could be taxed for the economic good, whereas drunken cowboys and destruction of property reflected badly on the community. Vice was a virtue in terms of filling the town treasury.

Gryden entered the courtroom shortly before nine o'-clock. His client was Miles Mix, a deputy sheriff in Masterson's office and the plaintiff in today's civil action. Mix was a bear of a man, noted for his ham-fisted enforcement of the law, and a loyal Republican. Yet he saw nothing irregular or disloyal about retaining Gryden, for party politics was not at issue in Mix's suit. Like many people, he simply thought Gryden was the smartest lawyer in town.

Mix was standing by a table near the jury box. He nodded as Gryden came down the aisle. "All set to bust some heads, Mr. Gryden?"

Gryden placed his leather portfolio on the table. "Miles, this is a lawsuit, not a prizefight. Let's try to keep it halfway civilized."

"Hoover's a horse's ass and a goddamn cheat. You want me to treat him like we're friends?"

"What I really want is for you to drop the suit. You won't recover enough to make it worthwhile. I've told you that before."

"No, I'm gonna sue," Mix said stubbornly. "Everybody needs to know Hoover's a liar and a cheat. I'm dependin' on you to prove that."

Gryden knew all along it was a matter of personal vindication rather than the monetary value of the suit. His client believed he'd been cheated, and what he was really after was revenge. Mix intended to humiliate Hoover in a public arena and have it reported in the newspapers. Pride, Gryden thought, often had little to do with common sense.

George Hoover entered the courtroom with his lawyer, David Swan. Hoover was a rotund businessman, with fleshy jowls and a bulbous nose. He owned the largest wholesale liquor company in western Kansas as well as a half interest in the Granger's State Bank. He was known as a shrewd operator, sometimes underhanded in his business dealings. His girth was a testament to his prosperity.

The lawsuit stemmed from the sale of a house. Hoover had built a new home, more befitting his social standing, in the Gospel Ridge residential area. He sold his old home, a modest dwelling at the west end of town, to Deputy Sheriff Miles Mix. When Mix took possession of the house, he discovered that the manual water pump in the kitchen had been removed. His suit contended that the pump was part of the permanent fixtures of the house. The pump was valued at twenty-five dollars.

Hoover seated himself at the defense table, avoiding eye contact with Mix. David Swan motioned to Gryden and moved to the side of the courtroom. Swan was a mild-mannered man, a longtime resident of Dodge City, and a respected litigator. He and Gryden had appeared as opposing counsel several times over the years, and like most lawyers, their relationship was one of mutual esteem. He nodded as Gryden crossed the courtroom.

"Good morning, Harry," he said affably. "I thought we might try once more to settle this matter in an amicable manner. The whole thing is ridiculous."

"Dave, I couldn't agree more," Gryden said. "All

Hoover had to do was replace the pump and we wouldn't be here today. If anything, it's become a comedy of errors."

"Suppose we offered twenty dollars in restitution? Would that satisfy Mix?"

"No, I'm afraid it's too late for any sort of settlement. My client is determined to have his day in court."

"But why?" Swan said. "It's such a picayune amount of money."

Gryden laughed. "I didn't say it made sense, Dave. I think it's come down to whose ox gets gored."

City Marshal Ed Masterson entered through a door at the rear of the courtroom. He was followed by Judge Rufus Cook, who presided over the municipal court. Cook was a sparrow of a man, thin and stoop shouldered, with frizzy gray hair and thick spectacles. He walked to the bench and seated himself.

"Court will come to order," Masterson said, taking his place before the bench. "First case on the docket is *Mix versus Hoover.*"

"Morning, gentlemen," Judge Cook said, squinting through his spectacles. "Everybody's here, so no need for delay. Mr. Gryden, call the first witness for the plaintiff."

Gryden stood. "The plaintiff is our only witness, Your Honor."

Miles Mix was sworn in by Masterson and took the stand. Gryden led Mix through a recounting of purchasing the house on Elm Street and later, after taking possession, discovering that the kitchen pump was missing. The testimony was brief, and as Mix left the stand Gryden presented a written statement from Wallack's Hardware Store noting the value of a replacement pump at twenty-five dollars. He ended with the argument that a water pump, like doors or windows, was an accepted part of a house sale.

George Hoover was called for the defense. After he was sworn in, Swan elicited testimony that the house had been sold in good faith, at a reasonable price. Hoover further testified that he had arranged a mortgage loan for Mix with the Granger's State Bank. Swan paused by the witness stand.

"Now we come to the matter of the water pump," he said. "Was there ever any understanding the pump was included with the sale of the house?"

"No, there wasn't," Hoover said adamantly. "Mix and me agreed the pump didn't go with the house."

"A verbal agreement?"

"Yes, it was."

"Why didn't you put it in writing?"

"We shook hands on it," Hoover said. "Guess it was my mistake to accept his word."

"You goddamn liar!"

Mix started out of his chair. Gryden grabbed his arm and forcibly pulled him back down. Judge Cook hammered his gavel, his jowls flushed with indignation. He peered down from the bench.

"Mr. Mix, I will not tolerate profanity in my courtroom. Any further outbursts and you will be held in contempt."

"We apologize, Your Honor," Gryden said quickly. "I assure you it won't happen again."

"See that it doesn't."

On cross-examination, Gryden was unable to shake Hoover's story. He went over it three times, and Hoover continued to insist that the pump was not included in the deal. Finally, with a scornful shrug, Gryden walked away from the stand.

Hoover started across the courtroom. As he went past the plaintiff's table, Mix rose and leaped across the table, bodily slamming Hoover to the floor. Mix slugged him in the jaw, then landed a blow to the mouth, cursing as he threw the punches. For all his bulk, Hoover was stronger than he appeared, and he somehow grabbed Mix in a vise lock. The scuffle quickly evolved into a wrestling match.

City Marshal Masterson jumped into the fray and managed to pry the men apart. Gryden and Swan took hold of their respective clients, and after a good deal of shoving and shouting the men were separated. Hoover's lip was split, leaking blood, and Mix's shirt was ripped down the front, exposing his hairy chest. Judge Cook hammered his gavel so hard the shaft splintered and broke. His face was purple with rage.

"Deputy Mix, you are a disgrace!" he shouted. "As an officer of the law, you have brought infamy on this court. I hold you in contempt."

Judge Cook awarded Mix twenty-five dollars' damages for the water pump. He then assessed George Hoover twenty-seven dollars for recording fees and court costs. Lastly, with a cold glare, he fined Mix a hundred dollars for contempt of court. Everyone stood as Cook stalked out of the courtroom.

"Jesus Christ," Mix muttered in dismay. "My salary's only seventy-five a month. How the hell am I gonna pay the fine?"

"You were awarded twenty-five," Gryden said. "Add

that to a month's salary and there's your fine. Think of it as a moral victory."

"Yeah, but I still have to pay you."

"You won the case and you got to punch Hoover a couple times. Was it worth it?"

"I dunno," Mix mumbled. "That's fifty dollars a punch."

"Yes, but was it worth it?"

"Well, yeah, maybe it was."

Gryden smiled. "I'll send you a bill."

ELEVEN

The cattle season got off to an early start. The weather was unseasonably warm, and Texas cattlemen pressed north along the Western Trail at the beginning of March. The first herds arrived on the Arkansas the afternoon of April 9.

On the holding grounds across the river, a sea of longhorns awaited shipment to Eastern slaughterhouses. More herds were expected daily, and the Santa Fe estimated that three hundred thousand cows would be driven to railhead by the end of trailing season. Texas cattlemen would collect upward of $8 million, and a good part of it would be spent in Dodge City. All of which promised a banner year for the Queen of Cowtowns.

The South Side was a carnival of vice. Some three hundred cowboys were in town, fresh off the trail and their pockets stuffed with over a month's wages. There was a riotous atmosphere along Second Avenue, drunken Texans crowding into whorehouses, saloons, variety theaters, and dance halls. As dusk turned to dark, the street was bathed in flickering lamplight and the discordant strain of banjos and rinky-dink pianos filled the night.

The sporting crowd went about the business of reducing the cowhands to instant paupers.

Ed Masterson and one of his deputies, Nat Haywood, patrolled the street. Already, with dark hardly upon the town, they had arrested three drunks and thrown them into the crude jailhouse just south of the tracks. The other two deputies on the force were assigned to guard the Deadline and ensure that none of the Texans tried to hoorah the uptown plaza. The boardwalks were jammed with rowdy cowboys as Masterson and Haywood passed the Lone Star saloon and crossed Locust Street. A block farther on they entered the red-light district.

Maple Street, which fronted the river, was home to the world's oldest profession. At the corner of Maple and Second Avenue, there were parlor houses offering young, attractive girls, where the charge was two dollars for ten minutes. Farther east and west were the brothels, where the women were older and jaded and the tariff was four bits a pop. A commotion broke out in one of the houses as Masterson and Haywood rounded the corner onto Maple. Women were screeching in caterwauling octaves as they hurried through the door.

The women were whores in flimsy shifts and peekaboo undergarments. Their anger was directed at two cowhands who smelled of sweaty horses and ripe manure. The whores had the men surrounded, hopping about in agitation and shaking their fists with loud shouts. Irene Baxter, the madam of the house, was the loudest of all.

"Alright, alright," Masterson said, wading into the melee. "What's the trouble here?"

"These yahoos"—Irene Baxter thrust a finger at the Texans—"say they been cheated."

"Cheated how?"

"They claim my girls popped their rocks too quick. The bastards want more pussy!"

"Do they?" Masterson turned to the cowhands. "What's your story, gents?"

The Texans shuffed their feet like naughty schoolboys. The taller one finally found his voice. "Four bits oughta get more'n a couple humps. Wham, bam, and they'd done us."

"Sounds like you boys were a mite randy. Couldn't hold it, that what you're saying?"

"Yeah, but it was still damn fast."

"Here's the deal," Masterson said. "Leave these ladies to their business or spend the night in jail. What'll it be?"

"Well . . ." The taller one exchanged a glance with his partner. "Reckon we'll just be on our way."

"Good idea."

The Texans went out the door muttering to themselves. Masterson turned to the madam. "Irene, try giving your customers a little more for their money. Send 'em away satisfied."

Irene Baxter laughed. "We'll give them three humps instead of two. How's that sound, Marshal?"

"Whatever it takes to make them happy."

Masterson led the way through the door. On the street, Haywood shook his head. "Four bits is half a day's pay for them cowboys. Small wonder they felt cheated."

"Nat, our job's to protect the whores, not the cowboys. We do what we're paid for."

"Yeah, I guess you're right."

"I usually am."

After touring the red-light district, they headed back up Second Avenue. As they approached the Lady Gay Variety Theater, they saw two trailhands standing in the middle of the street. The men were clearly tanked on rotgut whiskey and out to tree the town. A crowd of Texans was gathered three deep on the boardwalk, watching with amusement. One of the men in the street raised his pistol overhead and fired.

"Gonna shoot the stars outta the sky. Lemme howl!"

"Whooeee!" the other one bellowed, firing his gun into the air. "Let 'er rip!"

Masterson bulled a path through the crowd. Haywood was only a step behind, but the gap suddenly closed in a shoulder-to-shoulder wedge. He roughly shoved at the knot of men, trying to squeeze past. Four of them at the front held him boxed tight.

"Stay put, Deputy," one of the Texans said. "That's Jack Wagner and Alf Walker, and they're meaner'n tiger spit. You don't want no part of them boys."

"Move aside!" Haywood ordered. "Out of the way."

"Just tryin' to stop you from gettin' yourself killed."

"Goddammit, let me past!"

Masterson was in the center of the street. He slowed as he approached the cowhands, arms spread wide. "Fun's over," he said in a firm voice. "Nobody's hurt and I aim to keep it that way. Let's have those guns."

"Hell you say!" Wagner shouted. "I ain't fixin' to spend the night in jail."

"Mister, you broke the law when you fired that gun. Don't give me any trouble."

"You mess with me and you ain't got nothin' but trouble."

Masterson grabbed his gun arm. Wagner grappled with him and there was a muffled explosion. Shot in the stomach, his shirt on fire from the muzzle blast, Masterson staggered backward. He pulled his pistol, fire licking around his belt buckle, a ghastly expression on his face. The Texans were jarred out of their stupor as his pistol came level; an instant too late, they raised their guns. He fired four shots in a blinding roar.

A slug caught Wagner in the chest, and he went down with a strangled grunt. Walker was struck in the arm, the shoulder, and the chest, lurching backward under the impact. He somehow kept his balance, wobbling across the street, and collapsed on the boardwalk in front of Peacock's Saloon. Masterson stumbled in the opposite direction, flames still licking at his shirt, and the pistol slipped from his hand. He fell dead in the doorway of the Lady Gay.

Haywood finally broke through the crowd and rushed to Masterson's side. Charlie Bassett, the Assistant City Marshal, scattered onlookers as he sprinted down the street. A moment later Bat Masterson hurried along the boardwalk, his pace slowing as he saw the men huddled outside the Lady Gay. The sharp odor of blood mixed with burnt cloth steamed off the body as he moved closer, suddenly dropped to his knees. His brother's sightless eyes were fixed on the sky.

"They've killed him," he said hollowly. "Mother of God, they've killed Ed."

Bassett glared at Haywood. "Where the hell were you?"

"Them Texans held me back," Haywood said in a cracked voice. "Wasn't nothin' I could do."

"Who you talkin' about?"

"Them four over there."

Haywood nodded toward the cowhands at the front of the crowd. Bassett studied them a moment, then lowered his voice. "Follow my lead, Nat," he said quietly. "We're gonna arrest those boys."

"Why would we arrest them?"

" 'Cause if we don't, Bat will kill them sure as hell. Let's go."

They left Masterson hunched over his brother. Bassett moved forward, Haywood at his side, and stopped in front of the four Texans. "You boys are under arrest," he said coldly. "Don't give me an excuse to kill you."

"What the hell for?" one of the cowhands squawked. "We ain't done nothin'."

The crowd muttered angrily, and Basssett snapped his gun out of the holster. "Stand clear!" he ordered. "Anybody tries anything, you're dead."

Doc Milton arrived as Bassett and Haywood marched the Texans uptown. He knelt down beside Masterson and put a finger to the neck of the fallen marshal. He looked up with a sorrowful expression.

"There's nothing to be done, Bat. He's gone."

Masterson stared down at his brother with a vacant gaze. His voice was so soft it was almost a whisper. "Sonsabitches."

"How's that?" Doc Milton said.

"Dirty sonsabitches."

The town was in shock. The next morning every business establishment on the Front Street plaza draped its windows in black bunting. The city council met in emergency session and passed a resolution that was published in both newspapers.

> **WHEREAS, Edward J. Masterson, Marshal of the City of Dodge City, was on the night on April 9th, 1878, killed in the lawful discharge of his duties, be it RESOLVED by the Council of the City of Dodge City, that in his death the city has lost an officer who was not afraid to do his duty, and who never shrank from its faithful performance; a worthy servant and an upright citizen.**

The people of Dodge City were not satisfied that Jack Wagner and Alf Walker were dead. The town wanted a public sacrifice, the trial and punishment of the four men rumored to be accomplices in the death of Ed Masterson. Nor was Bat Masterson content that his brother, even in the moment of dying, had summoned the strength to kill his assailants. Undone by grief, the sheriff demanded retribution.

Mike Sutton, in his capacity as county attorney, had his ear attuned to the groundswell of public opinion. From a political standpoint, he was fully aware that a trial in open court would have significant impact on voters in the November elections. Early that morning, he filed a formal complaint against the cowhands with the Ninth District court. The charge was accessory to murder.

Judge Strang appointed Harry Gryden as defense counsel. The four Texans were all but penniless, and the court had the power to require any attorney to "volunteer" his services. Gryden met with the judge in chambers late that morning and expressed his displeasure at being drafted in an unpopular cause. The judge informed Gryden that he had no choice in the matter and, further, that the preliminary hearing would be held tomorrow morning. Gryden trudged off to the jail to interview his clients.

The burial was the most elaborate in the town's history. At three that afternoon, the funeral procession started from the First Methodist Church. The hearse was followed by Bat Masterson and members of the city council and directly behind, resplendent in their uniforms, the men of the Dodge City Fire Company. To the rear were twenty buggies and carriages with townsmen and their wives, many from the South Side. The cortege slowly wound its way to the Prairie Grove Cemetery, a peaceful spot on the plains northeast of town. There, the Reverend Orville Burton performed the graveside services.

The next morning many of the same people were seated in the Ninth District courtroom. Having attended the funeral, they were now on hand to see the men implicated in the murder of their marshal. Bat Masterson, with a squad of armed deputies, got the men seated at the defense table beside Gryden. Their names were John Hungate, Thomas Highlander, Thomas Roads, and John Reece. They were young and frightened, clearly terrified they would be bound over for trial after the preliminary hearing. Everyone stood as Judge Strang took his seat at the bench.

The first witness called was Dr. Benjamin Milton. Under Sutton's questioning, Milton explained that Marshal Masterson had died from a gunshot wound, the bullet entering above the navel and exiting near the spine. The next witness sworn was Deputy Marshal Nat Haywood, and Sutton led him through a recounting of the shooting itself.

Sutton then turned to the matter of the alleged accessories, and Haywood testified how he had been blocked
by the four Texans. He was adamant that the Texans had
deliberately stopped him from assisting the marshal.

"No further questions," Sutton said, walking away.
"Your witness, Mr. Gryden."

Gryden approached the stand. "Deputy Haywood,
what did Mr. Hungate—the man on the left at the defense
table—say to you at the time of the incident?"

"I ordered him to move aside," Haywood replied. "He
come back with how he was tryin' to keep me from getting killed. That's pretty close to his words."

"So neither Mr. Hungate nor his friends threatened you
or Marshal Masterson. Isn't that true?"

"Wasn't exactly a threat, I guess."

"There were only four of them in a crowd of forty or
fifty men. Why didn't you just go around them?"

"Happened too fast," Haywood said, averting his gaze.
"I was still yelling at them when the shootin' started."

"Come now, Deputy," Gryden said pointedly. "The
truth is, you were talking rather than thinking. You could
have easily gone around them. Isn't that so?"

"Yeah, lookin' back, that's what I should've done.
Course, you're talkin' hindsight."

"Or foresight, if you had taken two steps in either direction. Tell the court, are these men from the same cattle
outfit as Wagner and Walker? Were they friends?"

"I suppose not," Haywood admitted grudgingly. "Wagner and Walker rode for another outfit. We checked it out
yesterday."

"So there was no conspiracy?" Gryden pressed.
"These men were not involved in the murder of Marshal

Masterson. You found no evidence to that effect, did you?"

"No, we didn't."

"You questioned Marshal Bassett's decision to arrest these men. Why was that?"

Haywood looked startled. "Well, way it seemed to me, they hadn't had no part in the shooting."

"Yet Marshal Bassett insisted that they be arrested immediately, that very moment. What reason did he give you?"

"Uh . . . I'm not sure—"

"You're under oath, Deputy. What did he say?"

"Near as I remember," Haywood muttered, "he wanted them locked up so Sheriff Masterson wouldn't kill them. Think that's how he said it."

"I see." Gryden paused, as if surprised by the revelation. "So they were arrested as a matter of their own safety, not as accessories. Correct?"

"Yeah, you might say that."

"Deputy, I believe that is your testimony. These men were simply in the wrong place at the wrong time. Isn't that so?"

"They would've done better to be somewheres else."

"And Sheriff Masterson, overwrought with grief, might have mistakenly killed them. Isn't that true?"

"Well, that's what Charlie Bassett said."

"No further questions of this witness, Your Honor."

Sutton failed to undo the damage on redirect examination. When he called Bassett to the stand, Sutton was unable to solicit testimony that would overturn Haywood's version of events. On cross-examination, Gryden forced Bassett to admit he'd never thought the Texans would be charged as accessories. The decision to bring charges was made by County Attorney Sutton.

Gryden declined to call the Texans to the stand. Instead, he moved that the charges be dismissed. "By their own admission," he said, "the officers at the scene of the shooting never once thought my clients were involved. The charges are baseless and without foundation, Your Honor."

Judge Strang took a long moment to weigh the matter. In the end, albeit with a frown of deep reluctance, he ordered the four cowhands released from custody. He tried to salve the decision by noting that, based on the evidence, a trial would not serve the interests of justice. Few in the courtroom appeared to buy the argument.

Gryden saw a look of naked rage cross Bat Masterson's face. He turned to the Texans, who appeared bewildered by their sudden turn of fortune. He kept his voice low.

"I'm going to give you men some good advice. Get out of town and ride like your lives depend on it. Don't stop till you get to Texas."

"Why's that?" John Hungate said with a dopey grin. "You just proved we didn't do nothin'. Hell, we're free as birds."

"Yes, for now," Gryden said. "But if you're smart, you won't be caught in town after dark."

"C'mon, you really think somebody'd kill us?"

"Let me put it this way. Gamblers right now are placing bets on how long you live. Odds are you won't last the night."

"You're shittin' me!"

"No, actually, I'm betting you're a dead man."

The Texans rode out of town within the hour. Gryden thought they had escaped death twice over. Once if they'd faced a jury . . .

And twice at the hands of Bat Masterson.

TWELVE

The sheriff's office was on the ground floor of the courthouse. The morning after the release of the four Texans, Bat Masterson called a meeting of all peace officers in Dodge City. The summons was not one to be ignored.

Masterson was the top law enforcement officer in Ford County. He had been elected by a large plurality, and he'd served with distinction after pinning on the badge. In the five months since taking office, he had apprehended bank robbers, train robbers, and an assortment of livestock thieves. His record to date was that of a lawman who always brought the outlaws to justice.

Only twenty-five, Masterson was originally from Canada. His father, a farmer, had moved the family from Canada to Illinois, and finally, in 1867, to Kansas. In 1872, burned out on farming, Masterson followed the lure of fast money into the buffalo trade. Late in 1874, by then a seasoned plainsman, he served as an army scout in the Red River War against the Comanche and Kiowa. In 1876, after settling in Dodge City, he bought a saloon and began forming political alliances. He'd sold the saloon following his election as sheriff.

The newspapers credited Masterson with having killed between fifteen and twenty men. The truth, as only his closest friends knew, was that he'd killed only one man in a face-to-face gunfight. His reputation notwithstanding, he was a man of courage and grit, and his days as a buffalo hunter, army scout, and saloonkeeper had versed him in the ways of the rough life. His immediate friends were gamblers and gunmen, and his loyalties lay with the sporting crowd on the South Side. Political alliances gave him currency with the uptown crowd, but he knew his rightful place was below the Deadline. Like everyone on the South Side, he held Texans in the utmost contempt.

The release of the four cowhands yesterday left him embittered and filled with simmering anger. Privately, he cursed the quickness with which Charlie Bassett had arrested them; bent over his dead brother, he hadn't known of their involvement until they were in jail. Had he known, he would have killed them on the spot or died trying. Their savior, the silver-tongued Harry Gryden, might be blamed as well; but Masterson's anger was directed now at all Texans, not just the four who had escaped. His brother was in the ground only two days, and deep in his gut he still felt as if he had swallowed molten lead. He swore to himself that there would be retribution, payment exacted in full.

The meeting had been called for eight o'clock. Undersheriff Joe Bohannon and deputies Miles Mix and Walt Frazer were seated in the outer office. They were competent peace officers, brave in the face of danger, but they were unsettled by Masterson's sullen mood. Their boss was in his private office, staring out the window, and although they weren't sure as to the purpose of the meeting, they sensed a storm was brewing. Masterson had become withdrawn since his brother's death, his features rigid and his eyes hard. They knew whatever he was planning wouldn't be pleasant.

Charlie Bassett came through the hallway door. He was followed by deputies Nat Haywood and Larry Johnson, and there was a quick exchange of greetings. The morning after Ed Masterson's death, the town council had met in emergency session and promoted Bassett from Assistant Marshal to the post of City Marshal. Bassett stepped into the role without hesitation and without qualms; the job was daunting, but he felt equal to the task. A former troubleshooter for the Santa Fe, he had served as a deputy marshal in the cowtown of Newton before moving to Dodge City. As a peace officer, he relied more on wits than guns, and, when necessary, his fists. He prided himself on never having been whipped in a fight.

Masterson came out of his office. His expression was solemn and he waved the men to chairs. He stood for a moment looking from one to the other. His voice, when he finally spoke, was raspy.

"The reason I called this meeting was to set some new rules about law enforcement in Dodge. I want the sheriff's office and the marshal's office to operate in the same fashion."

Bassett looked at him. "What's the new rules you're talking about?"

"Here's the way I see it," Masterson said. "We've had two law officers killed in the last two months. Hiram McCarty was killed trying to talk a half-wit out of his gun. Ed was killed for damn near the same reason."

"Aren't you forgetting something?" Bassett asked. "Ed

killed them cowboys right there in the street. He sent 'em straight to hell."

"Charlie, he's still dead," Masterson said. "When men are shootin' up the town, you ought to come with your gun drawn." He paused, his gaze fixed on Nat Haywood. "And your deputy ought to be there to back your play."

"Hold on now," Bassett objected. "Nat didn't have no idea them cowboys was gonna shoot Ed. He tried to break loose from that crowd."

"Not hard enough," Masterson said curtly. "He should've busted some heads and forced his way through. You only have to buffalo one man to make the others stand aside."

To "buffalo" a man was a technique commonly used by peace officers. A man whacked upside the head with the heavy barrel of a Colt six-gun invariably went down, as if struck with a truncheon. Nat Haywood knew that was exactly what he should have done, and he couldn't meet Masterson's eyes. He stared down at his hands.

"Well that's done and past," Bassett said, trying to defuse the moment. "Nobody's arguing with you about bustin' heads. Course, you can't go about it willy-nilly. Got to pick your time and place."

Masterson grunted. "Charlie, I'm not just talking about busting heads. I'm sayin' that's only a start."

"What are you drivin' at?"

'When an officer is threatened, he's got every right to go whole hog. I'm sayin' shoot first and let the coroner sort it out later."

"Careful now," Bassett warned. "Don't let your feelings about Ed take you a step too far. You're liable to cross the line."

"Whose line?" Masterson said sharply. "Texans only understand one thing, and that's force. Wild Bill Hickok put the fear of God into them in Abilene. Worked there and it'll work here."

"Yeah, and Hickok killed his own deputy, too."

The story was legend in Kansas. In 1871, when Hickok was the marshal of Abilene, he killed a Texan gambler in a gunfight. Hickok's deputy, rushing to his aid, hurried around the corner of a building. Hickok, who thought he was being attacked from the side, instinctively fired two rounds. His deputy fell dead in the street.

Bassett shook his head. "A lawman can't shoot first, and you know it, Bat. He'd likely be brought up on charges himself."

"Not as long as I'm sheriff."

"Mike Sutton might disagree with you on that."

"To hell with Sutton!" Masterson bristled. "We've got to put a lid on the South Side once and for all. Sutton's not the one getting shot at."

"No, he's not," Bassett said. "But he wouldn't turn a blind eye if we killed somebody without proper cause. He'd file charges for manslaughter."

"There's a damn big difference between murder and defending yourself. The Texans have to be taught they can't defy the orders of a peace officer. I'm saying we crack down hard and fast."

"A minute ago, you said shoot first and let the coroner sort it out later. Sounds like you're sayin' something else now."

Masterson scrubbed his face with his hands. "I don't want any more lawmen killed." He looked around at the group. "Ed's badge didn't save his life and neither will yours. You've got to take the fight to the Texans."

"Yeah, you're right," Bassett agreed. "We've got to get the upper hand when trouble starts. Act faster and act smarter."

"And enforce it with a gun."

Masterson wasn't sure he'd convinced them. As the meeting broke up, he thought Bassett had won the verbal sparring match. The idea of being brought up on manslaughter charges was a strong argument for the cautious approach. Yet the solution, the only meaningful deterrent, was dead Texans. Lots of dead Texans.

Masterson wondered if Mike Sutton would actually bring charges.

The indigo sky was flecked through with stars. A southerly breeze brought with it the pungent smell of cow dung from the holding grounds across the river. The calliope of drunken laughter and carousing cowhands below the Deadline carried all the way to the plaza.

Mike Sutton returned to his office shortly after supper. Earlier that day, he'd sent messages to the Republican leaders of Ford County asking them to a meeting that evening. He was still chafing over his defeat in court yesterday and the release of the four Texans. He was even more galled by the death of Marshal Ed Masterson.

Fred Colborn was already in the office. He'd arrived early, lighting lamps and arranging chairs around a conference table sometimes used for clients. He turned as Sutton entered the room.

"Would you listen to the noise," Colborn said, jerking

a thumb at an open window. "It's business as usual on the South Side."

"Why are you surprised?" Sutton dropped his hat on his desk. "The festivities resumed ten minutes after Masterson was killed. No one from Texas mourned his passing."

"With a few exceptions, the same might be said of the sporting crowd. Their one concern is the almighty dollar."

"Fred, the concept of morality is foreign to the South Side. Death can never be seen as an impediment to commerce."

Voices sounded on the stairwell. Robert Wright, Jim "Dog" Kelley, and Nick Klaine moved through the anteroom to Sutton's office. Once they were seated around the table, the five men represented the county attorney, the state legislator, the mayor, the city attorney, and their partisan newspaper editor. They were, for all practical purposes, the Republican oligarchy of Ford County. Sutton was their acknowledged leader.

"I asked you here tonight," he said, "because I believe we are at the turning point. The murder of Ed Masterson convinced me that we must act with dispatch."

"Damn shame," Kelley said quietly. "Course we've got Charlie Bassett on the job now. He's a good man."

"No doubt," Sutton remarked. "But Masterson's death crystallized thoughts I've had for some while. We must formulate a strategy for the future of Ford County. Perhaps the future of Kansas."

Wright scrutinized him closely. "You've got our attention, Mike. What sort of strategy?"

"One that will sound the death knell on the Texas cattle trade."

Sutton went on to elaborate. The population of Ford

County was approaching eight thousand, the majority comprised of farmers. The cattlemen of the Stockgrowers Association were an influential group; but they and their cowhands were outnumbered fifty to one by homesteaders. The two factions nonetheless had a common enemy in Texas cattlemen. Or more to the point, longhorn cattle—and Texas fever.

The Shorthorn Breeders Association represented both farmers and ranchers throughout Kansas. The organization was already lobbying the legislature for a statewide embargo on Texas cattle. Longhorns were a menace to domestic stock because they carried a disease that killed shorthorn herds. The disease was borne by a tick that buried itself in the hides of longhorns. Over many generations, the longhorns, which were heavily infested with ticks, had developed an immunity to the disease. No one knew exactly how the ticks were transferred, but the end result was all too clear. Shorthorn cattle died soon after exposure to Texas fever.

Farmers and ranchers of Ford County were embattled on another front as well. The Western Trail, which was the artery for hundreds of thousands of longhorns, sliced through the southern quadrant of the county. Texas cattle, always skittish and prone to stampede, destroyed hundreds of acres of crops and inevitably became mixed with the herds of local ranchers. Grangers, as farmers were often known, and breeders of shorthorn stock shared both a common enemy and a common goal. They wanted longhorns banned from entry into Kansas.

"In addition to farmers and ranchers." Sutton continued, "there is another organization we should consider in our overall strategy. I refer specifically to the Kansas Temperance Union."

Earlier in the year, he noted, the first State Temperance Convention had been held in Topeka. The gathering was organized by Albert Griffin and it demonstrated the solidarity and strength of Prohibitionists throughout the eastern counties of Kansas. The convention denounced "lawless and immoral cowtowns" and directly targeted Dodge City as a "blot on the fair name of Kansas." There was consensus that the only way to restore decency was to close the saloons from border to border. In short, a statewide prohibition of alcoholic spirits.

"Hang on there," Kelley interrupted. "Maybe it slipped your mind I'm a saloonkeeper. You're talkin' about putting me out of business."

"Dog, you must look to the future," Sutton said. "Before too long, agriculture will be the economic lifeblood of Ford County. The cattle trade is on its way out."

"How do you figure that?"

"Five years from now, perhaps sooner, the railroads will extend into Texas. At that point Dodge City will have seen the last of the Texas herds."

"Maybe so," Kelley conceded. "But you're talkin' about hurrying it along. I could make a ton of money on a saloon in five years."

"Then you have a decision to make," Sutton said. "Do you wish to jump on the bandwagon of the future, a lifetime of prosperity? Or do you prefer to risk everything on a short-term gain?"

"Think about it, Dog," Wright interjected. "You could open a granary and make far more money off the farmers. Why hitch your star to a saloon?"

Klaine nodded. "The men in this room run Ford County, Dog. It's the old story of go along to get along."

Dog Kelley never doubted that his livelihood was directly linked to political connections. The men seated at the table could make him or break him, and it was his choice. "Maybe I'll open a granary," he said, looking at Sutton. "So what's your strategy for the future?"

"We form a coalition," Sutton said. "A working alliance of farmers, shorthorn cattlemen, and the Temperance Union. We start in Ford County and establish a groundswell movement that will spread across Kansas."

A moment of silence elapsed as the men considered the enormity of the scheme. "You've set a high mark," Wright finally said. "We'd have to bring the leaders of those groups together and kindle a spirit of cooperation. Not an easy task."

"Easier than you might think," Sutton assured him. "All of them agree that longhorns and Texas cattlemen are an evil that has to be eradicated. It's to their advantage to unite and work for the common good."

"Mike has a point," Klaine chimed in. "The Temperance Union's already got the churches in its pocket. And there's a shorthorn breeders association in every county in the state. All we have to do is organize the farmers."

"We'll create a Grangers Union," Sutton proposed. "Once we have it established in Ford County, the idea will take hold in other counties. Things will begin to snowball in no time."

Wright slowly nodded agreement. "I have influential contacts in the legislature. They'll get behind it once we've formed the coalition."

"Nick, you have to take the lead," Sutton said. "Write a

series of editorials and get people fired up. Make them think it's their idea."

Klaine laughed. "Don't worry, I'll sell it to them."

"By God, Mike," Kelly marveled. "You pull this off and there's no tellin' where it'll end. You're liable to wind up governor."

"Governor?" Sutton repeated incredulously. "Who in his right mind would want to live in Topeka? Dodge City suits me just fine."

Fred Colborn smiled to himself. He thought Sutton was at his best when he avoided telling a lie by evading the truth. Tonight was a case in point.

Mike Sutton would sell his soul to be governor.

THIRTEEN

A wagon trailed a wake of dust as it trundled along Front Street. The morning sun, slowly cresting the horizon, bathed the plaza in sparkling light. Shops and stores throughout the uptown district opened for business.

Gryden emerged from the hotel. The date was May 4, the first Saturday in the month, and he felt tired just thinking about it. Saturday was always the busiest day of the week and to him, the longest day. He wasn't sure he could deal with yet another land settlement suit. Or, God forbid, write someone's will.

Velma Oxmard looked up as he entered the office. She greeted him with a quick smile, then placed five file folders on the edge of her desk. He stared at the folders with a dour expression.

"What's the bad news?"

"Three land cases," she said. "and a small-claims action by Roger Brokaw against a carpenter. And Abigail Martin will be here at two to discuss a divorce suit."

"No kidding?" Gryden said. "Abigail's really going through with it?"

"Yes, when she came by to make the appointment, she

said she was through giving last chances, Mr. Martin has been carrying on with a chorus girl at the Lady Gay."

"Well, compared to land suits, adultery will be high entertainment. Abigail should get a very nice settlement."

"I should hope so," Velma said testily. "Her husband ought to be tarred and feathered."

"How about drawn and quartered?"

"Now you're making fun of me."

"Perish the thought."

Gryden went into his office and dropped the folders on his desk. As he seated himself, Thomas Jones came through the door with a copy of Friday's *Dodge City Times*. He placed the paper in front of Gryden.

"I just now got around to yesterday's *Times*. Did you read Klaine's editorial?"

"Read it last night," Gryden said. "More of the same on this idea of a coalition between farmers and ranchers."

"And it's not going away," Jones commented. "This is the third editorial in as many weeks."

"Klaine always was a bulldog when he's peddling Sutton's latest brainstorm."

"Interesting you should say that. I ran into Dan Frost on the way to work this morning. He said the rumor's around that Sutton met with a group of farmers in Spearville."

"Let me guess," Gryden said. "They're talking about forming a Grangers Union."

"Exactly," Jones affirmed. "Just as Klaine proposed in one of his editorials."

"So we'll have a Grangers Union working in concert with the Stockgrowers Association. Which makes a substantial bloc of votes for the Republicans in November."

"Do you think that's all there is to it? The November elections?"

"I can tell by the question that you don't. What's your educated guess?"

"I'm always suspicious when the obvious conclusion appears to be the only conclusion. Mike Sutton is too devious to publicize his true intent."

Gryden leaned back in his chair. "Sutton has more twists than a barrel of snakes. What do you think he's up to?"

"I wish I knew." Jones rubbed his nose. "Whatever it is, I don't like the smell of it."

Velma stuck her head in the door. "Mr. Gryden, sorry to interrupt. Waldo Finley is here from Judge Strang's office. He says it's important."

"Well then," Gryden said, "don't keep him waiting, Velma. Show him in."

Waldo Finley was the court clerk of the Ninth District court. He was a fussy little man, with a pinched expression and watery eyes. He nodded to Jones and stopped before the desk.

"Mr. Gryden," he said by way of greeting. "Judge Strang would like to see you in chambers. Posthaste."

"That soon, huh?" Gryden paused, but his humor fell flat. "Did the judge say what it's about?"

"No, sir, he just sent me to fetch you."

"I'm not in the habit of being fetched, Waldo."

"Mr. Gryden, I really don't believe it's in the form of an invitation. Judge Strang told me to bring you along, without delay."

"In that case, I guess I've just been fetched."

On his way through the anteroom, Gryden waved to

Velma. "Cancel my appointments until further notice. I have business before the court."

Velma sniffed. "What shall I tell your clients?"

"Tell them to get in line to see Colonel Jones."

"Harry, you're a card," Jones said with a chuckle. "Try not to take all day."

"I'm sure I've been shanghaied in some noble cause, Tom. Don't look for me until you see me."

Ten minutes later Waldo Finley ushered Gryden into the judge's chambers. Strang rose from behind a massive walnut desk and exchanged a handshake. He motioned Gryden to a chair.

"Sorry for the urgency, Harry," he said, seating himself. "But we have a situation of some delicacy. Early this morning, a man was arrested for murder."

"Have a heart, Judge," Gryden protested. "You're not going to draft me again, are you? Aren't there other lawyers in this town?"

"Not for a case of this nature."

"What's so different about it?"

"The accused is a Negro cowboy. A Texan but nonetheless a Negro."

"Who did he kill?"

"A white man . . . another cowboy."

Gryden sighed. "Judge, any number of lawyers could provide a good defense."

" 'Good' isn't good enough," Strang said. "The situation requires your expertise, Harry."

"Why me?"

"Kansas has always championed justice for Negroes. I intend to uphold that tradition in the Ninth District."

Gryden couldn't argue the point. The state was remembered as "Bloody Kansas" for its protracted struggle against slavery. John Brown, perhaps the most infamous abolitionist, conducted a guerrilla war in 1856, terrorizing proslavers and assassinating many of their leaders. Finally, in 1859, territorial delegates held a long and bitter constitutional convention, which defeated the proslavery faction and petitioned Congress for statehood. On the eve of the Civil War, in January 1861, Kansas entered the Union as a Free State.

The struggle between the Free State and proslavery factions became even more violent during the war. Kansas sided with the Union, fomenting still greater bitterness, and the state again ran red with blood. In 1863, Capt. William Quantrill raided Lawrence with a Confederate guerrilla force, killing 150 civilians and burning the town to the ground. Two Kansas Negro regiments distinguished themselves in battle, and following the war freed slaves from the Old South trekked west to a safe haven. Kansas emerged from the war as the Promised Land for Negroes.

"All right, Judge, you've got me," Gryden said at length. "Who's my client in the case?"

"His name is William Allen," Strang replied. "I understand the killing took place late yesterday, in a cow camp south of the river. Sheriff Masterson arrested him this morning."

"Who preferred charges?"

"The foreman of the cattle outfit."

"A Texan?"

"Yes."

"And the details of the killing?"

"You must discover that for yourself," Strang informed

him. "As you may appreciate, I cannot reveal the particulars, or express my opinion as to their merits. I must remain impartial in the matter."

Gryden sensed an unspoken message. Judge Jeremiah Strang was telling him—without putting it into words—that there was something peculiar about the case. He'd been subtly advised to dig deeper.

"I understand," he said, rising from his chair. "I'll go have a word with my client."

"Thank you, Harry," Strang said earnestly. "The people of Kansas are in your debt."

"I'll do my damnedest to get him off."

The sheriff's office was almost empty. On Saturdays, one deputy manned the office while the others walked the streets, particularly alert to trouble on the South Side. Miles Mix was cleaning his fingernails with a pocketknife when Gryden entered the office.

"Mornin', Mr. Gryden," Mix said, snapping the knife shut. "What brings you around?"

"Legal business, Miles. I'm representing William Allen."

"Jesus, don't tell me the judge roped you into that. You're gonna be fightin' a lost cause."

"In any event, I need to speak with the sheriff."

Mix waved him through. "Go ahead and announce yourself. He's in his office."

Gryden crossed the room to the sheriff's private office. The door was open and Masterson looked up from a desk littered with paperwork. His expression was neutral.

"What can I do for you, Harry?"

"Good morning to you, too, Bat. Mind if I sit down?"

"Grab a chair."

Gryden seated himself. "Judge Strang assigned me to defend William Allen. I'd like to hear the particulars of the case."

"Got suckered again, huh?" Masterson snorted a short stutter of a laugh. "Or maybe you're just quick to take the part of Texans."

"Why do I get the impression we're talking about Ed's murder? Do you blame me for getting those cowboys off?"

"No, I wouldn't say I hold it against you. But you didn't have to work so hard."

"Anyone who was there knows I didn't win the case. Mike Sutton lost it."

"Water under the bridge," Masterson said dismissively. "You're here about William Allen."

"Yes, I am," Gryden said. "Why is he charged with murder?"

"Well, Harry, he shot another man dead. I guess that's reason enough."

"Who was the other man?"

"One of the cowhands in the crew. His name was George Crawford."

"And the foreman preferred charges?"

"Jack Tuttle," Masterson said with a nod. "He brought a herd up the trail for the Circle X cattle company. Just after sunup, he rode across the bridge and rousted me out of bed. I went back with him and arrested Allen."

"Wait a minute," Grydon said. "Allen was still in the cow camp? He didn't try to escape?"

"No, he was squatted down by the fire with a cup of coffee. Came along peaceable as you please."

"How do you explain that?"

"Harry, I never try to second-guess what goes through a murderer's mind. Gave it up a long time ago."

"When did the shooting occur?"

"Just before dark last night."

"Am I missing something?" Gryden said. "Allen had all night to escape and he didn't make a run for it? Why did Tuttle wait until this morning to bring charges?"

"Only know what he told me," Masterson said. "Him and the rest of the crew like Allen, and they slept on it overnight. Finally decided they had to turn him in."

"Bat, I have to say, that sounds very implausible. They considered forgiving him shooting another man in the crew? What kind of story is that?"

"Texans are crazy as hell and they shoot people all the time. I've seen stranger things happen."

"What brought about the shooting?"

"Allen and Crawford got into an argument over who was supposed to ride midnight watch on the herd. Tuttle and the others swore Allen drew first and plugged him."

"Just like that?" Gryden said. "A petty argument and he kills a man? No other provocation?"

Masterson shrugged. "They told me he's got a real bad temper. Goes off like a firecracker."

"If we're to believe their story, he's more on the order of a volcano."

"Whatever he is, he's a damn good shot."

"You inspected the dead man?"

"Drilled straight through the heart," Masterson said. "I sent the undertaker to get the body."

"We'll see what the coroner says," Gryden allowed.

"Tell you the truth, I'm looking forward to the preliminary hearing. This may never go to trial."

"Harry, you don't have the chance of a snowball in hell. Tuttle and his crew aren't about to budge from their story."

"Perhaps they'll change their tune when they're placed under oath. In the meantime, I have to speak with my client."

"Tell Joe I said to let you into Allen's cell."

The county jail was in the basement of the courthouse. The place was damp and dank, and whenever Gryden went there it put him in mind of a medieval dungeon. Joe Kelsey, the daytime jailer, was a stout man who brooked no nonsense from his wards. He admitted Gryden through a door at the rear of the building.

"Good morning, Joe," Gryden said. "Sheriff Masterson authorized me to speak with one of your prisoners— William Allen."

Kelsey chuckled. "Gimme three guesses and the first two don't count. Judge Strang 'volunteered' you for the defense."

"Either you have a crystal ball or someone's been carrying tales."

"Tell you what my crystal ball does tell me."

"What's that?"

"You're finally gonna defend an innocent man."

"Why do you think so?"

"You'll see."

Kelsey walked Gryden back to the cell block. There were two cowboys in the first cell, sleeping off a hangover from the night before. At the end of the corridor,

Kelsey unlocked the door to a barred cell and swung it open. He motioned Gryden forward.

"Here's your man."

Gryden stepped inside and Kelsey locked the door. William Allen was seated on a bunk with a dirty mattress covered by a thin blanket. His skin was the color of dark mocha, his eyes veiled with sadness, as if he'd seen all the sorrow the world could offer. He was lean and muscular, with gnarled hands, a broad forehead, and short woolly hair. He stood, arms loose at his sides, head slightly bowed.

"Mr. Allen," Gryden said, extending his hand. "I'm Harry Gryden, attorney-at-law. The court has appointed me as your defense counsel."

"Well, suh, that's good," Allen said, hesitantly exchanging a handshake. "Reckon I needs defendin'."

Gryden got the impression that the cowboy had never before shaken hands with a white man. He sensed as well that Allen was mild mannered, almost subservient, hardly the quick-tempered hothead described by the men of the Circle X crew. He understood why Kelsey thought the black Texan might be innocent.

"You're charged with murder," Gryden observed, watching for a reaction. "They say you killed a man named George Crawford."

Allen ducked his head. "Yassuh, that's purty much so."

"Why did you shoot him?"

"'Cause he spit in my coffee."

"That's it?" Gryden said, astounded. "He spit in your coffee?"

Allen nodded. "That'n he called me a nigger. A no-good nigger."

"And you killed him?"

"Yassuh, I surely did."

Gryden thought there had to be more to it. For Allen's sake, he hoped there were mitigating circumstances that would justify a shooting. He was reminded that three days ago, with all appeals exhausted, Thomas O'Haran had been hanged at Leavenworth State Penitentiary. He didn't want another client to walk the gallows. Especially this one.

"William," he said, "I want you to tell me everything. Start at the beginning and tell me everything."

"You mean how I come to kill ol' George?"

"Yes, exactly how it happened."

"Well, suh, I reckon it was 'cause I whapped him a good 'un."

"You struck him with your fist?"

Allen grinned. "Knocked him flat on his butt."

FOURTEEN

There wasn't an empty seat in the courtroom. A murder trial was considered the highest form of entertainment, and spectators stood shoulder-to-shoulder along the walls. Outside, a line of people waiting for a seat extended onto the courthouse lawn.

The date was May 21, not quite three weeks following the shooting. A preliminary hearing had been held on May 5, the court ordering that William Allen be bound over for trial. The evidence established that George Crawford had died of a gunshot wound, and eyewitnesses had identified the killer. The charge was murder in the first degree.

Yesterday Sutton and Gryden had devoted a full day to jury selection. Sutton favored ranchers and cowboys, for the defendant was accused of murdering one of their own. Gryden preferred farmers and townspeople, who were generally less biased in matters of race. By late afternoon, when all preemptive challenges had been exhausted, twelve men were seated. The jury was composed of three townsmen, four cattlemen, and five farmers.

Sheriff Masterson brought William Allen into the courtroom. After the manacles were removed, Allen took a seat beside Gryden at the defense table. Early that morning, Gryden had arranged for a barber to visit the jail, where he gave the accused a trim haircut and a shave. Gryden had also provided a shirt and tie, new boots, and a store-bought suit in charcoal gray. Allen looked anything but a Texas cowboy.

On the bailiff's command, everyone stood as Judge Strang entered and seated himself at the bench. He then nodded to the bailiff, and the jurors were brought in from a rear door, taking their chairs in the jury box. The courtroom quieted as the bailiff read the charges in *The State of Kansas versus William Allen.*

Judge Strang peered down at opposing counsel. "Are you gentlemen ready to proceed?"

Sutton stood. "The state is prepared, Your Honor."

"The defense is prepared," Gryden said.

"Very well," the judge replied. "You may proceed with your opening statements."

Sutton walked to the jury box. His thumbs hooked in the pockets of his vest, he subjected the jurors to a grave stare. "We are here today," he said, 'to hold a man accountable for the most heinous of crimes—murder in cold blood."

The jurors returned his stare with solemn expressions. Sutton went on to relate a brutal version of the killing, the eyewitnesses he planned to call, and the sterling character of the deceased, George Crawford. He spoke in a measured tone, his manner somber, shoulders squared like a drill sergeant. Finally, his features stern, he turned sideways to the jury.

"We will prove beyond a shadow of a doubt"—he paused, thrust a forefinger at the defense table—"that

William Allen is guilty of murder as charged. The evidence, gentlemen, will tell the tale."

Sutton returned to his chair. Gryden rose, crossed the courtroom, and nodded to the jurors with an open gaze. " 'Fourscore and seven years ago,' " he said, " 'our fathers brought forth on this continent, a new nation, conceived in Liberty, and dedicated to the proposition that all men are created equal.' Abraham Lincoln spoke those words at the Gettysburg National Cemetery in 1863."

Everyone in the courtroom stared at him, waiting. "Fifteen years later," he said in a ringing voice, "Abe Lincoln would be sad to learn that, in certain parts of our nation, the war he fought and won was fought in vain. Fifteen years later in Texas, *some men are still more equal than others.*"

A thunderous silence settled over the courtroom. "Texas fought for the Confederacy," Gryden said, "and Texans *still* uphold the traditions of the Old South. A black man, a *Negro,* was not and will never be considered the equal of a white man. And therefore, in Texas, it is perfectly acceptable to falsely accuse a black man of murder. After all, what's a little lie when it involves only a *nigger?* "

The word brought a numbing stillness over the spectators. "Listen closely to the testimony," Gryden told the jurors. "You will hear lies foisted off as truth by men who see the world *only* in black-and-white. You will be forced to decide whose word you accept here today."

The jurors seemed to hold their breath. "In his Second Inaugural Address," Gryden declared, "Abraham Lincoln said, 'With malice toward none, with charity for all, with firmness in the right, as God gives us to see the right.' And today, gentlemen, I ask nothing more nor less from each of you. Follow your conscience as God gives you to see the right."

Gryden walked back to his chair. There was a prolonged moment of silence as jurors and spectators alike dwelled not on murder but on the ugly specter of racism and prejudice. The eyes of every man and woman in the courtroom were involuntarily drawn to William Allen. He sat with his head slightly bowed, a black statue with sorrow etched on his face. Judge Strang finally broke the silence.

"Mr. Sutton, you may call your first witness for the state."

Dr. Thadius McCabe, the county coroner, was called to the stand. He related that the deceased had suffered a single gunshot wound to the heart; in his opinion, death had been instantaneous. Gryden waived cross-examination, and Bat Masterson was called as the next witness. He testified that the killing had been reported the morning of May 4 by the Circle X foreman, Jack Tuttle. Perhaps an hour later, Masterson recounted, he rode to the cow camp south of the river and arrested the defendant.

Sutton turned away from the stand. "No further questions, Your Honor."

Gryden rose, his features perplexed. "Sheriff Masterson, when did the shooting take place?"

"According to witnesses," Masterson said, "it happened just about dusk on May 3."

"Where was Mr. Allen when you reached the cow camp the morning of May 4?"

"By the cook fire, drinkin' a cup of coffee."

"I'm confused, Sheriff," Gryden said with a puzzled

frown. "Twelve hours or more elapsed between the time of the shooting and the time you arrived in the cow camp. Mr. Allen could have escaped during those twelve hours and fled to Indian Territory. Correct?"

"Yeah, I suppose."

"But as we now know, he made no effort to escape. In fact, when you arrested him, he offered no resistance whatever. And he was still armed at the time. Isn't that true?"

"I told him he was under arrest and he surrendered his gun. There wasn't any trouble."

"Why didn't he escape? Why did he surrender peacefully? Have you ever known a murderer who didn't flee? Or try to fight if caught?"

Masterson shrugged. "No, that was a new one on me."

"Given all that, when you arrested him, you thought he was innocent. Didn't you?"

"Objection," Sutton said. "Calls for speculation."

"Sustained," Judge Strang said. "Jury will disregard the question."

"Let's move on," Gryden said. "Sheriff Masterson, on the night of May 14, three prisoners overpowered the night guard and escaped from your jail. Is that correct?"

"Yeah," Masterson said sheepishly. "But they didn't get far. We caught them the next day."

"Nonetheless, there were four prisoners in your jail that night. One of whom was the defendant, William Allen. And he took no part in the jailbreak. Nor did he attempt to escape. Instead, he stayed in his cell throughout the incident. Isn't that so?"

"Near as I can figure, that's the way it happened."

"Tell the court and this jury," Gryden said. "If a man were guilty of murder, wouldn't he seize on the opportunity to escape? Wouldn't he run for his life?"

The story of the jailbreak had appeared in the newspapers, and everyone knew Allen had bypassed the chance to escape. Sutton still felt obliged to enter an objection for the record, and the judge ordered the jury to disregard the question. Gryden walked away.

"I have nothing further of this witness."

Jack Tuttle, the Circle X foreman, was called to testify. Under Sutton's questioning, Tuttle related that he had been out checking on the herd when the shooting occurred. He went on to say that three men in the crew were riding night guard at the time and four were in camp. Upon hearing the gunshot, he had returned to the camp and found George Crawford dead. Anson Polk, the chuckwagon cook, and Luther Hunsaker, one of the cowhands, told him William Allen had murdered Crawford. Sutton passed the witness for cross-examination.

Gryden moved forward. "Do I understand you correctly, Mr. Tuttle? William Allen told you he fired in defense of his life. Yet you chose to believe the story of Polk and Hunsaker. Why is that?"

"Why wouldn't I?" Tuttle knuckled his mustache. "Two says one thing, and the man that done the shootin' says another. Who would you believe?"

"So you were convinced it was murder?"

"Course I was."

"Then enlighten us, if you will." Gryden fixed him with a stare. "Why did you wait until the next morning to ride into town and press charges? If you truly believed it was murder, why didn't you go for the sheriff that night?"

"No special reason." Tuttle fidgeted in his chair. "Just figgered mornin' was soon enough."

"Come now, Mr. Tuttle. Weren't you pressured into it by the men in your crew? Didn't it take the night for five white men to convince you to act against a black man? Isn't that how it happened?"

"No, that ain't how it happened. I done told you what went on."

"Have you?" Gryden said with wry sarcasm. "There was a man lying dead and you didn't notify the sheriff. You didn't even disarm Mr. Allen, or place him under guard. Why is that?"

"Didn't see no need," Tuttle said weakly. "Allen wasn't trying to run off or nothin'."

"No, he wasn't, was he, Mr. Tuttle? Instead, he calmly waited—*all night*—for you to bring the sheriff to arrest him. Why did he just sit there and wait?"

"I don't rightly know."

"You don't know because you and your men concocted a story that has no bearing on the truth. Isn't that the case, Mr. Tuttle?"

"Objection," Sutton said loudly. "Argumentative."

Judge Strang nodded. "Objection sustained."

"No further questions," Gryden said, turning away. "Mr. Tuttle has told us all we need to know."

Luther Hunsaker, one of the Circle X cowhands, was the next prosecution witness. He testified that Allen and Crawford had gotten into a fistfight and Allen knocked Crawford to the ground. Sutton then led Hunsaker to recount that Allen drew his pistol and fired while Crawford was still down. He swore that Crawford never had a chance to draw his gun.

"You're positive of that?" Sutton insisted. "Crawford never touched his gun?"

"Yessir, I am," Hunsaker said. "George never even got to his feet."

"And the defendant, William Allen, shot him while he was helpless, lying on the ground. Is that correct?"

"Yessir, he did."

"Murdered him in cold blood?"

"Coldest thing I ever saw."

"No doubt," Sutton said with a satisfied smile. "Your witness, Mr. Gryden."

"Indeed he is," Gryden said, glancing at the jury. "After Tuttle heard the gunshot, he rode back to the camp. You and Tuttle and Polk had William Allen outnumbered three to one. Why didn't you disarm him and take him prisoner, Mr. Hunsaker?"

"I dunno," Hunsaker muttered. "Guess me and Polk was waitin' for Tuttle to make the first move."

"None of you made the first move. The truth is, you didn't take him prisoner because you wanted him to escape. Isn't that a fact?"

"Nope, wasn't that way a'tall."

"You wanted him to run and make the law believe it was murder rather than self-defense. That is the truth, isn't it?"

"I done told—"

"You weren't sure you could make a murder charge stick in a court of law. You gave him all night to run and lend credence to your phony charge. Tell the truth for once!"

"Objection!" Sutton shouted. "Counsel is badgering the witness, Your Honor."

Gryden walked off. "I have nothing further."

Anson Polk, the camp cook, was the prosecution's last witness. He was an older man, grizzled and balding, something astringent in his manner. His testimony was a virtual duplicate of that given by Hunsaker. Sutton led him to the most damning point.

"Was Crawford on the ground when he was shot?"

"Shore was," Polk said. "Flat on his back."

"And you saw William Allen fire the fatal shot?"

"Saw him with my own eyes."

"So Crawford was killed—murdered—with no chance to defend himself?"

"Just plain slaughtered, that's what he was."

"Like a pig in a pen," Sutton said, nodding pointedly to the jury. "No further questions."

Gryden approached the stand. "In the late war, did you fight for the Confederacy, Mr. Polk?"

Polk grinned. "I'm proud to say I did."

"And you are currently a member of the Ku Klux Klan. Isn't that correct?"

"Sonny, you'd play hell provin' that."

"In all candor, you don't like black people, do you?"

"I can take 'em or leave 'em. Don't make no never-mind to me."

"In other words," Gryden persisted, "a coon's a coon except when he's a nigger. Would you agree?"

Polk smirked. "You said it, not me."

"George Crawford was your friend, isn't that so?"

"Just as good a friend as a man could want."

"And William Allen was never your friend. Correct?"

"Well, you know, he's pretty sold on himself. Sorta standoffish."

"An uppity nigger?"

"Don't go puttin' words in my mouth."

"How about this?" Gryden said. "I submit you would have done anything to avenge the death of a friend. Including falsifying a charge of murder. Isn't that true?"

"No, it ain't true," Polk said hotly. "I only told what I saw."

"On the contrary, Mr. Polk, this jury knows exactly who and what you are. Nothing further of this witness, Your Honor."

Sutton rose with a smug look. "Mr. Gryden should not presume to lecture the jury. If it please the court, the state rests its case."

"Very well," Judge Strang said. "Is the defense prepared to proceed?"

"We are, Your Honor," Gryden said. "The defense will present only one witness. We call William Allen."

Allen took the stand and was sworn in by the bailiff. He settled into the chair, his demeanor placid and his eyes alert. Gryden took a position by the jury box.

"Mr. Allen, were you born a free man?"

"No, suh, my whole family was slaves."

"And freed by Abe Lincoln?"

"Yassuh," Allen said, with a big smile. "I'm good with horses, and after the war, I got work as a cowhand. Mighty good job."

"How long have you worked for the Circle X?"

"Well, come spring, I signs on with outfits for the trail drives. This my first time for the Circle X."

"Let's talk about the night of the shooting," Gryden said. "What caused the argument with George Crawford?"

"Come on sudden," Allen said ruefully. "Crawford was after me to take his turn ridin' herd at midnight and I wouldn't do it. He spit in my coffee and called me a no-good nigger."

"What happened then?"

"I knocked him down and he jumped up and went for his gun. I beat him to it."

"So he was on his feet?" Gryden asked. "And he went for his gun first?"

"Yassuh, he surely did," Allen said. "I ain't never pulled a gun on no man 'fore that night."

"Anson Polk and Luther Hunsaker testified that Crawford never tried for his gun. Why would they accuse you of murder?"

"'Cause they don't care much for black folks, and Crawford was white. They wants to see me hung."

"Did they say anything about seeing you hang?"

"Well, they was whisperin' and such, but I still hears 'em. They spent the night talkin' Mr. Tuttle into goin' for the sheriff."

"That would be your foreman, Jack Tuttle. And it took all night to convince him?"

"'Nigh on to dawn 'fore they argue him into it."

"Tell me," Gryden said. "Have you ever before been called a nigger?"

"Oh, sure," Allen replied. "Lotta times."

"What was different about this time?"

"Well, most white folks calls you a nigger, they don't mean nothin' by it. They just sayin' it 'cause that's the way they was raised. George Crawford was plumb mean about it."

"Mean in what way?"

"Called me a *no-good* nigger," Allen said. "And he already spit in my coffee."

"Have you ever struck a white man before?"

"Wouldn't think of doin' no such a thing. Not till that night, anyways."

Gryden held his gaze. "And you fired your pistol only in protection of your life? Only after George Crawford drew his pistol? Isn't that true?"

"Yassuh," Allen said firmly. "Done swore on the Bible, and God hear me. I'm tellin' the truth."

"You could have escaped the night of the shooting and again the night of the jailbreak. You were accused of murder, and you knew the odds were stacked against you. Why didn't you run for Indian Territory?"

"'Cause if I run, folks gonna think I'm guilty. I ain't no murderer."

"So you chose to plead your innocence rather than escape?"

"Yassuh, wasn't no other way for me."

"No other way indeed." Gryden turned away. "Your witness, Mr. Sutton."

Sutton moved forward. "You say you've never before pulled a gun on a man. Is that right?"

"Yessuh," Allen said. "Never had no call to."

"Then how do you explain beating George Crawford to the draw?"

"Guess he was a mite slower'n he thought."

"Or he was still sprawled on the ground. And you shot him while he lay defenseless. Isn't that more like it?"

Allen shook his head. "Wouldn't shoot no man 'lessen he's tryin' to shoot me."

"Wouldn't you?" Sutton said derisively. "We have two eyewitnesses who swear otherwise. Do you expect us to believe they would conspire and perjure themselves—simply because you are a black man?"

"Partly 'cause of that and partly 'cause they's friends of Crawford. White folks stick together."

"Mr. Allen, I think you are more clever than you would have us believe. You distract us with black versus white, when all the time it's just man against man. Regardless of their color! Isn't that so?"

"No, suh," Allen said flatly. "Killed him 'cause he was tryin' to kill me. Ain't nothin' else to it."

"Of course there is," Sutton retorted. "You say Anson Polk and Luther Hunsaker are persecuting you solely because you are a black man. Isn't that your one and only defense?"

"Time comes, Polk and Hunsaker are gonna be judged by the Lord. I'm only askin' this here jury to judge me on the truth."

"Mr. Allen, you will most certainly get your wish. And the truth shall convict you."

Sutton ended on what he considered a high note. The defense rested its case, and in closing argument Sutton hammered the theme of murder at its foulest. He reviewed the testimony of Polk and Hunsaker and stressed how the preponderance of evidence led to a verdict of guilty. He asked the jury to render the death sentence.

Gryden, in closing argument, underscored the many

inconsistencies in the prosecution's case. He urged the
jury to employ logic in considering the testimony of Tuttle, Polk, and Hunsaker. Again and again, Gryden touched
on the absurdity of men waiting overnight to report a
murder to the authorities. All the more when they made
no effort to disarm or restrain the man they accused. He
ended with an eloquent plea.

"Abe Lincoln once said, 'You may fool all the people
some of the time, you can even fool some of the people
all the time; but you can't fool all of the people all the
time.' Don't allow these Texans to fool you with their bigotry, their hatred of a man's color. William Allen was
freed from the bonds of slavery in 1865. I ask you to free
him from injustice here today."

The jury was out slightly more than an hour. When
they were brought back into the courtroom, the jury foreman rose and rendered a verdict of not guilty. Judge
Strang ordered the defendant released from custody and
nodded his approval to Gryden. William Allen, his eyes
damp with tears, shook Gryden's hand profusely. His
voice froggy, Allen swore he would never return to Texas.

Later, on his way to the hotel, Gryden reflected over
the course of the trial. He felt quite certain he'd saved an
innocent man from the hangman's noose. Yet the thought
uppermost in his mind was one of wry admission.

Abe Lincoln was the advocate who had won acquittal.

FIFTEEN

A full moon flooded the town with spectral light. Trailing season was at its peak, with over fifty thousand longhorns on the holding grounds across the river. Cowhands swarmed the South Side in search of devilment and loose women.

Gryden crossed the Deadline shortly before eight o'-clock. The date was June 11, three weeks following the murder trial of William Allen. Below the railroad tracks, Gryden was still the toast of the South Side, something of a celebrity. His defeat of Mike Sutton in court greatly endeared Gryden to the sporting crowd, saloonkeepers and whores alike. His victory was looked upon as a triumph for vice.

The newspapers were predictably partisan in their coverage of the trial. The *Dodge City Times* characterized the verdict as a "gross miscarriage of justice" and lambasted Gryden as the "attorney of choice for murderers, evildoers, and women of fallen virture." The *Ford County Globe* lauded him as the "champion of the downtrodden" and blasted Sutton as the "Little Caesar swamped in a Rubicon of perfidy." The editorial went on to praise Gryden for securing a job for William Allen as a cowhand with a Ford County rancher.

Texans were understandably angered by the abuse heaped on them during the trial. In an interview with the *Dodge City Times,* Abel "Shanghai" Pierce, one of the largest ranchers in the Lone Star State, pointed out that over 20 percent of trailhands were Negroes. He adamantly insisted that Negroes were hard workers, always dependable, and treated as fairly as white cowboys. Despite their resentment of Gryden, many Texans still sought him out when they ran afoul of the law. Over the past three weeks he had defended several rowdies for disturbing the peace and whorehouse brawls.

Texans jammed the boardwalks as Gryden made his way downtown to the Comique. Tonight was opening night for Eddie Foy, a popular song-and-dance man from the variety circuit back East. Foy traveled to Dodge City every summer for the trailing season and shared co-billing as a star attraction with Belle. Opening night was always an event, and Gryden had quit a poker game to catch Foy's act. Ever the diplomat, he'd made it a point to arrive in time for Belle's big number. Had he missed her onstage only to show up for Foy's opening, he knew he might sleep alone tonight.

Lloyd Franklin, owner of the Comique, greeted him as he entered the theater. "Evening, Harry," he said. "Here to see Eddie Foy?"

"Bite your tongue," Gryden quipped. "Ardent admirer that I am, I have eyes only for Belle."

"Don't blame you in the least, Harry. In your shoes, I'd say the same thing."

"Lloyd, if by chance I happen to catch Foy, it's pure coincidence. That's my story and I'll stick to it."

"You're a wise man, even if it's all horseapples."

Franklin escorted him to a reserved table down front. The house was packed with cowhands, soldiers from Fort Dodge, and townspeople drawn by the frivolity of nightlife. A waiter appeared with a shot glass and a bottle of bourbon and placed them on the table. Gryden poured himself a drink as the curtain went up.

A line of chorus girls exploded out of the wings. Belle was in the lead, her eyes bright and her golden locks flying, as the orchestra thumped through a rousing dance number. The theater vibrated with shrill whistles and wild cheers as the chorus line went high-stepping across the stage. Belle raised her skirts, revealing a shapely leg, and joined them in a prancing cakewalk. The girls squealed and Belle flashed her underdrawers and the tempo of the music quickened. The audience went mad.

Cowboys were on their feet, spurs jangling in time to the music, and soldiers shouted themselves hoarse. Belle pranced down to the footlights, throwing Gryden a bawdy wink, which every man in the house thought was for him alone. They cheered louder, calling out her name, as the orchestra went into the finale with a blare of trumpets and a clash of cymbals. The chorus line, in a swirl of raised skirts and jiggling breasts, went cavorting into the wings. Belle flashed her underdrawers one last time as she danced offstage.

The applause was thunderous. As the girls disappeared into the wings, the orchestra segued into a sprightly tune, with the horns muted and the strings more pronounced.

Eddie Foy skipped onstage, tipping his derby to the audience, and went into a shuffling soft-shoe routine. The sound of his feet on the floor was like velvety sandpaper, and halfway through the routine he began singing a ribald ballad. The lyrics, which were just short of lewd, brought hoots of laughter from the crowd. He ended the number at center stage.

The orchestra fell silent with a last note of the strings. Foy was short and wiry, with ginger hair and an infectious smile. Framed in the footlights, he walked back and forth with herky-jerky movements, delivering a rapid comedic patter that was at once risqué and hilarious. Waves of laughter rolled over the theater, and on the heels of a last, riotous joke the orchestra suddenly blared to life. Foy nimbly sprang into a high-stepping buck-and-wing routine that took him gyrating around the stage.

Toward the end of the number, his voice raised in a madcap shout, he belted out a naughty tune involving a girl and her one-legged lover. Foy's rubbery face stretched wide in a grin, he whirled, clicking his heels in midair, and skipped offstage with a final tip of his derby. The audience whistled and cheered, rocking the walls with a deafening ovation. Foy, bouncing merrily onto the stage, took three curtain calls.

Gryden was on his feet with the rest of the crowd. He applauded so hard his hands stung, and he thought Eddie Foy was the finest entertainer ever to play Dodge City. Then, with sudden insight, it occurred to Gryden that the comedian was only second best.

Belle's underdrawers would always be the hit of the show.

◆ ◆ ◆

Outside the Comique, the cheers from the crowd could be heard on the street. With the onset of nightfall, even more cowhands were released from the camps across the river. The boardwalks teemed with men "out to see the elephant."

Assistant City Marshal Wyatt Earp and Deputy Marshal Jim Masterson stood near the doors of the Comique. Neither of them knew the derivation of "out to see the elephant," probably something to do with traveling circus shows. But they understood only too well what it meant to Texans fresh off a grueling cattle drive. The cowhands were intent on a night of busthead whiskey and frisky whores.

Earp was a veteran peace officer. In 1875, when Wichita was in its heyday as a cowtown, he had served as a deputy marshal. The summers of 1876 and 1877, he'd worked as a deputy on the Dodge City police force. He was a tall man, with a blacksmith's shoulders and a brushy mustache, and known for his rough handling of lawbreakers. On June 1, the city council had hired him as second-in-command to Charlie Bassett.

Jim Masterson was the younger brother of the sheriff. He had worked with his brothers as a buffalo hunter in the early 1870s, and later returned to the family farm. After Ed Masterson's murder by Texas cowhands, Jim had begun pestering Bat for a job in law enforcement. Finally, earlier in the month, Bat had relented and secured a position for him as a deputy city marshal. He was handy with his fists and no slouch with a pistol, but he'd never before worn a badge. To gain seasoning as a lawman, he had been assigned to work with Earp.

"Sounds like a good show," Masterson said, hooking a thumb back at the Comique. "Wouldn't mind seeing Eddie Foy myself."

Earp nodded. "We'll wait for a slow night and catch the show. Tonight's not the night."

"Why? You expectin' trouble?"

"Jim, when there's this many Texans in town, I'm always expectin' trouble. Hardly ever fails."

"Well, they've been half-civilized so far. Maybe we'll get lucky."

"Don't bet your bankroll on it. The night's still young."

Five Texans spilled out the door of the Comique. They were staggering drunk, stumbling into one another, their eyes bright with liquor. Scarcely noticing Earp and Masterson, the Texans turned in the opposite direction, wobbling along the boardwalk. Their voices were raised in merriment.

"Gawdalmightydamn!" one of them whooped. "That little runt's the funniest sonovabitch I ever seen. Like to split my sides."

"Laugh a minute," another one said. "Course, let's not forget he's a gawddamn Yankee."

"Well, Alvin, he's a *funny* gawddamn Yankee."

"Frank, he'd have to be with a name like Foy."

The Texans stopped by the hitch rack in front of Peacock's saloon. Their voices were indistinct at a distance, but Earp and Masterson could tell a drunken argument of some sort had broken out. The ones named Alvin and Frank were laughing and gesturing uptown, and the word "hurrah" came out of the jumble of voices. The other three cowhands kept shaking their heads, and then, breaking off the argument, they pushed through the doors of the saloon. Alvin and Frank unhitched their horses and clumsily swung themselves into the saddle. They rode toward the railroad tracks.

"Those boys are up to no good," Earp said. "Looks to me like they're gonna cross the Deadline. Let's just tag along."

"Guess we better," Masterson said. "You think they aim to shoot up the plaza?"

"We'll find out soon enough."

Earp led the way along the boardwalk. The Texans reined to a halt short of the Deadline, gesturing and arguing as they stared north at the plaza. Alvin apparently won the argument; they rounded the corner and rode east beside the railroad tracks. Earp and Masterson hurried to the corner.

The cowboys spurred their horses into a gallop. Two blocks east, just south of the railroad tracks, were the stockyards. There, in large slat-sided pens, cattle were held for loading into boxcars. Directly south of the stockyards was a spur line, where trains were backed in parallel to the holding pens. A train with twelve boxcars and a caboose was waiting to be loaded in the morning. The only light was a lantern on the end of the caboose.

The two Texans were drawn by the glow of the lantern. Whooping and shouting, their horses at a gallop, they bore down on the caboose. Their six-guns roared in a volley of gunfire and the lantern exploded in a splatter of fiery coal oil. The deck at the rear of the caboose was engulfed in flame as slugs drilled holes through the door. The cowboys emptied their guns, wheeling their horses, and rode back toward Second Avenue. Their voices filled the night with the yowling Rebel yell of Confederate soldiers in the late war.

Yipping and laughing, swaying drunkenly in the saddle, the Texans rounded the corner onto Second Avenue. Earp and Masterson leaped into their path, spooking their horses, and dragged them out of the saddle. Earp roughly collared Alvin, slamming him to the ground, and whacked him over the head with a Colt Peacemaker. Masterson grabbed Frank by the shirt and hammered him with three splintering blows to the jaw. The cowboys flopped limply onto the dusty street, out cold.

City Marshal Bassett and Deputy Nat Haywood crossed the Deadline from the plaza at a run. The flames quickly spread over the rear of the caboose, and the train crew, asleep inside only moments before, was now battling the blaze. As a crowd of Texans gathered around the lawmen and the fallen cowboys, Bassett sent Haywood to assist the train crew with the fire. Bassett ordered the crowd to stand back as Earp and Masterson hauled the addled cowboys to their feet. Alvin's forehead was split open, leaking blood, and Frank's nose was blossomed like a rotten plum.

A moment later Haywood sprinted back from the train. "The brakeman's dead!" he yelled, huffing for breath. "Bullet went through the door and caught him in his bunk. Killed him outright."

Alvin and Frank were woozy from liquor and the blows they'd suffered from the lawmen. They gaped at Haywood, their eyes glazed, unable to comprehend the news. Bassett turned to them with a cold expression.

"There's hell to pay now," he said tersely. "You boys are under arrest for murder."

The crowd muttered a protest. Bassett cleared the way as Earp and Masterson seized the prisoners with brute force. Haywood brought up the rear.

Alvin and Frank were marched off to the county jail.

Shanghai Pierce owned the AP cattle spread in Texas. He was six feet four, with a booming voice, and his ranch covered almost a half-million acres. He was a man accustomed to getting his own way.

Early the next morning Pierce walked into the law offices of Gryden & Jones. Velma was taken aback by Pierce's towering presence, all the more so when she asked if he had an appointment and he ignored the question. He informed her in blunt terms that he was there to see Harry Gryden.

Gryden came to the door of his office. He was familiar with Pierce's name, and since he had no pressing appointments, he invited the rancher to step inside. Pierce gripped his hand in a meat-grinder handshake and gave Velma an indignant glance as he moved into the office. Gryden motioned him to a chair.

"What can I do for you, Mr. Pierce?"

"You heard about the ruckus last night?" Pierce said. "That railroad man gettin' shot?"

"Everyone has," Gryden said, seating himself behind his desk. "The story's all over town."

"The boys they arrested work for me. Their names are Frank Norton and Alvin Sawyer."

"I see."

"What I want you to do is get 'em off."

"That's no small matter, Mr. Pierce. They've been charged with murder."

"You got that darkie off for murder. What's the difference with white men?"

The reference to a "darkie" involved the trial of William Allen. Gryden knew it would be a waste of breath to lecture a Texan of Pierce's stature on bigotry. He let it pass.

"There's a big difference," he said. "The Santa Fe has inordinate influence with the town and with the court. Your boys killed one of their brakemen."

"To hell with the railroad," Pierce said curtly. "Them boys was drunk and havin' a little fun. They didn't mean to kill nobody."

"Even if it was an accident, the law still treats it as negligent homicide. I can assure you they will be tried for murder."

"Goddammit, I don't want them boys hung! Thought you was supposed to be a smart lawyer."

"I don't perform miracles, Mr. Pierce."

"Well, what the blue-billy-hell can you do? There's got to be some way."

Gryden was thoughtful a moment. "I might be able to save their lives. No promises, but there's a chance."

"What're you sayin'?" Pierce demanded. "They'd serve time in prison?"

"That's exactly what I'm saying."

"How long?"

"Twenty or thirty years, minimum."

"Jesus Crucified Christ," Pierce said with a dark scowl. "Them boys'll be old men when they get out."

"Yes, they will," Gryden agreed. "But it's better than being hanged."

"Alright, what's your fee?"

"A thousand dollars and no guarantees. I'll do the best I can."

"Just don't let 'em swing."

Pierce wrote a bank draft for the full amount. When Gryden showed him to the door, the rancher wrung his hand again. His booming voice dropped by a couple of octaves.

"Alvin and Frank are good Christian boys. Do right by them."

"I fully intend to, Mr. Pierce."

Later that morning, Gryden requested a conference with Mike Sutton and Judge Jeremiah Strang. The preliminary hearing for the cowboys was that afternoon, and Gryden wanted to cut a deal before the case went to court. He knew the Santa Fe would exert great pressure for a swift trial and a speedy hanging. A courtroom was not the place to bargain for mercy.

The meeting was held in Judge Strang's chambers. Gryden opened by informing Sutton and the judge that he now represented Frank Norton and Alvin Sawyer. He then stepped off the proverbial cliff.

"If we can come to terms," he said, "perhaps we can avoid going to trial. I believe that would be in everyone's best interests."

"Not in a month of Sundays," Sutton told him. "They're going to stand trial and I'll ask for the death sentence. I'll get it, too."

"On the contrary, Mr. Sutton, I might easily win acquittal."

"I'd be very interested in hearing your rationale, Mr. Gryden. However you gild it, murder is still murder."

"Not at all. I have a dozen witnesses who will swear

that Norton and Sawyer were senseless with liquor. Moreover, they had no way of knowing the train crew was asleep in the caboose. It was simply a tragic accident."

"Tommyrot," Sutton said. "Being drunk does not mitigate the act of homicide. You need to brush up on your law."

"There's more," Gryden went on. "This has all the appearances of the Santa Fe pressuring the county attorney's office to put my clients on the gallows—"

"That's a damn lie!"

"And as you know, farmers and ranchers loathe the Santa Fe for its exorbitant freight rates. I really think I could persuade a jury to see it my way."

"Try it!" Sutton blurted. "Nobody will believe that tripe."

Judge Strang cleared his throat. "Harry might have something there, Mike. The Santa Fe is hardly beloved by farmers and cattlemen."

"And pardon the pun," Gryden added, "but the prosecutor could very well be seen as railroading a couple of delinquent drunks."

"Not to mention," Strang observed, "the political ramifications could be very damaging. People take exception to a public official who appears to be the toady of the railroad."

Sutton suddenly realized that Strang was indirectly speaking for himself. A judge, as well as a county attorney, risked his political future if he was perceived as partial to a monolith such as the railroad. A moment slipped past as Sutton weighed the consequences.

"What are you saying?" Sutton asked, looking directly at the jurist. "Are you recommending I strike a deal?"

Judge Strang nodded sagely. "Given the circumstances, I believe that would be most judicious."

Sutton was almost apoplectic, yet he knew better than to ignore political wisdom. He ground his teeth, his eyes veined red with anger. But in the end, he cut a deal with Harry Gryden. The charge was reduced to manslaughter.

That afternoon, Frank Norton and Alvin Sawyer were sentenced to twenty years in Leavenworth. That night, Texans on the South Side celebrated the deliverance of their pards. There was, after all, justice in Dodge City.

Shanghai Pierce figured it was the best thousand he'd ever spent.

SIXTEEN

Cecil Wheeler stepped off the morning train from Topeka. He was met by Leonard Parker, the Santa Fe General Superintendent for western Kansas. Parker's greeting was of the sort reserved for visiting royalty.

Wheeler was the vice president of the Santa Fe. A man of imposing bearing, he was on the sundown side of forty, with salt-and-pepper hair and a neatly trimmed mustache. He was second only to the railroad's founder and president, Cyrus Holliday. His attitude was as if he expected people to snap to attention when he walked into a room.

Parker escorted him through the depot. A stairway at the east end of the waiting room led to the division offices on the second floor. There clerks and bookkeepers toiled over company business affairs extending to the Colorado line and beyond. Parker's private office was on the northwest corner, overlooking the town plaza.

Wheeler hooked his hat on a coatrack. Then, like a general assuming command of a distant outpost, he seated himself behind Parker's desk. He was attired in a severe black suit, with a gold watch chain draped across his vest; he gave the impression that he routinely sent men to stand before a firing squad. Parker dutifully took a chair before his own desk.

"Your wire was most disturbing," Wheeler said. "Have you arranged a meeting as I instructed?"

"Yessir," Parker said in a deferential tone. "Sutton will be here at nine, along with the mayor. Just as you requested."

Late yesterday, Parker had telegraphed company headquarters. In the wire, he informed Wheeler that the county attorney, in some sort of backroom deal, had reduced the charges to manslaughter. Parker went on to report, in language so apologetic it was almost servile, that the murderers of the Santa Fe brakeman had been sentenced to twenty years. Wheeler had wired back that he would take the overnight train from Topeka.

"I require candor," Wheeler said stolidly. "Did you, or did you not, convey my wishes to Sutton?"

Parker bobbed his head. "I met with Sutton early yesterday morning in his law offices. I told him the Santa Fe demanded justice in this affair."

"A public trial and conviction?"

"Yessir."

"The death sentence?"

"Yessir."

"And his reply?"

"I came away with the understanding that he would press the case to the limit. He was in complete agreement."

Wheeler frowned. "In short, he betrayed us."

"Nothing less," Parker said. "For whatever reason, he made a deal with the defense counsel. The moment I learned of it, I telegraphed you."

"Have you spoken with him as to his decision?"

"I thought it better to await your arrival. I sent a messenger to inform him of today's meeting."

"Politicians are a detestable lot," Wheeler said, as if thinking out loud. "Even when they're bought and paid for, they sometimes rebel at taking orders. They have the ethics of a snake-oil salesman."

The Santa Fe was experienced at under-the-table deals with politicians. Over the past ten years, the railroad's lobbyists had bribed lawmakers in Congress, several state legislatures, and dozens of towns across the West. The bribes sometimes came in the form of cash, sometimes in gifts of Santa Fe stock, and sometimes in lavish trips aboard a private railway car. The company's deepest involvement in graft had taken place in the halls of the capitol in Topeka. The Santa Fe virtually owned the Kansas state legislature.

Cyrus Holliday was one of the great Robber Barons of the era. In 1868, with wealth accumulated from other ventures, he formed the Atchison, Topeka & Santa Fe Railroad. The original plan was to build a railway line throughout Kansas and extend track to Santa Fe, New Mexico Territory. The Santa Fe, known simply by its truncated name, spread through western Kansas and reached Pueblo, Colorado, in 1876. The revised plan was to bypass Santa Fe for Albuquerque in New Mexico and lay track to the Pacific Coast.

Ever more ambitious, Cyrus Holliday then envisioned a transcontinental railway line. The Santa Fe reached Kansas City in 1875, arrived in Saint Louis a year later, and even now, under a cloak of secrecy, was acquiring right-of-way for extending track to Chicago. The line currently leased track from smaller railroads for the run to

Chicago, operating passenger trains as well as freight service. The company nonetheless had a monopoly in many areas and openly gouged shippers with exorbitant freight rates. The profits generated were more than adequate to bribe an army of politicians.

Cecil Wheeler was Cyrus Holliday's right-hand man. He oversaw the operations of the railway from Chicago to New Mexico, and his authority within the company was that of a feudal lord. On a routine basis, he dealt with congressmen and senators in the nation's capital, as well as lesser politicos at the state level. He felt confident that he could deal with the outland hacks in Dodge City.

Sutton and Mayor Kelley arrived at the stroke of nine. Neither of them had ever met the Santa Fe's second-in-command, but they knew they'd been summoned by one of the most powerful men in Kansas. Parker performed the introductions, and Wheeler granted them perfunctory handshakes. His expression was stern as he motioned them to chairs.

"Let me be blunt," he said, his eyes locked on Sutton. "Leonard tells me you agreed to prosecute those Texans to the fullest. I've no use for a man who goes back on his word."

Sutton flushed at the insult. "Mr. Wheeler, I found myself in an untenable position. I had no choice but to reverse course at the last minute."

"Untenable in what way?"

"You have to understand the nature of things in Ford County. The Santa Fe has its detractors. Farmers and cattlemen, mostly."

"The world's full of whiners. How does that affect the case at hand?"

"Judge Jeremiah Strang advised me to reduce the charges. In his opinion, no jury would convict for murder."

"I care nothing for opinions," Wheeler said harshly. "Two thugs murdered one of our employees and they received a slap on the wrist. Your job was to get them hanged."

"The risk was too great," Sutton said. "A hostile jury, and an acquittal, could have cost me the election in November. I'm of no use to you if I'm turned out of office."

"Just to add my two cents' worth," Kelley interjected. "This mess could've blown up in our faces easy as not. Every Republican in Ford County might've been hurt."

"You have a short memory, Mr. Mayor," Wheeler countered. "The Santa Fe contributes ten thousand a year to Republican campaign funds. Would any of you win an election if I withhold those funds?"

"Probably not," Sutton said. "But then you'd have to deal with the Democrats. They have no love for the Santa Fe."

"You test my patience, Mr. Sutton."

"I'm only trying to point out the reality of the situation."

Wheeler steepled his fingers. "Here is a reality," he said gruffly. "We planned to build a roundhouse in Dodge City, at a cost of one hundred thousand dollars. Does that pique your interest?"

A roundhouse was a enormous circular structure, with a gigantic mechanical turntable in the center, used for storing, repairing, and switching locomotives. The railroad already stimulated the town's economy, with trade goods being transshipped by wagon caravans to outlying settlements, the Texas Panhandle, and army posts in Indian Territory. The prospect of a roundhouse held the promise of transforming Dodge City into a hub of transportation for the greater Southwest.

"Mr. Wheeler, you know our views," Sutton said. "We believe the future of Dodge City is in transportation and farming, not cattle. We would be vitally interested in having a roundhouse built here."

"Any town would," Wheeler said with heavy irony. "We could just as easily build it in Wichita as Dodge City. Do you take my point?"

"No, sir, I'm not sure I do."

"We are hesitant to make such an investment in a town that cannot guarantee law and order. A town where the murderers of a Santa Fe brakeman are allowed to escape the gallows. Does that clarify it for you?"

Sutton and Kelley understood that bribes came in various forms. They were already the beneficiaries of yearly campaign contributions to the Republican Party. Now, they were being tantalized with the prospect of the major transportation facility between Topeka and New Mexico. Yet the offer came with conditions.

"You have our guarantee," Sutton said seriously. "No murderer, Texan or otherwise, will ever again be treated with leniency. I will prosecute them to the full extent of the law."

"That's a good start," Wheeler said. "I will also require a concerted effort to suppress vice and clamp down on violence. Dodge City has the reputation of a pesthole."

"We share your concerns in that regard, Mr. Wheeler. We'll take immediate steps to correct the situation."

"No two ways about it," Kelley quickly added. "Our lawmen can make the Texans toe the mark. You'll see a change."

"Do not disappoint me again," Wheeler warned them. "If you do, there will be no further campaign contributions. Nor will the proposed roundhouse be built in Dodge City. Understood?"

Sutton and Kelley understood perfectly. They were dismissed with another round of handshakes and hurriedly made their way from the office. After they were gone, Wheeler stared at the door a moment. Then he slowly rose from his chair.

"Well, Parker, do you think they got the message?"

"Yessir, I do," Parker said. "They had the look of men who'd just been baptized."

Wheeler smiled. "I rather like the analogy. Quite apt indeed."

Sutton convened an emergency session of the Republican hierarchy. His law clerk raced around town, summoning the men, and an hour later they gathered in Sutton's office. Present were Dog Kelley, Bob Wright, Nick Klaine, and Fred Colborn.

Once they were seated, Sutton recounted the meeting with Cecil Wheeler. He told them of Wheeler's outrage over the murdered brakeman, and the intimidating tactics employed with respect to campaign contributions and construction of a roundhouse in Dodge City. His anger mounted as he spoke, and at the end he could scarcely contain himself.

"Damn the man," he said in a hard voice. "He treated us like we were dirt on his shoes."

"More like cowshit," Kelley amended. "Never had a man talk down to me that way."

Earlier, Bob Wright was somewhat offended that he

hadn't been invited to the meeting with Wheeler. He'd thought it an intentional slight that Ford County's state representative was shown so little respect, But now he felt relieved for having been excluded.

"Don't take it personally," he said. "Wheeler's known for his heavy-handed methods with politicians. He talks the same way to the governor."

"Well, he probably pays the governor more," Klaine said drily. "Who knows how much money the Santa Fe spreads around?"

"Speaking of which," Colborn remarked. "We can't afford to lose ten thousand in campaign funds. Without it, we'd never win another election."

"And don't forget the roundhouse," Kelley said. "Operation that big would bring a lot of money into town. Not to mention it'd put us on the map."

"No question of it, Dog," Wright agreed. "As a transportation center, we wouldn't be so dependent on the Texas cattle trade. That dovetails nicely with our plans for the future."

"How's that going?" Kelley said, glancing at Sutton. "You making any headway with the Grangers Union?"

Sutton sighed heavily. "Farmers are long on talk and slow on action. Getting them to agree on anything will take time."

"Unfortunate, but true," Wright said. "Those I've talked with see the benefits of a coalition with the Temperance Union and shorthorn breeders. But they refuse to be rushed."

There was a long silence as the men considered what seemed a thicket of problems. Kelley finally wagged his head. "One thing's for damn sure," he said. "The Santa

Fe's got us and the town over a barrel. Like it or not, money talks."

"We don't really have a choice," Colborn said. "We're in a position of having to satisfy Wheeler's demands. Otherwise, we're out in the cold."

"Way it looks to me," Klaine said, "the South Side is our most immediate problem. Where do we start?"

"We start by enforcing the law," Sutton said. "I want a crackdown on the Texans that makes the point. No more gunplay in the streets."

"High past time, too," Kelley said emphatically. "Tell Charlie and Bat to take off the kid gloves."

"Dog, I intend to do exactly that."

Sutton's law clerk was again dispatched on messenger service. Not quite an hour later, Charlie Bassett and Bat Masterson were ushered into Sutton's office. He closed the door and got them seated and then briefed them on the meeting with Cecil Wheeler. Sutton's features were stony.

"Understand me," he said. "You and your deputies are to bring the Texans into line. I hold you responsible."

Masterson stared at him. "Sounds like you're sayin' we're not doing our jobs."

"When a Santa Fe brakeman is killed in his sleep, someone must be held accountable. You men are the ones wearing the badges."

"To hell with that," Bassett growled. "We caught them cowboys and brought 'em in for murder. You're the one that let 'em off with a prison sentence."

"Charlie's right," Masterson said. "You let Harry Gryden swift-talk you into a deal that stinks to high heaven. Everybody in town knows about it."

"You know nothing," Sutton said stiffly. "I did the expedient thing in the interests of justice. Judge Strang approved the . . . arrangement."

Bassett snorted. "Call it anything you want, but it still smells. How the hell are we supposed to police the South Side when you go light on murder? Answer me that."

"Let's all calm down," Sutton said. "We're fighting among ourselves when we should be fighting the Texans. I have the solution."

"Well, Bat and me would sure like to hear it."

"I intend to ask the city council to pass an ordinance against carrying firearms. Only law officers will be allowed to carry a gun within the city limits."

Masterson and Bassett were agog with shock. A leaden moment slipped past before Bassett recovered his senses. "You're plumb daft," he said. "We'd have a goddamned war on our hands."

"Talk about gettin' yourself killed!" Masterson huffed. "Quickest way on earth is to try and disarm three or four hundred drunk Texans. Might as well commit suicide."

"Bat, it's the only solution," Sutton protested. "We'll never civilize this town while men are allowed to carry guns. The Texans *must* be disarmed."

"You want them disarmed, do it yourself."

"Damn right," Bassett jumped in. "You pass that ordinance and every deputy I've got will quit. You can have my badge, too."

Masterson nodded. "Same goes for the sheriff's office."

"Good God," Sutton said wearily. "Do you understand that Dodge City lives in a state of anarchy? There has to be a solution."

"There is," Masterson said. "Wild Bill Hickok proved it in Abilene."

"What are you talking about?"

"Anytime a lawman is threatened, it's shoot first and ask questions later. That's how you put the tame on Texans."

"Are you serious?" Sutton said. "You're asking me to condone summary execution?"

"No, I'm telling you," Masterson said. "Texans hot off the trail and tanked on rotgut whiskey aren't like normal people. You want to control them, you convince them gunplay will get them killed. Then they'll act halfway civilized."

"Bat's got a point," Bassett said. "I don't go along with shootin' men unless there's good cause. But if it's them or us . . . I vote for us."

Sutton looked at them as if through a cloudy prism. He finally lowered his head in acceptance. "Do whatever it requires to control the South Side."

"Let's be clear now," Masterson said. "One of our officers kills a man a little too quick, you won't bring charges. Agreed?"

"Yes, agreed."

Sutton stared down at his hands. He thought back to the meeting that morning and his assurances to Cecil Wheeler. The campaign funds and the certainty of a Santa Fe roundhouse being built. The future of Dodge City.

He told himself he'd just made a pact with Satan. And the Santa Fe.

SEVENTEEN

Fourth of July was one of the major holidays of the year. Otherwise known as Independence Day, the date the Declaration of Independence was adopted in 1776, the event was celebrated by towns throughout Kansas. There was a shared sense of patriotism in the air.

The day was sweltering, heat waves rising off the plains in the distance. The sun was lodged like a brass ball in the cloudless sky, searing everything in a noonday blaze. A warm southerly breeze brought the rank scent of cow dung from the holding grounds across the river.

On the South Side, the saloons were open and horses stood hipshot at the hitch racks. Texans looked upon themselves as sons of the Confederacy, and Fourth of July was something of a dubious holiday. Yet any celebration was an excuse to drink, and as the sun reached its zenith the saloons were full. Piano players, in deference to Texans, occasionally belted out "Dixie."

The uptown celebration was planned for one o'clock on the plaza. Farmers and ranchers from the courtryside were on hand, and Front Street was already crowded with buckboards and wagons. Even though it was a national holiday, shops and stores were open to accommodate the throngs of people. A parade was scheduled, followed by speeches from dignitaries, and the boardwalks were jammed with spectators. A spirit of jubilee prevailed along the plaza.

Gryden and Belle emerged from the Dodge House. He was attired in a navy suit with a red foulard tie, and she wore a royal blue gown and carried a silk parasol. She snapped the parasol open to shield her from the sun as they stepped off the hotel veranda. Her mouth dimpled in a playful smile.

"Aren't we the spiffy pair?" she said. "Yankee Doodle Dandy had nothing on us."

"Former Confederate that I am," Gryden replied satirically, "I should be on the South Side celebrating with the Texans. I feel a bit of the turncoat."

"Who do you think you're kidding, sugar? You're so patriotic you could be wrapped in the flag."

"Yes, but I'm still a Rebel at heart."

"I hope you won't mention it in your speech. The voters of Ford County are true-blue Yankee."

"I almost wish I hadn't agreed to run. I'm not liar enough to be a politician."

"Just tell the truth," Belle said happily. "They'll be floored by an honest candidate."

"Wouldn't that be a novelty?"

Only a week ago the Democrats had offered Gryden the nomination for county attorney. Flattered, he nonetheless thought defending criminals was far more entertaining, and lucrative, than prosecuting them. He proposed instead that Col. Thomas Jones stand for the position; he noted that Jones was a man of impeccable character and unimpeachable credentials. But the Democratic caucus

argued that Gryden's experience as a defense attorney
made him the perfect choice for prosecutor; he had in-
sights into the criminal mind that few possessed. Even
more, they urged, he was the one Democrat who could
defeat Mike Sutton.

Gryden was only partly persuaded by their arguments.
What finally pushed him off the fence was his intense
personal dislike of Sutton. In his view, Sutton was an
overbearing elitist, a man who saw himself as superior in
intellect to the common people. All the more damning,
from Gryden's standpoint, was that Sutton fully intended
to stamp out the cattle trade and transform Dodge City
into a bucolic farm town. Gryden couldn't tolerate the
thought of life without the iniquitous frivolity of the
South Side. He reluctantly accepted the nomination.

On notable occasions, particularly the Fourth of July,
politicians were expected to deliver entertaining and up-
lifting speeches. A holiday forum was the ideal showcase
where candidates could display their oratorical talents
and impress voters with their vision of prosperity and
public service. The townspeople, as well as the country
folk, wanted to see their leaders in action and hear them
express their convictions in spirited words. Gryden and
Sutton, as rival candidates, were the featured speakers at
today's celebration

A grandstand constructed of ripsawed lumber had
been erected at the corner of Front Street and Second Avenue. The structure was festooned with red, white, and
blue bunting, and Old Glory was raised on a flagstaff at
the rear. The crowd was gathering on the plaza, and Bat
Masterson and Charlie Bassett were stationed in front of
the grandstand. Over the past three weeks they'd clamped

down on the South Side, and while no Texans had been killed, cowboys with busted heads were a more frequent sight. The lawmen expected Texans at the celebration and had hired extra deputies to prevent a disturbance. The deputies were posted on the fringes of the crowd.

Gryden and Belle mounted the steps to the grandstand. Mayor Dog Kelley was on the platform, although his paramour, Dora Hand, was notably absent. Bob Wright, Judge Strang, and City Court Judge Rufus Cook were there with their wives, and everyone exchanged courtesies in the spirit of the day.

A row of chairs was arranged at the rear of the platform, and Sutton and City Attorney Fred Colborn were seated with their wives. Gryden thought to offer Sutton a handshake, but then he saw Florence Sutton dart a venomous glance at Belle and point her nose in the air. He turned away with Belle and looked out over the crowd,

The festivities got under way at one o'clock. The Dodge City Brass Band led the parade, trumpets blaring and drums pounding as they marched past the grandstand. The band was followed by the fire brigade, with a team of black geldings, their harness polished to a luster, pulling the fire wagon. A company of mounted cavalry from Fort Dodge brought up the rear, the brass buttons on their uniforms glittering in the sunlight. The fire brigade and the cavalry troop wheeled about and halted in formation at the end of the block. The band marched back, halting beside the grandstand, and thumped into the "Battle Hymn of the Republic."

There were almost two thousand people assembled on the plaza. Toward the rear, near the railroad tracks, a group of some thirty Texans broke out in a strident chorus of "The Bonnie Blue Flag." The deputies converged on them from all points, jostling and shouting, until finally the Texans fell silent. Only the people at the back of the crowd were aware of the disturbance, for the noise from the band drowned out the commotion. The Texans held their position by the railroad tracks, faced now by a line of watchful deputies. A moment later the band ended the stirring marching song with a clash of cymbals.

Amid whooping cheers, Dog Kelley stepped to the podium. He greeted the crowd as mayor, welcoming them to the festivities, and launched into a patriotic harangue. He was loud, though not a gifted speaker, and the crowd listened politely as he underscored the historic significance of Independence Day. There was polite applause when he closed with a non sequitur involving Betsy Ross and George Washington. Kelley then urged everyone to turn out and vote in November and went on to say that the first speaker of the day would be County Attorney Michael Sutton. The Democratic candidate, Harry Gryden, would speak next.

The crowd greeted Sutton warmly. He moved to the podium, staring out across the throng. "In 1776," he announced in a clear voice, "the founders of our country declared independence from England. Today, with equal fortitude and valor, the people of Ford County must declare their independence from Texas!"

The statement drew cheers from the farmers in the crowd. The Texans by the railroad tracks booed and loosed catcalls. Sutton waited for the noise to subside. "We must determine," he said, "that our future prosperity lies with agriculture and ranchers who raise shorthorn cattle. We must resolve that Dodge City will not remain a frontier boomtown but, rather, a settled, civilized community. A hub of commerce where we can trade in peace without fear of being gunned down in the streets. A town free from the yoke of the Texas cattle trade!"

Sutton went on for several minutes, hammering home the evils of longhorns and Texas trailhands. When he finished, a burst of applause drowned out jeers from the Texans. Dog Kelley then introduced Gryden, lauding him as a man of integrity and a member of the legal profession. Gryden walked to the podium.

"On the Fourth of July," he said with a sweeping gesture, "we come together to celebrate the courage of our forefathers. Brave men all, they put their lives in harm's way so that we might be born free men. Among their many attributes, our forefathers were practical, hardheaded realists, and we must follow their example."

Gryden went on to say that Ford County enjoyed unheralded prosperity only because of the cattle trade. One day, he noted, the railroads would expand into Texas and longhorns would no longer be trailed to Dodge City. But that day was many years away, perhaps a decade in the future. Texans, he declared, brought millions of dollars into the community, and that was the reality. Anything else was a fairy tale.

"Welcome the Texans and their cattle," he ended. "Welcome them as long as it lasts, and hope it lasts forever. These are high times, my friends, the best of times. Grab hold and never let go!"

The Texans by the tracks roared their approval. Some of the townspeople in the crowd applauded with genuine enthusiasm. The farmers stared at him in doleful silence.

Gryden returned to his seat. Bob Wright, the Ford

County state representative, was scheduled to deliver the keynote address. After Kelley gave Wright a flowery introduction, he launched into a stem-winder on the significance of Independence Day and the visionary wisdom of the founding fathers. Gryden seemed lost in his own thoughts.

Belle leaned closer. "Where are you off to, lover?"

"Trying to be honest with myself," Gryden said. "I think Sutton got the most applause."

"Well, with all the farmers in the crowd, does that surprise you?"

"No, it's fair to say I'm not their candidate."

"And never will be," Belle whispered. "Farmers don't know the truth when they hear it."

Gryden slowly nodded in agreement. It occurred to him that Sutton was always quick to exploit people's moral high-mindedness for political advantage. He thought it was too bad the Texans couldn't vote.

He'd win by a landslide.

The sun went down along the Arkansas in a splash of molten gold. As twilight faded into dark, lamps throughout the garrison flooded windows with a cider glow. The strains of an orchestra drifted from the officers' mess.

Fort Dodge was on a wide plain overlooking the river. To the immediate front was the parade ground; and beyond that, the regimental headquarters. Close by were the hospital and the quartermaster's depot; and farther on, the quarters for married officers. Along a creek intersecting the river were the stables, and nearby, the enlisted men's barracks. Everything looked spruce and orderly, quite military.

The officers' mess had been cleared of furniture for the Fourth of July ball. Gaudy streamers decorated the ceiling, and several coats of wax, buffed since early morning by a guardhouse detail, had brought the floor to a mirror polish. The regimental band, attired in gold-frogged uniforms, played sedately under the baton of a stern-eyed master sergeant. At the far end of the floor, soldiers in white jackets tended the punch bowl.

Col. William Lewis, the post commander, held Florence at arm's length and guided her around the dance floor. Although perfectly tailored, resplendent in a uniform bedecked with sash and medals, Lewis was nonetheless overshadowed by his partner. She wore a satin gown, teal blue with a frilly neckline, and her hair was arranged in a coiffuer with ribbons and flowers. She loved the pomp and circumstance of a military ball.

When the number ended, Colonel Lewis bowed, extending a crooked elbow, and escorted her to the refreshment table. There they were joined by Sutton and the colonel's plain dumpling of a wife. Sutton was perspiring lightly from the exertion, and he surrendered his partner almost too eagerly. Florence moved to his side with an engaging smile.

"What a wonderful evening," she said. "Thank you so much for inviting us, Colonel."

"Not at all," Lewis replied. "Delighted you could join us on such an auspicious occasion."

The Fourth of July ball at Fort Dodge was one of the social highlights of the year. The military maintained cordial relations with their civilian counterparts, and the town leaders were always invited to the ball. Bob Wright, Fred Colborn, and Judge Strang were all in attendance with their wives. Dog Kelley, who never took Dora Hand to social events, was absent. He was spending the evening at the Lady Gay Variety Theater.

"Mayor Kelley sends his regrets," Sutton said discreetly. "He was otherwise engaged this evening."

Lewis nodded, waiting as the attendants served the ladies glasses of punch. "I heard about your speech," he said. "You've taken a bold approach to civic reform."

"Colonel, I felt it was time," Sutton said. "Dodge City's future is directly linked to agriculture and transportation. Our community is infested with Texans and the unsavory element that caters to them. We must rid ourselves of both."

"A noble endeavor, Mr. Sutton. The avarice of the 'unsavory element' all too often impedes progressive reform. I've seen it in many postings with the army."

Lewis was a graduate of West Point. As a young lieutenant he had fought two Indian wars, first against the Seminole and later against the Navajo. During the Civil War, assigned to New Mexico Territory, he was brevetted major for gallantry at the Battle of Apache Canyon and, a month later, brevetted lieutenant colonel at the Battle of Peralta. His bravery in action ensured a brilliant military career.

After the war, Lewis served as post commander of Fort Steele, Wyoming, through 1870. For the next three years, he was billeted as Special Inspector for the Department of Dakota Territory. In 1874, after being promoted to colonel, he was posted to Fort Dodge. His command included the 4th Cavalry Regiment and the 19th Infantry Batallion. He was on the short list for promotion to brigadier general.

Sutton admired Lewis as a man of intellect and worldly experience. As post commander, Lewis had watched Dodge City grow from a buffalo hide trade center to the largest cowtown on the Western plains. He had emerged victorious from every war he'd fought, and he was an astute observer of men and events. He was an ally worth courting.

"We have a hard fight ahead," Sutton observed. "The sporting crowd is firmly entrenched on the South Side, and they'll resist reform to the bitter end. Your advice would be most welcome."

"Progress never comes easy," Lewis said. "I've served on many frontiers, and the struggle of good versus evil was remarkably the same. The decent people of a community are hard-pressed to oust the undesirables."

"Is it your experience that the decent people win out?"

"Yes, but not without great difficultly. Evil has a perverse appeal to the baser instincts of men."

"So how does good overcome evil?"

"Obstinacy," Lewis said with a dry chuckle. "Decent people draw strength from their moral convictions, and they never quit. Their struggle may take years, but no matter. They will not be denied."

"Attrition, is that it?" Sutton asked. "They outlast their opponents, wear them down?"

"Like water inevitably conquers stone, Mr. Sutton. In the end, constancy overwhelms any obstacle."

"Oh, Michael has constancy!" Florence said, fluttering her fan with an animated smile. "He simply doesn't accept the possibility of defeat."

"I'm confident he will carry the day, Mrs. Sutton. A righteous man has no equal in war or politics."

The band segued into a waltz and the colonel went stumping away with his wife in tow. Sutton watched after them with a look of triumphant revelation. His eyes positively glittered.

"Nothing like an old soldier for wisdom," he said. "War and politics are very much akin."

"Of course they are," Florence said brightly. "And you are the Christian soldier in a righteous cause. You cannot be denied."

"Yes, my dear," Sutton said with a broad grin. "As the colonel so aptly put it, like water on stone."

They danced the night away in carefree gaiety. Neither of them doubted for a moment that Sutton would win in November. Nor were they any less certain of the inevitable outcome.

Dodge City would one day be just as they wanted it.

EIGHTEEN

Fifty to play."

Doc Holliday studied the dealer's hand. On the table were an eight, a jack, an eight, and a jack. He figured it for two pair, with nothing of consequence in the hole. Jake Keifer, the dealer, was a tinhorn gambler who fancied himself a high roller. He waited to see if Holliday would call the bet.

The poker game was at a table in the Lone Star saloon. The stakes were fifty-dollar limit, and the other players were Harry Gryden and Ben Thompson and two Texas ranchers, Shanghai Pierce and Hugh Goodale. Everyone had dropped out of the hand except Holliday and Keifer.

Keifer stared across the table with a sly smile. The game was five-card stud, and Holliday's hand revealed a king, a three, a king, and a jack. In the hole he had another king, but it was the jack that impressed him most. With three on the board, Keifer would have to hold the case jack to make a full house. Or an eight.

"Your fifty"—Holliday fluttered greenbacks onto the center of the table—"and raise fifty."

"Think you're bluffin', Doc."

"You have only to call to catch me out."

"I'll do even better," Keifer said. "Call your raise and bump it another fifty."

"I do like a sport," Holliday said, thumbing bills from his stack. "Allow me to take the last raise. Fifty more."

The other players watched with amused looks. Keifer fidgeted a moment, then pushed bills into the pot. "You're called," he said. "What've you got?"

Holliday turned over the third king. Keifer glowered at the cards with an expression of dumb disbelief. "Jesus Christ," he cursed. "How'd you know I only had two pair?"

"You are an open book, Jake."

"Says you."

"I believe I just did."

Holliday raked in the pot. The deal passed to Shanghai Pierce, and as he began shuffling he called draw poker. The players anted ten dollars and he dealt each of them five cards. Gryden found himself looking at a hand where nothing matched. When the bet came around, he tossed his cards into the deadwood. Goodale bet twenty and Thompson raised the limit.

Gryden checked his pocket watch and saw it was almost three in the morning. He realized that tomorrow—today, actually—was July 26 and a Saturday, the busiest day of the week in the office. Yet he wasn't about to quit the poker game, even though he probably wouldn't make it into the office on time. Nor did he particularly care, for he hadn't had a criminal case in six weeks and he was bored with civil suits. The thought of another one made him wince.

The political arena was hardly more encouraging. Four weeks had passed since he'd announced his candidacy for county attorney, and public response had been somewhat lukewarm. On successive weekends, he'd campaigned in Spearville and Dighton, where the townspeople proved to be an attentive audience. But as he crisscrossed the countryside, the farmers he spoke with were cool and distant, solidly in Sutton's camp. So far, Gryden's major constituency was the sporting crowd on Dodge's South Side.

Earlier in the evening, after catching Belle's show at the Comique, he'd gone in search of a poker game. There were games in every dive on the South Side, but he was looking for high rollers, the stimulant of high stakes. He found the game in Ham Bell's Lone Star saloon, a watering hole frequented by wealthy Texas ranchers. Shanghai Pierce and Hugh Goodale would deliver ten or twelve herds to railhead before the end of the season, and they were rolling in money. They were also inveterate poker players.

To Gryden's surprise, there were three professional gamblers in the game. Men who made their living at the tables usually butted heads only when there were no pigeons to be plucked. From all appearances, Pierce and Goodale were so awash in cash that there was more than enough to go around. Jake Keifer was a sleezy tinhorn, one cut above a cardsharp, and excited no one's interest. But Pierce and Goodale were apparently intrigued by the idea of going up against two of the most notorious gamblers in the West. Gryden was intrigued as well and took a chair in the game.

Ben Thompson was a Texan who spent most of the trailing season in Dodge City. He was a blocky man, not quite six feet tall, with square, broad shoulders and rugged features. His gray eyes were alert and penetrating, and even with a full mustache, he looked younger than his thirty-six years. Beneath his suit coat he wore a spring-clip shoulder holster, the leather molded to the frame of a Colt pistol. He was reputed to have killed fourteen men in gunfights.

A dandy of sorts, Thompson was an impeccable dresser. His normal attire was a Prince Albert suit, with a somber vest and striped trousers, and a diamond stickpin in his tie. He was a regular on the Western gamblers' circuit, and over the past decade he had played poker from the Mexican border to the Dakotas. In the Kansas cowtowns, during trailing season, he never failed to find a high-stakes game with wealthy Texas cattlemen. His name alone brought high rollers to the table.

By contrast, John Henry "Doc" Holliday looked older than his twenty-six years. A southerner by birth and a dentist by profession, he was a man of breeding and education. Incurable tuberculosis had brought him West in 1873, seeking a drier climate. Yet there was small demand for a dentist who coughed blood, and he'd drifted into the life of an itinerant gambler. An ungovernable temper, coupled with his physical frailty, had transformed him into a mankiller. For him, a Colt six-gun was the equalizer, and he killed men because it was the sole means of defending himself. He took sport in wagering life against life.

Tall and emaciated, with ash-blond hair and a grenadier's mustache, Holliday was doomed by galloping consumption. His visage was that of a sallow-faced undertaker, sober but not really sad. His attitude toward his fellowman was an inimical union of gruff sufferance and thinly disguised contempt. Speculation had it that he'd killed nine men in five years on the frontier, and his manner left no question that he was equal to the task. He impressed people as someone who could walk into an empty room and start a fight.

Holliday had shown up in Dodge City shortly after the Fourth of July. He was traveling with his mistress, a tawdry woman named Kate Elder, and they had taken up residence in the Dodge House. There were rumors that Wyatt Earp, several months before, had saved Holliday from a lynch mob somewhere in Texas. Why Earp was in Texas and why he would save the life of a virtual stranger was still somewhat of a mystery. But rescuing a man from being hanged seemed as good a reason as any for their friendship. Holliday was understandably wary of undermining his friend's position as Assistant City Marshal. He'd taken an oath he wouldn't kill anyone while in Dodge City.

Gryden looked upon Holliday and Thompson as one might watch circus tigers leap through burning hoops. He'd seen them around town, occasionally exchanged pleasantries, but tonight was the first time he had faced them in a poker game. For all their reputation as mankillers, he was more fascinated than fearful, intrigued by their skill at cards. Over the course of the night he was down slightly more than a hundred dollars and not particularly concerned by the loss. He thought of it as the price of admission for observing professionals at work.

Goodale dealt a hand of draw poker. Holliday and Pierce checked, and Thompson opened for fifty dollars. Gryden slowly squeezed his cards apart, hardly able to keep a straight face. He was looking at four sevens and a queen.

"Your fifty," he said, straining to control his excitement, "and raise fifty."

Keifer and Goodale quickly folded, and Holliday and Pierce tossed their cards into the deadwood. Thompson gazed across the table with a look of appraisal.

"Well now, Harry, holding a winner, are you?"

Gryden shrugged. "Tell you after the draw."

"Let's just see," Thompson said, counting out bills. "Raise you another fifty."

"I'll have to take the last raise, Ben. Fifty more."

"You're a sneaky one, Harry. How many cards you taking?"

"Just one."

"Got two pair, huh?" Thompson laughed, discarding a single card. "Well, wouldn't you know, so do I. We're both drawing to a full house."

Gryden knew he couldn't be beat by a full house. In some Eastern casinos the traditional rules of poker had been revised to include straights, flushes, and the most elusive of all combinations, the straight flush. The highest hand back East was now a royal flush, ten through ace in the same suit. By all reports, the revised rules lent the game an almost mystical element.

Poker in the West was still played by the original rules, observed in earlier times on riverboats. There were no straights, no flushes, and no straight flushes, royal or otherwise. There were two unbeatable hands west of the Mississippi. The first was four aces, drawn by most players only once or twice in a lifetime.

The other cinch hand was four kings with an ace, which precluded anyone holding four aces. Seasoned players looked upon it as a minor miracle or the work of a skilled cardsharp. Four kings, in combination with one of the aces, surmounted almost incalculable odds. Gryden thought four sevens would do just as nicely.

Goodale dealt one card to Thompson and one to Gryden. As the opener, it was Thompson's turn to bet. He looked at the card he'd drawn and grinned like a wolf. "You're in deep shit, Harry," he said. "Gonna cost you fifty to play."

Gryden saw that he'd drawn a nine. "I'm forced to raise."

"I'll bump it another fifty. Do yourself a favor and run for the hills. I've got my full house."

"Ben, I still have you beat. Your fifty and fifty more."

"You're called, sport." Thompson spread his cards to reveal three tens and a pair of kings. "Told you I caught the full house."

"Not good enough." Gryden turned over his cards. "Four little sevens."

The other players leaned forward to look at the cards. "I'm a sonovabitch!" Thompson croaked, glaring at Goodale. "You dealt me into quicksand."

Gryden raked in over four hundred dollars. "Hugh, you can deal for me anytime."

"Me, too," Pierce said. "Damnedest thing I ever saw."

Thompson shook his head. "Shanghai, get yourself an eyeful. You won't likely see it again."

The deal passed to Holliday. "Never say never," he commented lightly. "Perhaps I can deal someone four of a kind. The game is draw poker."

After he dealt, the men fanned their cards. Pierce opened for twenty and Thompson and Gryden folded. Keifer raised fifty, Goodale tossed in his cards, and after looking at his hand, Holliday raised fifty. Pierce muttered softly and folded.

"Got your number, Doc," Keifer said. "Cost you another fifty."

"Call the raise," Holliday said. "How many cards would you like?"

"I'll take three."

Keifer discarded three cards. Holliday dealt him three replacements, then flipped one of his own cards into the deadwood. "One card to the dealer," he said. "I believe it is your bet."

From the play, it seemed apparent that Keifer had started with one pair and Holliday was drawing to a full house. "Well, lookee here," Keifer said, glancing up from inspecting his cards. "Doc, your two pair's not gonna cut it."

Holliday was suddenly seized by a coughing spasm. He jerked a handkerchief from his coat pocket and wiped a wad of reddish phlegm from his mouth. He wheezed harshly, took a slow, deep breath as the other men pretended not to notice. A glass of whiskey sat by his elbow and he knocked it back at a gulp. He looked across at Keifer.

"It is still your bet."

"Got that right," Keifer said. "Fifty bucks."

"Call," Holliday said. "Raise fifty."

"Fifty right back at you."

"And the last raise is mine."

Keifer called the raise with a sly smirk. Holliday turned over his cards "Three aces."

"Bullshit!" Keifer flung his cards on the table, revealing three kings. "You held four and sandbagged me with three aces? That what you're sayin'?"

"Exactly," Holliday said, pulling in the pot. "It's called poker, Jake."

Keifer stood, kicked back his chair. "Maybe you dealt yourself three aces off the bottom. That'd be my bet."

A pall of silence descended on the table. To call a gambler a cheat was an open invitation to a gunfight. Yet the men in the game knew Holliday had given his word not to kill anyone in Dodge City. A gentleman's oath, taken to avoid embarrassing Wyatt Earp.

"You're a lucky fellow," Holliday said. "Under normal circumstances, you would be a dead man. Tonight, I choose not to kill you."

"What a load of crap!" Keifer snarled. "I think you tuned yellow."

"Back off," Thompson said in a hard voice. "You know why Doc won't fight."

"I'm not talkin' to you," Keifer said sullenly. "Just mind your own business."

"Let me rephrase it." Thompson snapped the pistol out of his shoulder holster. "Turn around and walk away or I'll shoot your ear off."

"Go fuck yourself!"

Thompson fired. The slug clipped Keifer's left earlobe in a spray of blood. He screeched like a schoolboy stung by a wasp. "You sonovabitch!" he yelled, clutching his ear. "You shot me!"

"Yessir, I did," Thompson said deliberately. "Now get your sorry ass out of here or I'll shoot your balls off."

Keifer backed away, blood dripping from his ear. He

turned and hurried toward the door. Holliday chuckled softly.

"Ben, you are a marksman of some distinction."

Thompson laughed. "Tell you the truth, Doc, I missed. I meant to take his ear off."

"Nonetheless, close enough. I thank you for coming to my aid."

"Why, hell, I saved his life. Except for Earp, you would've killed the bastard,"

"Yes," Holliday said quietly. "I would have indeed,"

Gunfire erupted from the street. Horses galloped past the Lone Star, the reverberation of gunshots rattling the windows. A Rebel yell pierced the night as the horses thundered south toward the bridge across the Arkansas. A few moments later the staccato roar of four gunshots, one upon the other, echoed off buildings. The night abruptly fell silent.

A man stuck his head in the open door. His face was red with excitement and his voice boomed through the saloon. "Earp and Masterson killed a cowboy!"

Doc Holliday shoved out of his chair. He strode rapidly toward the door, followed closely by Gryden and the other cardplayers. Outside, the boardwalks were crowded with drunk Texans, staring at the shadowy forms of men gathered near the bridge. Holliday led the way along the street.

Wyatt Earp and Jim Masterson were a few yards from the north side of the bridge. A loose horse stood with its reins dragging, and a man in range garb lay sprawled at their feet. The lawmen still had their guns drawn, and Masterson stooped down and pressed a finger to the cowhand's neck. Earp turned as Holliday and the others hurried forward.

"Damn fools," Earp said hollowly. "This one and five more shot out some street lamps. We ordered them to halt and they fired on us."

Masterson got to his feet. "By God, he won't be shootin' at anybody else. One of us plugged him square through the shoulder blades."

"Hope it was you," Earp said. "I don't care to take the credit."

"Me, neither," Masterson said dully. "Wonder who he is?"

"His name's George Hoy."

Hugh Goodale stepped forward, "George worked on one of my trail crews. Their herd just got in this morning."

"Time enough to get drunk," Masterson said. "There'll be a coroner's inquest, probably sometime tomorrow. We'll need you to make identification."

"I'll be around," Goodale said, shaking his head. "Don't know what gets into these boys."

"John Barleycorn," Masterson replied. "Too much, too fast, and they start thinkin' they can whip the world."

"Or outrun fate," Holliday said, staring down at the body. " 'As flies are to wanton boys, are we to the gods; They kill us for their sport.' "

Earp looked at him. "What's that you say, Doc?"

"A line from *King Lear*," Holliday said. "The Bard wrote epitaphs for all eternity. And drunk cowboys."

Later, on his way to the hotel, Gryden reflected back on the senseless death of George Hoy. Yet his greater wonderment was at the friendship of a cowtown marshal and a mankiller who casually quoted the Bard. He thought they lived in strange times, dangerous times, a random world. Where gods killed wanton boys for their sport.

Shakespeare might have been writing about Dodge City.

NINETEEN

August in Kansas was often compared to a slow journey through hell. A merciless sun seared the plains by day, and the nights were cloaked by oppressive heat. Everyone in town prayed for rain.

Yet the sizzling temperature hardly fazed the Texans. By now, the trailing season was far enough along that herds were arriving from the lower Rio Grande valley. The cowhands were accustomed to the blistering desert of southern Texas, and the plains of Kansas did nothing to moderate their spirits. They caroused through the South Side with the abandon of men splashing about in an oasis.

Wyatt Earp and Jim Masterson walked their usual beat through the sporting district. Dark was upon the town, and even with a breeze from the river, their shirts were damp with sweat. As they passed the Lady Gay, they heard the sounds of boisterous Texans mixed with squeals of laughter from the saloon girls. The cowboys were celebrating end of trail at the bottom of a whiskey bottle. No night was complete if they ended it sober.

Three weeks had passed since the death of George Hoy. Oddly enough, the killing of a trailhand hadn't put a damper on the carnival atmosphere of the South Side.

The cowboys still roamed the streets drunk and rowdy, but for Texans their behavior was almost civilized. There were no further attempts to hurrah the town, and a gunshot hadn't been heard since the night of Hoy's death. The carnage was now limited to occasional fistfights.

Earp and Masterson were lionized by Mayor Dog Kelley and the city council. Neither of them sought credit for the killing, and they still hadn't resolved between themselves who fired the fatal shot. In newspaper interviews, they were quick to note they'd been under fire by six mounted cowhands and they had both returned fire. Hitting a mounted man at night, they observed, was all but a toss of the dice.

County Attorney Sutton and Sheriff Bat Masterson were positively delighted a Texan had been killed. Sutton saw it as an object lesson for all Texans and received congratulations from Santa Fe officials for having brought law and order to the South Side. Masterson, who was almost gleeful in talks with other lawmen, thought it affirmed his contention that brute force was the key to suppressing violence by the Texans. He secretly hoped that it was his brother who had fired the fatal shot.

On their first patrol of the evening, Earp and Masterson rounded the corner of Second Avenue and Maple Street. The red-light district, despite the scorching heat, swarmed with trailhands looking to get their wicks dipped. Torrid weather apparently inflamed the Texans' lust, and with money in their pockets and love for sale, they were on the prowl. The two-dollar parlor houses were busy, and the slam-bam cathouses were doing a land rush business. Whores were the sirens' call for cowboys far from home.

A caterwauling howl suddenly split the night. Earp and Masterson turned west on Maple and hurried along the boardwalk. Halfway down the block, they saw a cowhand in filthy long johns being chased by a naked whore. The girl was screaming like a banshee and pounding the Texan over the head with a metal chamber pot. The cowboy reeked of whiskey, and as the whore whacked him again across the back of the skull he lost his footing. He fell spraddle legged into the street.

Earp and Masterson arrived as the whore drew back her arm for another blow. Earp grabbed the chamber pot out of her hand and Masterson took her roughly by the arm. Her name was Hattie Mauzy and they knew her as a woman with a firecracker temper. Her breasts were pendulous, a thatch of black hair between her legs, and her eyes blazed with anger. She cocked her fist and slugged Masterson in the jaw.

Masterson's response was one of sheer reflex. He backhanded her across the mouth, and she went down on her rump beside the cowboy. She screamed a curse, arms windmilling as she tried to lever herself off the ground, and Masterson swatted her again. She stayed down, still glaring at him, her lip split and blood leaking off her chin. The cowboy was bleeding about the head, his eyes dazed. He scooted away from the whore.

Earp grinned, the chamber pot under his arm. "Think you can handle her, Jim?"

"I'll manage," Masterson said, towering over the girl. "Hattie, what the hell's the matter with you, anyway? Why are you beatin' this man with a piss pot?"

" 'Cause he's a rotten cocksucker," she said, her eyes wild. "You know what the sonovbitch tried to do?"

Masterson was almost afraid to ask. "What'd he try?"

"Told me he wanted to ride me like a horse. From be-hind!"

Earp smothered a laugh. "Maybe that's how they do it in Texas."

"Let's go, Hattie," Masterson said, unamused. "You're under arrest."

"Arrest!" she screeched, scrambling to her feet. "What the hell for?"

"Indecent exposure and assaulting a police officer."

"You're just a great big asshole, Jim Masterson. You got no right to arrest me!"

"C'mon or I'll give you another fat lip."

"Better get her dressed," Earp said. "It'd cause a riot if we tried walkin' her to jail buck naked."

"Yeah, guess we'd better," Masterson agreed.

They marched her toward the whorehouse. The Texan slowly pushed himself off the ground, testing the knot on the back of his head. He thought Dodge City was even wilder than its reputation and a whole lot weirder, too. He'd never before been chased by a naked whore.

Or beat half-dead with a piss pot.

Early the next morning Gryden entered the municipal courtroom. Fred Colborn, the city attorney, was seated at the prosecutor's table. He offered no greeting as Gryden came down the aisle.

"Hello, Fred," Gryden said, pausing by the table. "How's the docket this morning?"

"The usual," Colborn replied, thumbing through a stack of papers. "These Texans never learn, no matter how stiff the fine. Are you representing someone?"

"Hattie Mauzy."

"The prostitute?"

Gryden nodded. "I'd appreciate it if you could call her case first. I have a busy day at the office."

Colborn sighed heavily, as if the request was an imposition. At best, he and Gryden maintained a relationship that was barely civil. The election campaign for county attorney had degenerated into a mudslinging contest, with Sutton and Gryden trading insults in the newspapers on a daily basis. Colborn was Sutton's law partner, as well as a staunch Republican, and bitterly resented Gryden. He finally waved a hand dismissively.

"I'll ask the judge to hear your case first. Don't interpret that to mean you have special privileges in this court."

"You're a prince of a fellow, Fred."

Gryden took a seat at the defense table. That morning, when he'd arrived at the office, Sally Maxwell was waiting in the anteroom. She was the madam of the brothel where Hattie Mauzy was employed, and she'd begged Gryden to take the case. She explained the charges and went on to elaborate on how Jim Masterson had repeatedly struck the girl. Gryden saw it as an opportunity to hold law enforcement—and, by association, Mike Sutton—to public scrutiny. He agreed to act as defense counsel.

The street door swung open. City Marshal Charlie Bassett herded seven Texas cowhands and Hattie Mauzy into the courtroom. Assistant City Marshal Wyatt Earp and Deputy Marshal Jim Masterson, acting as rear guard, got the prisoners seated in a pew down front. Gryden spoke with Bassett and then escorted the girl to the defense table. He explained that Sally Maxwell had retained him to handle her case.

Hattie wore a gingham dress that was wrinkled and soiled from a night in jail. Her bottom lip was scabbed over with dried blood, and her hair looked like a bird's nest. She was nonetheless relieved to have a lawyer, and she dropped wearily into a chair beside Gryden. She darted a venomous look over her shoulder at Jim Masterson.

Judge Rufus Cook entered by a rear door. Bassett called the court to order and everyone rose to their feet as Cook seated himself behind the bench. He peered over his spectacles at Colborn.

"Alright, let's get to it, Mr. Prosecutor."

"Yes, Your Honor," Colborn said. "We call the case of one Hattie Mauzy, charged with indecent public exposure and assaulting a police officer. Our first witness is Deputy Jim Masterson."

Masterson took the witness stand. Colborn rose from his chair. "Good morning, Deputy," he said. "Would you tell the court what transpired with the defendant last night?"

"Marshal Earp and myself," Masterson said, "were making our rounds on Maple Street. We saw Hattie beatin' a cowboy over the head with a chamber pot."

"How was she dressed at the time?"

"Why, she wasn't dressed at all. She was stark naked."

The Texans in the first pew laughed, looking at Hattie in a different light. "Very well," Colborn said. "What happened next?"

"Marshal Earp got hold of the chamber pot," Masterson said, "and I pulled her off the cowboy. She'd beat him to the ground by then."

"Go on."

"Well, she hauled off and slugged me with her fist. Packs a pretty good wallop for a woman."

"And you arrested her?"

"Yessir, on the spot."

"One last question," Colborn said. "What is the defendant's occupation?"

"Hattie's a whore," Masterson said simply. "Works in Sally Maxwell's house."

"Your witness, Mr. Gryden."

Gryden approached the stand. "Why didn't you arrest the cowboy?"

"Nothin' to charge him with," Masterson said. "No law against visiting a whorehouse."

"Isn't it true he demanded a lascivious act of Miss Mauzy?"

"What's that mean, 'lascivious'?"

"Indecent and improper," Gryden told him. "Offensive to a young women's sensibilities."

"You talkin' about Hattie?"

"I am indeed."

"Hattie's a four-bit whore," Masterson said. "Have to go a long way to offend her anywhichahow."

"Let's move on," Gryden said. "Did you or did you not strike Miss Mauzy?"

"Only after she'd punched me."

"And then you struck her again, after she was on the ground. Isn't that correct?"

"She come off the ground swingin' and I gave her a little tap. Just enough to put her down."

"Take a look at her face, Deputy." Gryden waited for everyone to inspect her split lip. "Is it your practice as a peace officer to brutalize defenseless young women? To punch them in the face—*repeatedly*?"

"Only hit her twice," Masterson said curtly. "And she wasn't exactly what I'd call defenseless. Not if you'd saw what she done to that cowboy with her chamber pot."

"Yet you didn't attempt to restrain her or overpower her with your superior strength. Instead, you struck her forcefully and hard in the face. Isn't that true?"

"Wasn't near as hard as I could've hit her. But yeah, I put her down."

"No further questions."

Wyatt Earp was next called to the stand. Colborn led him through a recital that corroborated Masterson's testimony in every detail. On cross-examination, Gryden again underscored that Hattie had been struck twice, and forced Earp to admit that she could have been restrained. When he finished, Colborn rested the case for the prosecution. Gryden called Hattie Mauzy for the defense.

"Tell the court, Miss Mauzy," he said. "How long have you been a prostitute?"

"Oh, I don't know," Hattie said, reflecting on it a moment. "I was at Wichita before I come here. Maybe five years, I suppose."

"In your line of work, I would imagine you've seen some strange things from clients? What they ask of women?"

"Yessir, I just guess I have. Real strange things."

"Now be truthful," Gryden said. "Have you ever had a customer demand what that cowboy demanded of you last night? Even once?"

"Nossir, not ever."

"And what was it he tried to force upon you?"

"Well . . ." Hattie blushed, lowered her eyes. "He tried to ride me like a horse. You know . . . from behind."

The Texans in the front pew guffawed and hooted, rollicking with laughter. Judge Cook hammered them into silence with his gavel and admonished Bassett to keep them quiet. Hattie was still blushing when the judge ordered Gryden to continue.

"So you were offended?" Gryden asked. "You were outraged by the indecency of his demands?"

"I was mortified," Hattie said angrily. "And when he wouldn't quit, I grabbed my chamber pot and chased him out of the house. The sorry devil deserved it, too!"

"And you gave no thought as to your state of undress?"

"Well, no, I guess I wasn't thinkin' of that. I was just blind mad at what he'd tried to do to me."

"And in that same mindless outrage, you accidentally slapped Deputy Masterson. Isn't that so?"

"Yessir, it is," Hattie said sheepishly. "I've known Jim Masterson ever since he come to town. Me and some of the girls even let him have a little free nooky now and then. I didn't mean to—"

The courtroom erupted in laughter. Masterson turned the color of a ripe beet and slunk down in his chair. Judge Cook pounded his gavel until the uproar subsided, and waved Hattie and Gryden back to the defense table. In a hectoring voice, Cook lectured Masterson on the proper duties of a law enforcement officer. He then dismissed the charges and ordered Hattie Mauzy released from custody.

Gryden thought it was one of his finer days in a courtroom. He grinned at Colborn and wished he could be a fly on the wall when Sutton heard the news. Gryden couldn't wait to see the reports in the newspaper.

A soiled dove exonerated by the lawman she'd slugged.

A meeting of the town's leading Democrats was held in Gryden's office that afternoon. The primary issue under discussion was the November election for the post of county attorney. They were gathered as well to select a delegate to the Democratic state convention in September.

Gryden chaired the meeting. Seated around the room were his law partner, Thomas Jones; Dan Frost of the *Ford County Globe;* Deacon Cox, who owned the Dodge House; and Ham Bell, proprietor of the Lone Star saloon. Fred Zimmerman, the owner of Zimmerman's Mercantile, was the last to arrive. He was one of the few merchants who supported a Democratic ticket.

"Harry, you're a newspaperman's dream," Frost said, playfully wagging a finger at Gryden. "You turned that courtroom on its ear this morning."

"Damned if he didn't!" Bell enthused. "It's all over town about Jim Masterson humpin' a whore. Sutton and the Republicans will never live it down."

"I can't take all the credit," Gryden said. "I had no idea Masterson frequents a whorehouse. Hattie just blurted it out."

Jones laughed. "However it happened, it's a feather in your cap. You're the defender of wayward girls who are brutalized by corrupt lawmen. The voters will sit up and take notice."

"Will they ever!" Frost hooted. "Wait till you see my story in tomorrow's paper on the hypocrisy of reformers. I'll do everything but put *Sutton* in that whorehouse."

"Yes, but it's a marginal victory," Gryden said, his tone

suddenly serious. "In November, I doubt that I'll carry ten percent of the farm vote. That's a deficit we have to overcome."

Zimmerman cleared his throat. "Many people are privately against reform," he said. "They fear the end of the cattle trade will be the end of prosperity for Dodge City. By the same token, they are concerned about law and order on the South Side."

"The way I see it," Cox said, "Harry needs to broaden his base. Tag Sutton and the Republicans as Prohibitionists whose hidden goal is to outlaw liquor. And at the same time, steal some of Sutton's thunder—stress the need for law and order."

"Damn good idea," Frost chimed in. "I'll write some articles along the same lines. Position Harry as the candidate for *all* the people. The man who will save Dodge from the reformers' meddling."

"Try not to lay it on too thick," Gryden said. "You might make me sound like a reformer myself."

"How's this for an angle?" Bell said. "There's a Republican in the White House and he's about to start an Indian war in our own backyard. Let's make Sutton the whipping boy for the president's tomfoolery."

"Wait a minute," Frost said, confused. "What Indian war?"

"Down in Indian Territory," Bell said. "I was talkin' with a cattleman in the saloon this morning. He just brought a herd off the trail and he told me there's big trouble brewing down there."

The Texan, according to Bell, had been approached by an army officer and a squad of cavalry in Indian Territory. The officer was acting on orders from the commander of

Fort Supply, and he'd paid top dollar for fifty steers. From what the Texan gathered, the Indian Agent for the Cheyenne had shorted them on rations and the tribe was threatening to go on the warpath. The fifty steers were a peace offering to prevent a rebellion.

"See where I'm headed?" Bell concluded. "The president and Sutton are both Republicans, and it's the Republicans that got the Indians riled up. Lay some of the blame on Sutton."

"That's a little thin," Frost said. "We have only the Texan's word, and for all we know, it's an isolated incident. Besides, no one gives a hoot in hell for the Indians."

"Sad but true," Jones added. "The only concern people have about Indians is that they be confined to the reservation. Out of sight, out of mind, and largely forgotten. It's hardly a campaign issue for Harry."

"Don't be too sure," Gryden said. "President Hayes is a die-hard Prohibitionist, and he almost didn't get elected. We might use that and the Indian scare to undercut support for Sutton."

Rutherford B. Hayes advocated national prohibition on the sale of alcoholic beverages. In the 1876 presidential election, he'd run against Democrat Samuel Tilden in the most controversial contest in American history. Hayes won by a razor-thin 185-184 margin in the Electoral College.

"Harry has a point," Zimmerman said thoughtfully. "The Democratic state convention begins September 20, hardly more than a month away. We could start beating the drum there."

"Why not?" Deacon Cox paused, looking around at

the group with a sly smile. "So who do we send to Topeka?"

"Who else?" Frost said, deadpan. "We send Harry."

"Excellent suggestion," Jones said quickly. "I second the motion."

"Hold on now," Gryden protested. "I'm in the middle of an election and I've got a law practice to run. Pick someone else."

"How could we?" Cox said. "You're the smooth talker of this bunch, Harry. The convention will give you a forum to link Sutton to our toss-out-the-whiskey president."

"No doubt about it," Frost jumped in. "And everything you say will be reported in newspapers across the state. You couldn't ask for better publicity."

"Hell, who knows?" Bell said wryly. "You might come home a hero, Harry."

"Gentlemen, enough talk," Zimmerman prompted them. "Let's put it to a vote."

The vote was unanimous, with Gryden abstaining. Though it was the democratic way, he was nonetheless a reluctant delegate. His mood was hardly tempered by a repugnant thought.

He wondered how the hell he would contend with all those politicians in Topeka. Just the idea of it spoiled his day.

TWENTY

Gryden stepped off the overnight train from Topeka. The early morning sun cast brilliant streamers of light over the plaza. He hefted his valise and started across the depot platform.

The town was in a state of chaos. A fortnight past, the Northern Cheyennes had broken out of the reservation in Indian Territory and headed toward Kansas. Farmers and their families, fearful of being massacred by a savage horde, sought sanctuary in Dodge City. Over five hundred settlers were camped at the west end of the plaza.

Late yesterday, after receiving a wire from Thomas Jones, Gryden had caught the last train out of Topeka. He'd traveled there four days past for the Democratic state convention, fully convinced the Cheyennes posed no threat to Dodge City. But Jones implored him to come home, and he had jumped at an excuse to leave the convention three days early. He'd long since had his fill of politicians.

According to Jones, the community was gripped by panic. The townspeople and the floodtide of refugees from southern Ford County were terrified the Cheyennes would attack Dodge City. However the rumor got started, the alarm spread within hours, and a sense of impending disaster took hold. In the cowcamps across the river, the Texans formed armed patrols to safeguard their herds. The general feeling was that an attack could occur at any moment.

Gryden saw Edgar Mohler, the stationmaster, standing outside the depot and moved across the platform. "Good morning, Edgar," he said. "What's the latest on the Cheyenne?"

"Not good," Mohler said glumly. "Yesterday, they were sighted about twenty miles west of town. Lots of folks think they're headed this way."

"Was it the army that sighted them?"

"Harry, I don't rightly know. One story has it they were seen crossing the Arkansas and moving northwest. Another has it they turned east and started in our direction. Depends on who you talk to."

"Have any new skirmishes been reported?"

"No, but there's reports of more settlers being massacred. The red devils are killing people right and left."

Gryden thought how easily it might have been avoided. In early 1877, eight months after the Battle of the Little Big Horn, the Northern Cheyennes had surrendered in Montana. The Bureau of Indian Affairs, with typical bureaucratic insanity, dictated that the tribe be removed from its ancestral homelands. The Northern Cheyennes were marched from Montana to Indian Territory, where they were joined with their distant kinsmen, the Southern Cheyennes. The reservation, located near Fort Reno, was some two hundred miles southeast of Dodge City.

Food was in short supply. Congress never appropriated adequate funds, and the Indian Agent routinely shorted the tribe on food allotments. Once a month, the Cheyennes were given slat-ribbed steers that equaled less than half the meat they'd consumed when they hunted buffalo. During the winter of 1877–78 fifty-one children died of malnutrition, and just that summer eighty-three more died in a measles epidemic. The Southern Cheyennes, confined to the reservation since the Red River War of 1874, were inured to such treatment. The Northern Cheyennes finally rebelled.

On September 9, Little Wolf and Dull Knife, chiefs of the Northern Cheyennes, led their people from the reservation. Their announced intention was to return to the center of their universe, the Sacred Mountain, located in the Black Hills of Dakota Territory. Gen. John Pope, commander of the Department of the Missouri, ordered units into the field from Fort Leavenworth, Fort Hays, Fort Wallace, Fort Lyon, Fort Dodge, Fort Reno, and Fort Supply. The strategy was to entrap the tribe in a multi-pronged pincer movement, denying them escape in any direction. The pursuit began on September 10.

On September 12, the Northern Cheyennes crossed the Cimarron in Indian Territory. There were 350 in the band, including men, women, and children, and they made camp on the north side of the river. The following morning, shortly after dawn, a cavalry battalion from Fort Reno attacked the encampment. The Cheyennes were prepared to die rather than surrender, and the battle raged through the day and into the night, with three warriors lost and eleven troopers killed. On the morning of September 14, the cavalry commander ordered a general retreat.

The Northern Cheyennes crossed the border into

Kansas on September 17. A day later, just fifty miles south of Dodge City, they outfought a cavalry unit at the Battle of Bluff Creek. On the morning of September 21, at the Battle of Sand Creek, the warriors again routed a cavalry battalion. The following day, only twenty miles south of Dodge City, a Cheyenne scouting party killed a rancher and his wife and two cowhands. The army units were scattered and in disarray, and the Northern Cheyennes advanced deeper into Kansas. The latest report put them twenty miles west of Dodge City or perhaps riding east to attack the town. No one really knew.

The date was September 24. Gryden reflected that the Cheyennes, in fifteen days, had fought three battles, routing the army at every turn, and killed well over thirty soldiers and civilians. As a former cavalryman he felt a grudging admiration for their tactical genius, and at the same time he sympathized with their determination to return to their ancestral homelands. The fault, he told himself, lay with the bureaucrats who had forcibly removed the Cheyennes to Indian Territory. Any man, red or white, would fight if his children were starving.

Gryden rounded the corner of the depot. He angled across Railroad Avenue to the opposite corner and entered the Dodge House. In the lobby he waved to the desk clerk and took the stairs to the third floor. When he opened the door to the suite, Belle was seated on the sofa, still dressed in a nightgown and peignoir. A room service tray was on a side table, with a pot of coffee, biscuits and jam, and a plate of crisp bacon. She looked around as Gryden closed the door and dropped his valise on the floor. She hurried across the room.

"You're home!" She laughed, throwing her arms around his neck, and kissed him soundly. "I've never been so happy to see you."

"I should go away more often," Gryden said, holding her in a tight embrace. "How'd you know I was coming in?"

"Tom Jones told me last night. I got up early and ordered a little breakfast. I thought you might be hungry."

"I'm starved."

She got him seated on the sofa and poured coffee. Gryden spread jam on a biscuit and wolfed it down with cold bacon. He drained his coffee cup and she poured again as he reached for another biscuit. Her features suddenly turned serious.

"Isn't it terrible about the Indians? Everyone's just sick with worry we'll be attacked."

"I tend to doubt it," Gryden said between bites. "The Cheyennes are too smart for that."

"What do you mean?"

"There are only three or four hundred of them. It doesn't make sense they'd attack a town this big. Especially with Fort Dodge just five miles away."

"How can you be so sure?" she said. "The whole town's talking about nothing else."

"Take my word for it," Gryden said, pausing for a sip of coffee. "The Cheyennes are doing their best to avoid the army. They're not looking for a fight."

"Then why did you rush home in such a hurry?"

"To be with you."

"Oh?" She gave him a curious look. "I think you're a big fibber."

"Matter of fact . . ." Gryden studied her outfit. "I've

been away four days and here you are wearing next to nothing. I'm starting to get ideas."

"Now I know you're fibbing."

"What makes you say that?"

"Because I know you, Harry Gryden. You only came home because Tom wired you."

"Well, maybe I should talk with him and see what's what. We could always continue this later."

She gave him a vixen smile. "Later will be just fine, sugar. I'm not going anywhere."

"Don't change clothes, either."

She laughed a throaty laugh and walked him to the door. Gryden kissed her as he went out, then hurried down the stairs and onto the street. He moved along the boardwalk, aware of a tense quiet that had settled over the plaza. A few minutes later he turned into the office.

Velma gave him a quick once over. "You look like you slept in those clothes."

"You are the soul of perception, Velma. Next, you'll tell me I need a shave."

"That, too."

"Thanks."

Gryden crossed the anteroom to Jones's office. Jones rose from behind his desk. "Well, Harry," he said. "I see you caught the night train."

"Your wire brought me running, Tom. What's all this nonsense about an Indian attack?"

"Sutton and his pals have everyone convinced we're under imminent threat of being scalped. In my opinion, they're alarmists, but they actually believe it could happen. Personally, I think the Cheyennes won't come anywhere near Dodge City."

"Then why did you call me back from Topeka?"

"Politics, plain and simple," Jones said. "As a candidate for county attorney, you have to appear concerned with the people's safety and welfare. Just as concerned as Mike Sutton."

"You're talking about pretense," Gryden said. "You want me to pretend I believe the town is in danger? All for appearances' sake?"

"I just want to see you elected, Harry. No one ever said politics is clean-cut and aboveboard."

"Well, I suppose there's nothing for it but to play the game. I'll have to talk with Dog Kelley."

"Why Kelley?"

"When you rally round the flag, who else would you go to but the mayor? He's the defender of our fair town."

"Except that he takes orders from Sutton."

"I won't let him know that I know."

A swamper was emptying spittoons when Gryden came through the door of the Alhambra. One bartender was stocking shelves while the other rolled in a keg of beer. Kelley was seated at a poker table toward the rear, drinking a cup of coffee. He nodded amiably.

"Mornin', Harry," he said. "Thought you were in Topeka."

Gryden took a chair. "I caught the night train when I heard the Cheyennes are about to attack. I've come to volunteer my services."

"What services is that?"

"Dog, I was a cavalry officer in the war. I feel fully qualified to fight Indians."

Kelley looked uncomfortable. "Mike Sutton has set

himself up to command whatever militia we raise. You'd have to serve under him."

"Of course," Gryden said with a straight face. "I'm here to help defend our town. Who commands isn't important."

"Well, that's damn good of you, Harry. I'll tell Mike you said so."

"Sound the bugle and I'll be there, Dog. I won't let you down."

On the street again, Gryden walked next door to the *Ford County Globe*. He thought the likelihood of an Indian attack was somewhere between slim and none. But he was all too aware that politics was a matter of perception, much like a magician's sleight of hand. The voters needed to be told about his intrepid return from Topeka. How he stood between them and the Cheyennes.

Dan Frost was just the man to write the story.

Fort Dodge was in the midst of preparing for battle. Horses were being saddled by cavalrymen, and infantry units were forming on the parade ground. Troops were rushing everywhere.

Late that morning, Sutton and Kelley arrived in a buggy. They left the horse tied to a hitching post and entered regimental headquarters. The orderly room was staffed by a burly sergeant major, a corporal, and three privates. The sergeant major stepped forward.

"Gentlemen," he said in a rumbling voice. "Can I help you with something?"

"I'm County Attorney Sutton," Sutton replied, "and this is Mayor Kelley. We're here to see Colonel Lewis."

Sgt. Major John Quincannon was barrel-chested, with

no neck, his head fixed directly on his shoulders. "The colonel's a mite busy just now," he said. "What would be the nature of your business?"

"A matter of some urgency," Sutton said. "If you will, just tell him we're here."

Quincannon drilled them with a hard stare. He abruptly wheeled around, crossed the orderly room, and disappeared through a door. Some moments later the door opened and he stepped out with a stolid glare. He motioned them forward.

"The colonel will see you."

Sutton and Kelley moved through the door. Col. William Lewis was seated at his desk, signing documents with a quick stroke of his pen. He was dressed in campaign blues and his manner was harried. He looked up with an impatient frown.

"Gentlemen," he said. "I haven't much time this morning. Please be brief."

There was no offer of chairs. Sutton and Kelley remained standing before the desk, hats in hand. Sutton gestured out the window. "Colonel, from the look of things, you're taking to the field."

"We depart momentarily," Lewis said. "I intend to pursue and engage the hostiles. Anything else?"

"What about Dodge City?" Sutton said. "You're leaving the town defenseless."

"The field command will consist of the 4th Cavalry and three companies of the 19th Infantry. A company of infantry will remain in garrison."

"Infantry won't be of any use if we're attacked. They'd never make it to town in time."

"Mike's right, Colonel," Kelley added. "You've got to leave at least a troop of cavalry."

Lewis set aside his pen. "Why do you think you'll be attacked?"

"We can't take any chances," Sutton said. "We heard the Indians were only twenty miles away."

"That was yesterday, Mr. Sutton, and it was my scouts who made the report."

Lewis stood and moved to a large map framed on the wall. He pointed to a spot on the winding Arkansas. "The sighting was here," he said. "The Cheyennes crossed the river and moved off to the northwest. Dodge City is in no danger."

"We don't know that for sure," Sutton protested. "The Indians have already fought the army to a standstill in three battles, and escaped each time. They're killing civilians, Colonel."

"I am aware of the casualties," Lewis said in an icy tone. "The hostiles will not escape my command."

"Let's pray to God you run them down and halt this madness. But what if they slip past you and double back in this direction? What then?"

Lewis was all too aware of the task before him. Little Wolf and Dull Knife, the Cheyenne war chiefs, seemed fiendishly clever at outwitting and outfighting the army. Gen. Phil Sheridan had once declared the Cheyennes "the finest light cavalry in the world," and over the past two weeks they'd again proved the point. Until now, the mission of subduing the Cheyennes had been assigned to company grade officers, and that had been a costly mistake. Lewis planned to lead his command himself, with an entire regiment in the field. Little Wolf and Dull Knife were about to meet their master.

"The Cheyennes will not turn back," he said. "They are resolutely determined to reach Dakota, but that will not happen. I intend to defeat them in the field."

"Never hurts to be careful," Kelley said tactfully. "How about leavin' us one troop of cavalry . . . just in case?"

"No, Mayor Kelley, I cannot," Lewis said. "I plan to overpower the hostiles by strength of force. I cannot spare a cavalry unit."

"Then give us rifles," Sutton insisted. "We'll form a militia to defend the town. We need rifles to arm everyone."

"Sorry, but that isn't possible. We have emptied the armory to supply the regiment for an extended campaign. Have you tried the hardware stores in town?"

"Drop in the bucket," Kelley said. "Hardware stores don't carry anywhere near enough rifles. We need at least six hundred."

"*Six hundred,*" Lewis repeated incredulously. "You could defend Saint Louis with six hundred men."

"Colonel, it's as you said," Sutton observed. "Strength of force will carry the day. If the Indians double back, we will not allow Dodge City to be overrun. We have a responsibility to the people."

Lewis wondered if Sutton was pandering to the public's fear of marauding Indians. He thought Sutton sounded very much like a demagogue, a politician positioning himself to be the hero of the hour. The idea took on added currency given the situation in the field. The Cheyennes were no threat to Dodge City.

"I suggest you contact Governor Anthony," Lewis said. "Perhaps he can provide the arms you require."

Sutton shook his head. "Even if he could, it would be too late. We need those rifles today."

"You don't need them at all," Lewis said sharply. "How many times do I have to tell you, Mr. Sutton? The Cheyennes will not attack Dodge City."

"You can't guarantee that, Colonel," Sutton retorted. "No disrespect intended, but so far, the army's done little to stop this uprising. We have to look to our own defense."

Lewis stiffened. "I have a campaign to conduct. Good day, gentlemen."

Sutton and Kelley understood that they had been dismissed. Lewis stared them down and they backed away, moving into the orderly room. Sgt. Major John Quincannon ushered them out of the building with a tight scowl. They climbed into their buggy without a word and drove off toward town. The Dodge City militia now seemed a stillborn idea.

Not quite an hour later, the post bugler sounded "Boots and Saddles." The 4th Cavalry rode out from Fort Dodge, guidons fluttering, followed by the 19th Infantry. Supply wagons brought up the rear of the column.

Col. William Lewis led his command west along the Arkansas.

TWENTY-ONE

"A cup of coffee, a sandwich, and you
A cozy corner, a table for two
A chance to whisper and cuddle and coo
With lots of loving and hugging from you"

Belle was a vision of loveliness. She stood before the footlights, exquisite in a gown of teal blue. The bodice was cut low and cinched tight at the waist, displaying her sumptuous figure. Her flaxen hair was upswept and drawn back, with a soft cluster of curls fluffed high on her forehead. The effect was one of lost innocence and smoky sensuality.

Her clear alto voice filled the theater, pitched low and intimate. She acted out the song with poignant emotion, and her sultry delivery somehow gave the lyrics a haunting quality. The crowd was captivated, all eyes on the stage, caught up in a ballad all the more touching because of her beauty.

"I don't need music, laughter, or wine
Whenever your eyes look into mine

A cup of coffee, a sandwich, and you
A cozy corner, a table for two"

A moment slipped past, frozen in time. Then the crowd
roared to life, the theater vibrating to thunderous applause and wild cheers. Belle took a bow, then another
and another, and still the house rocked with ovation. The
maestro signaled with his baton and the orchestra segued
into the final bars of the ballad. The curtain swished
closed as Belle stood bathed in the glow of the lights.

Gryden watched her with a look of warm approval. A
slow smile touched the corners of his mouth, for he knew
she'd played it for all it was worth. The ballad was the last
number of the night, and the musicians began packing
their instruments. The crowd of cowhands and soldiers
started drifting toward the door as Gryden sipped his
bourbon. He planned to wait and walk Belle to the hotel.

There were fewer Texans in the audience than a week
ago. The date was October 4 and trailing season was
drawing to a close, less than twenty thousand cows on the
holding grounds across the river. Eddie Foy had long
since departed for New York, and Belle was once again
the stellar attraction of the Comique. The pace of the
South Side slowed by degree, as though the scarcity of
Texans was a barometer. Winter was not far away.

Gryden was in a reflective mood. The end of trailing
season, and the departure of the Texans, always made him
maudlin. As he sipped his bourbon, he was reminded that
the county elections were only a month away. By his
reckoning, Sutton had gained ground posturing as the defender of Dodge City. Few people realized it was all nonsense, even when the governor refused to provide rifles

for the stillborn militia. Nor had the attack Sutton pre-
dicted come to pass. The Cheyennes were long gone from
Kansas.

The whole affair, in Gryden's mind, seemed the stuff
of tragedy. After a pursuit of three days, Col. William
Lewis had overtaken the Indians seventy miles northwest
of Dodge City. On September 27 Lewis and his command
had engaged the Cheyennes along the bluffs and canyons
of White Woman's Creek. The Indians made their stand
behind stone breastworks in a canyon, and the army's attack was blunted against a fortified position. Colonel
Lewis rode to the front of the skirmish line and rallied his
men in a headlong charge. He was shot from his horse by
the Cheyennes.

Capt. Clarence Mauck, the second-in-command,
halted the attack. Colonel Lewis was carried to the rear,
the femoral artery in his left leg severed by a rifle ball. As
darkness settled over the canyon, the soldiers withdrew
and the Cheyennes slipped off into the night. Colonel
Lewis was placed in an ambulance wagon, still bleeding
despite a tourniquet on his leg, and began the journey to
Fort Wallace, the nearest army post. On the Smoky Hill
River, just fifteen miles from Fort Wallace, he died from
loss of blood. His remains were shipped by train to Fort
Leavenworth.

The Cheyennes eluded the 4th Cavalry for the next
week. On October 1, desperate for food and fresh horses,
they raided settlements throughout northwest Kansas. In
the course of the raids, forty-one settlers were killed and
over twenty women were brutally ravished by warriors.
The Cheyennes had fought four pitched battles with the
army in their odyssey through Indian Territory and

Kansas and had yet to be defeated. On October 3, they crossed into Nebraska.

The Cheyennes' escape had occurred only yesterday, and it created a furor. The newspapers sensationalized the news with jingoistic prose, demanding revenge for the killings and the barbaric treatment of women. Dan Frost, in the *Ford County Globe,* damned the "brutal lust" of the Cheyennes and castigated "Eastern highbrows who dish up a lot of slush concerning the nobility of the savages." Nick Klaine, in the *Dodge City Times,* suggested that it was time "Kansas took a contract for missionary work, in which companies of frontiersmen should civilize or exterminate the red butchers." Mike Sutton was quoted as saying "the U.S. Army failed utterly in protecting the lives and property of the people of Ford County."

Gryden refused all requests for a quote. The bloody conflict seemed to him as tragic for the Cheyennes as it was for the settlers. The Indians would ultimately be caught and punished, perhaps slaughtered, by an army bent on retribution. He was bothered as well that the newspapers had printed only a cursory and altogether too sketchy obituary of Colonel Lewis. In Gryden's mind, a valiant officer who rode into the jaws of death deserved, at the very least, a heroic eulogy. He felt no less sympathetic for the settlers and their families, but he still refused a quote. He simply wasn't politician enough to trade on suffering for political gain.

Belle appeared from backstage. She'd changed into a taffeta gown, her hair still upswept, a shawl thrown over her shoulders. As she approached the table, she caught him staring into his whiskey glass. "Why the sad face?" she said. "You look like you just lost the trial of the century."

Gryden got to his feet. "Nothing that bad," he said, summoning a smile. "Just woolgathering on this and that."

"Well, sugar, I'm here to cheer you up. What say we grab a bite to eat somewhere? I'm famished."

"I wouldn't doubt it after the show you put on. That last song was a little gem."

"Did you like it?"

"You had the cowboys crying in their beer."

"How about you?"

"I still have a lump in my throat."

"That'll be the day!"

They walked from the theater through the saloon and gaming parlor. The cowhands and soldiers lining the bar turned to stare, envy for Gryden written across their faces. Outside, Gryden nodded to Wyatt Earp and Jim Masterson, who were posted by the front window. He led Belle to a café a few doors down from the Comique.

"Damn lawyers," Masterson said ruefully. "They have all the luck with women."

"No, not lawyers," Earp said. "Just Harry Gryden."

"Well, hell, Wyatt, you know what I mean. You and me make do with whores now and then. He's got Belle London to keep him warm."

"I suppose some men were just born to frolic with whores. Have a look and see what Kennedy's doing."

Masterson peeked through the window. His gaze went to a lanky cowhand with a soup-strainer mustache and buscadero holsters with a brace of pistols. The Texan stood at the bar, drinking and talking with a couple of cowboys. He signaled the barkeep for another round.

"Still sousing whiskey," Masterson said, turning from

the window. "Way it looks, he's the one buyin' the drinks."

"Guess he can afford it," Earp said. "His daddy's got more money than God."

"Yeah, but that don't explain why he's hangin' around town."

"I'd just bet it's got to do with Dog Kelley."

The Texan was James "Spike" Kennedy. He was the son of Miflin Kennedy, one of the largest ranchers in Texas and the partner of Richard King, of the fabled King Ranch. A week ago, during a drunken night on the town, Spike Kennedy had caused a disturbance in the Alhambra Saloon. Dog Kelley attempted to eject him, but Kennedy, who was an obstreperous hell-raiser, put up a fight. Kelley often acted as his own bouncer and he promptly decked Kennedy with a clubbing blow to the jaw. He tossed the young Texan into the street.

Kennedy left town the next morning. The consensus was that he'd thought better of further fisticuffs with Mayor Kelley, which would have landed him in jail. Everyone assumed he had returned to Texas, for the season was ending and the last of his father's herds had been trailed to railhead. Late yesterday, after a five-day absence, he reappeared on the South Side, drifting from saloon to saloon and buying drinks for fellow Texans. The rumor quickly surfaced that he was back to settle the score with Dog Kelley.

Marshal Charlie Bassett, after hearing the rumor, assigned Earp and Masterson to keep an eye on Kennedy. No one was particularly concerned, for Kelley had been rushed to the Fort Dodge hospital three days ago, where he underwent an emergency appendicitis operation. Still,

Spike Kennedy was a troublemaker, clearly carrying a grudge, and Bassett thought he would bear watching. Earp and Masterson had trailed him around town since yesterday evening, never worried that he might spot them. They wanted him to know he was being watched.

The door of the Comique swung open. Kennedy stepped outside, a cigarette dangling from the corner of his mouth. He paused on the boardwalk, wobbly with liquor, thumbs hooked in his buscadero gun rig. He glanced at Earp and Masterson with a drunken smirk.

"Figgered you boys'd get tired of ridin' herd on me."

"Not just yet," Earp said. "We're waiting for you to try something dumb."

"Well, sir, you got yourself a long wait. I'm headed out of town."

Kennedy walked to the hitch rack. He mounted his horse, flipping a drunken salute to the lawmen, and rode south toward the bridge. Two blocks down Second Avenue, he turned east on Maple Street, into the red-light district. Earp and Masterson exchanged a glance.

"What d'you think?" Masterson said. "Maybe he wanted a little nooky before he heads out."

"Maybe," Earp allowed. "But our orders were to watch him as long as he's in town. And that includes whorehouses."

"Guess we ought to go have a look, then."

"You're readin' my mind."

They walked off toward the red-light district.

Gryden and Belle came out of the Silver Star Café shortly after two o'clock. The South Side was closing for the night as they turned north on Second Avenue. She took his arm with a gentle squeeze.

"Thanks for supper," she said. "Nothing like a steak to perk a girl up."

"The question is . . ." Gryden paused, his mouth crooked in a grin. "How perky are you?"

"Take me back to the room and find out."

"Does that mean I'm in for a long night?"

She laughed softly. "A very long night."

"Hmmm," Gryden said with a low growl. "I hope I'm up to it."

"I'll see to that, sugar."

A gunshot echoed from somewhere uptown. Then, in rapid succession, three more gunshots split the night. Footsteps sounded on the boardwalk behind Gryden and Belle, and an instant later Earp and Masterson sprinted past them at a dead run. The lawmen had their guns out.

In the silty light of the street lamps, a horseman suddenly rounded the corner of Second Avenue. He spotted Earp and Masterson pounding along the boardwalk and jerked his mount to a skidding halt. Earp shouted something and the horseman winged a shot that shattered the front window in Peacock's saloon. Earp and Masterson returned fire and the man spurred his horse into a gallop, headed west out of town. The thud of hoofbeats faded into the night.

Somewhere in the distance, a woman's scream brought the lawmen to a halt. By then, they were at the corner, and they turned, looking east along the railroad tracks. The woman screamed again, a bloodcurdling scream of terror, and the lawmen hurried in that direction. City Marshal

Bassett and Deputy Haywood crossed the railroad tracks from uptown and followed them at a run. Gryden and Belle turned the corner as the woman screamed yet again, and saw the officers rushing toward a small house south of the tracks. Belle clasped a hand to her mouth.

"Oh, my God," she breathed. "Dora and Fannie are staying there."

The house belonged to Dog Kelley. Belle quickly explained that Fannie Garretson, one of the chorus girls at the Lady Gay, was staying with Dora Hand while Kelley was in the hospital. As they approached, someone lit a lamp in the front room, and they saw Fannie outside in her nightgown, shrieking and pointing inside the house. Earp and Masterson were visible in the lamplight, moving through the house. Bassett and Haywood stood with Fannie by the door. Fannie rushed toward Belle.

"Oh, God, Belle," she gasped in a quaking voice. "Somebody's shot Dora."

Belle started into the house. Earp stepped through the door and blocked her path. "Don't go in there," he said. "It's not anything you want to see. She's dead."

Belle burst into tears and Gryden pulled her into his arms. She buried her face in his shoulder, sobbing uncontrollably, and he gently stroked her hair. Fannie suddenly sat down, her nightgown hiked over her knees, her face buried in her hands. The four lawmen stared at the women, uncomfortable with the display of emotion. Bassett finally nodded toward the house.

"What happened?" he said. "Any idea who shot her?"

"Spike Kennedy," Masterson said. "Wyatt and me saw him up at the corner, and he fired on us. He took off headed west."

Earp went on to explain how they had lost track of Kennedy in the red-light district. "Guess nobody told him Dog's in the hospital," he concluded. "Way it looks, he shot up the house hoping he'd kill Dog."

"And he got Dora, instead," Bassett said. "Let's have a look inside."

The house had a sitting room leading to a bedroom, and another bedroom at the rear. Their investigation revealed that Kennedy had fired four shots through the window of the front bedroom. Fannie Garretson had been asleep in that room; one shot tore a hole in the bedclothes and two plowed into the floor. The fourth slug pierced the wall partition into the back bedroom, where Dora Hand was sleeping. The ball struck her in the breast and she appeared to have died instantly. Her face was composed in death.

Bat Masterson arrived as Belle and Gryden led Fannie across the tracks to the hotel. Bassett briefed him on what they'd found in the house and how Kennedy had fired on the deputies at the corner of Second Avenue. Masterson looked at his brother and Earp.

"No doubt in your mind?" he asked. "You're sure it was Kennedy?"

"We got a good look at him," Earp said. "I'd swear to it in court."

"Wyatt, if we're lucky, you won't have to."

Masterson considered a moment before nodding to Haywood. "Nat, fetch the undertaker and have him move Dora to the funeral parlor." He turned to his brother. "Jim, go find Bill Tilghman and have him meet me at the courthouse. Tell him to bring a horse."

"Tilghman's not a deputy," Bassett said. "What do you want with him?"

"Charlie, he's the best tracker in Ford County. I'll deputize him before we leave."

Haywood and Jim Masterson walked off in opposite directions. Bassett scuffed his toe in the dirt. "You aim to go after Kennedy, that it?"

"Come first light," Masterson said. "Tilghman will pick up his trail."

"Alright with you, I'll ride along. I always liked Dora."

"Same goes for me," Earp said. "Feel like I owe it to Dog."

"Suit yourself," Masterson said, glancing at Bassett. "With you and Wyatt gone, who'll look after the town?"

"Haywood's the next in line," Bassett said. "Some of your deputies could give him a hand."

"I'll take care of it."

"Kennedy's got a helluva head start. Not gonna be easy to run him down."

"Doesn't matter," Masterson told him. "I'd track the sonofabitch to hell and back twice over. He won't get away."

"Dog's gonna be heartbroke," Bassett said pensively. "He thought the world of that girl."

"Charlie, there's nothing worse than a woman killer. We'll see to it that Dog gets his revenge."

"You saying what I think you're saying?"

"Yeah, he is," Earp interjected. "That's why he told me not to worry about testifying in court. I knew it the minute he said it."

"Bat, what about it?" Bassett said. "You really plan to kill him?"

"I'm not bringing him back alive."

"What if he don't put up a fight?"

"What do you think?"

"I guess you'd shoot him anyway."

"No guess about it, Charlie."

"Wouldn't it be better to see him hung?"

"Why leave it to a court?"

"You tell me."

Masterson smiled. "I just did."

TWENTY-TWO

Harry, you have to get out into the county more."

"Talking to farmers is a waste of breath and we both know it."

"You're not going to win with the South Side vote."

"Tell me something I don't know."

Gryden paced the office with his hands behind his back, shoulders stooped like a thoughtful priest. Thomas Jones was seated in a chair before the desk, his features fixed in a somber expression. The election was less than a month away, and they were discussing campaign strategy. The situation appeared bleak.

"I should never have run," Gryden said. "You were the better candidate, and I told you so all along."

"No, you're wrong," Jones replied. "I lack the ability to galvanize people, or move them with words. All the things that make you a good trial lawyer."

"Well, Tom, even if it were a trial, I'd still be in bad shape. Sutton and his damned coalition have stacked the jury."

"Yes, the timing couldn't have been worse."

Mike Sutton had finally orchestrated an alliance of farmers, shorthorn cattle breeders, and Prohibitionists.

Albert Griffin, the president of the Kansas Temperance Union, had traveled to Dodge City for a meeting with Ford County ranchers and the newly formed Grangers Union. Sutton chaired the meeting and cobbled together a working alliance with a collective purpose. The publicized goal of the coalition was to rid Ford County of Texas longhorns and Texans.

"Sutton's flying high," Gryden said bitterly. "He's brought all the do-gooders together in a crusade against Texans. Not to mention demon rum."

"Quite shrewd, really," Jones observed. "Demon rum and Texans are synonymous in the minds of many people. Eradicate one and you abolish the other."

"And worst of all, it plays well with the voters."

"Yes, but looking at it another way, Sutton's coalition sounded an alarm. Your supporters finally woke up."

The sporting crowd on the South Side quickly united with news of the coalition. Ham Bell organized a fundraising effort that added more than two thousand dollars to Gryden's campaign war chest. Gryden began running full-page advertisements in the *Ford County Globe* and plastering the countryside with posters. He wondered if it was too little, too late.

"Money and politics," Gryden said, shaking his head. "I have an idea it was Santa Fe money that bought Masterson and Bassett."

Jones nodded soberly. "Their endorsement of Sutton certainly didn't help. As to whether they were bought, who knows?"

"Bought or not, they've got their thinking caps on backwards."

Gryden was puzzled by the endorsement. Masterson

and Bassett were intelligent men, so they couldn't fail to understand that they worked for the wrong side. The group they were aligned with—Sutton and his cohorts—was determined to halt the Texas cattle trade and close down the South Side. When that happened, when Dodge City ceased to be a wild and woolly cowtown, Masterson and Bassett would be out of jobs. Once the saloons and whores were gone, the voters would no longer have need of lawmen who maintained the peace with fists and guns. Gryden couldn't comprehend why they hadn't figured it out for themselves. Reform, the end of the South Side, meant the end of Masterson and Bassett.

"You need a larger constituency," Jones said thoughtfully. "It occurs to me that you might find it among the railroad workers. They're easily twenty percent of the vote here in town."

"Tom, that's a corker of an idea!" Gryden stopped pacing, his manner suddenly invigorated. "Railroad workers like their whiskey, and they've probably got no use for reformers. They'd jump on the bandwagon to save the South Side."

"And I seriously doubt they would vote the Santa Fe party line. They strike me as an independent lot."

"By God, I'll start glad-handing them today. They've got more in common with cowhands than they do with these prissy do-gooders."

"Indeed," Jones said. "I suspect there are many workingmen who would vote in favor of open liquor laws. The railroad workers might just be a start."

"I'll tell them a vote for me is a vote for John Barleycorn. How's that sound?"

"Harry, I think you've found your campaign slogan."

"None too soon, either!"

Velma stuck her head in the door. "Mr. Gryden, there's a man here to see you. He says his name is Miflin Kennedy."

"Kennedy?" Gryden said. "Any relation to Spike Kennedy?"

"I'm sure I don't know. Should I ask him?"

"No, Velma, it was a rhetorical question. Show him in."

"I'll be in my office," Jones said, moving toward the door. "Need I warn you of powder kegs?"

"Don't give it a thought, Tom."

Jones was no sooner out the door than Kennedy entered the office. He was tall, with iron gray hair and a snowy mustache, dressed in a serge suit and a high-crowned Stetson. He extended his hand.

"Mr. Gryden, I'm Miflin Kennedy," he said with a firm handshake. "I'm here to see you about my son."

"Have a seat," Gryden said, motioning him to a chair. "I assume your son is James Kennedy."

"Sometimes I wonder. Be that as it may, I'm told you're the best lawyer in Dodge City. I'd like to hire you to defend my boy."

"I'm afraid I can't do that, Mr. Kennedy. Dora Hand was a friend of mine."

"I've just come from the jail," Kennedy said. "Jim swears he had nothing to do with that girl's death."

"In his shoes, I'd swear the same thing," Gryden said. "I was there the night Dora was killed. All the evidence points to your son."

On the morning of October 5, a coroner's inquest concluded that Dora Hand had met her death by a single gunshot, fired by James Kennedy. Late the same afternoon,

Kennedy had been captured by a sheriff's posse sixty miles southeast of Dodge City, near a crossing of the Cimarron River. He was arraigned the following day in the court of Judge Jeremiah Strang and bound over for trial. He'd been locked in the county jail for the past week.

"Pardon my curiosity," Gryden said. "How did you get here so fast from Texas?"

"I humped my butt," Kennedy said. "Took a steamship from Corpus Christi to New Orleans, and several trains from there. I got in this morning."

"Well, so far as I'm concerned, you've come a long way for nothing. There are other lawyers in town."

"I made it my business to check you out, Mr. Gryden. Shanghai Pierce tells me you defended his men, the ones charged in the killing of Marshal Masterson. Have I got it right?"

"Yes, I represented them."

"You also defended the nigra cowhand, didn't you? The one charged with murder."

"Come to the point, Mr. Kennedy."

"Glad to," Kennedy said, fixing him with a hard stare. "When you agreed to represent those men, you didn't know if they were innocent or guilty. Fact is, you went on the assumption they were innocent. Tell me it isn't so."

"Yes, it's so," Gryden admitted. "The law presumes every man innocent until proven guilty."

"Then you've got to presume my son innocent and handle his case. Otherwise you violate whatever oath it is you lawyers take."

"You should have been a lawyer yourself, Mr. Kennedy. You make a strong argument."

"I mean to save my boy from the hangman."

Their eyes locked in a staring contest. Gryden realized too late that he'd been trapped by a skillful negotiator. If he refused, he violated the oath every lawyer lived by, the canon of his profession. And in the bargain, he would know himself to be a hypocrite. He found the notion unacceptable.

"All right," he said stiffly. "I'll represent your son."

"I'm much obliged," Kennedy said. "And you can name your own fee, Mr. Gryden. I'm rich as Midas."

"The fee will be one dollar, Mr. Kennedy."

"One dollar?"

"Just enough to make it legally binding."

Kennedy arched an eyebrow. "A man who works for nothing doesn't have his heart in the job. How do I know my son will get a proper defense?"

"I'll defend him," Gryden said, "solely as a matter of principle. Anything else and I'd feel like a whore. It's not open to discussion."

"You're a man of high values, Mr. Gryden."

"Or perhaps no values at all."

The trail was scheduled for October 22, only ten days away. Gryden promised to interview the younger Kennedy that afternoon and begin formulating a defense. After Miflin Kennedy left, Gryden explained the situation to his partner. Jones was stunned.

"Harry, you've just cost yourself the election. Defending a woman killer won't get you many votes."

"Probably not, but I have to live with myself. I couldn't refuse any man a defense."

"You'll lose," Jones said sharply. "You know yourself the town's already convicted him. What's the point?"

"Tom, I suppose that *is* the point. No man should be convicted by public opinion."

"You sound a little like Don Quixote."

"I always was a sucker for lost causes."

Gryden went from the office to the hotel. Dora and Belle had been best friends, and he could only hope she would understand. He dreaded telling her, but he couldn't allow her to hear the news from anyone else. He had to do it himself.

Belle had just finished dressing for the day. When he told her, she looked stricken, as if he'd betrayed her trust. Tears welled up in her eyes, and she walked from the bedroom to the sitting-room window, staring out over the town. He waited, hesitant to press her, hopeful she would come to terms with it. Instead, she turned on him, her face ugly with anger.

"How could you?" she said stridently. "Dora was my best friend in the world. And that man *killed* her!"

"I feel the same way," Gryden said. "Dora was my friend, too. And so is Dog."

"Then why in God's name would you do this?"

"I know you're upset, but try to look at it logically. The law entitles every man to a defense, and I'm a lawyer. I couldn't refuse."

"Why?" she demanded. "You and your precious law aren't the last resort. There are other lawyers."

"The case was brought to me," Gryden explained. "I didn't want it—I still don't—but his father made a compelling argument. In good conscience, I couldn't turn him away."

"Your conscience! Who gives a damn about your conscience? We're talking about Dora's killer!"

"C'mon, honey, try to understand. As a lawyer, I don't always have a choice. I'm bound by ethics."

"To hell with your ethics, Harry Gryden. And to hell with you!"

She rushed into the bedroom and slammed the door. Gryden started after her, but then he heard the lock click shut. She was overwrought with emotion, grief for Dora and anger at him, and he knew he'd lost the moment. He thought, given patience on his part, she would reconcile herself to the situation. She just needed time.

The old adage popped into his mind, about how time heals all wounds. He wondered if she would forgive him, too.

The courtroom was mobbed. Apart from the sporting crowd, few townspeople recalled ever having seen the accused killer of Dora Hand. Yet they knew his name and the newspapers had informed them that he was an assassin, a maddog Texan. They were there to see James Kennedy convicted and sentenced to hang.

There was a general feeling of loathing toward Harry Gryden. By now, everyone had heard the story of how his client, in an attempt to murder Mayor Kelley, had killed an innocent young girl. Common wisdom had it that Miflin Kennedy, who was reported to own half of Texas, had paid Gryden a fortune to defend a cowardly rich boy. The atmosphere in the courtroom was thick with tension.

Gryden was weary of the whole affair. Barring a miracle, it seemed a foregone conclusion that he would lose the election. His fellow Democrats were in shock, and many of his friends on the South Side were outraged that he would defend the murderer of Dora Hand. Belle hadn't moved out of the suite, but she was distant, barely able to hide her anger, and spoke to him only when the occasion demanded. For the last ten nights he'd slept on the sofa in the sitting room, and there was no indication he would be allowed back in her bed. His one consolation was that he was doing what he believed to be correct, if not entirely right. He told himself, with no small irony, that he was an ethical leper.

All day yesterday he and Sutton had trudged through the voir dire process of selecting a jury. Seemingly there was no one in Ford County who hadn't heard of the death of Dora Hand and formed a strong opinion. Many panel members were excused for their predisposed bias, and many cleverly masked it in hopes of being chosen. Gryden and Sutton both exercised their three peremptory challenges, weeding out men potentially sympathetic to the other's case. Neither of them was fully satisfied with the jury.

A murmur rippled through the crowd as Sheriff Masterson brought James "Spike" Kennedy into the courtroom. Kennedy's left arm was in a sling, and he moved gingerly, still experiencing pain from his shoulder wound. He nodded to his father, who was in the front pew behind the defense table, then took a chair beside Gryden. The bailiff called the court to order as Judge Strang entered from the rear and mounted the bench. The jurors were shepherded in by a deputy and shuffled to their seats in the jury box. The trial got under way.

In his opening statement, Sutton outlined the prosecution's case. He first covered the gory details of the killing, noting that the intended victim was Dodge City's mayor. Then he elaborated on the pursuit by the sheriff's posse and how the fugitive had been captured only a few miles from Indian Territory. His voice husky, he ended with the harsh declaration that the state would seek the death penalty.

Gryden's opening statement was somewhat briefer, almost nonchalant in tone. He casually denounced the circumstantial nature of the state's case and urged the jurors to look for inconsistencies in the testimony. He reminded them that reasonable doubt alone was sufficient reason for acquittal.

Sutton presented his case with zeal and confidence. His first witness was Dr. McCabe, the county coroner, who explained that a single bullet had struck the deceased in the breast and penetrated her heart. Assistant City Marshal Wyatt Earp testified next; he recounted the rumor of a threat on the mayor's life and how Kennedy had been trailed around town. Sutton then led Earp through the night of October 4 and the sequence of events that ended with the shooting. The final question went to identification of the defendant.

"Yessir," Earp answered. "Right after the shooting, Deputy Masterson and me saw Kennedy at the corner of Second Avenue. Saw him clear as day in the lamplight."

"And when he saw you," Sutton said, "what did he do?"

"Fired a shot at us and rode off at a gallop."

"In short, he tried to kill you, isn't that correct?"

"That's exactly what he tried to do."

"No further questions."

Gryden approached the stand. "This rumor?" he said. "The one that Mr. Kennedy intended to harm Mayor Kelley. How did you confirm it?"

Earp shrugged. "No way to confirm a rumor."

"So you didn't trace it to Mr. Kennedy? In fact, you have no proof that he ever threatened the mayor. Isn't that true?"

"Well, there was lots of talk."

"Gossip, as we all know, is notoriously unreliable. A simple yes or no, Marshal. Did you have proof?"

"No."

"Now, as to the shooting itself," Gryden said. "Did you see James Kennedy at or near the mayor's house?"

"No," Earp said. "But he come riding from that direction."

"Be honest now, Marshal. You can't swear who was at the mayor's house. Nor can you *prove* who fired the shots. Isn't that so?"

"No, I didn't see Kennedy. But—"

"And so far as you know, anyone could have fired those shots. Fired into the house and then ridden in the opposite direction. Away from you, into the dark. That's entirely possible, isn't it?"

"Possible, but not likely."

"Yet the truth is, you don't know, do you, Marshal? Mr. Kennedy just happened along and you jumped to the conclusion—"

"Objection!" Sutton said. "Argumentative."

Gryden walked away. "Nothing further, Your Honor."

Deputy Jim Masterson was called to the stand. Sutton took him through the night of the shooting, soliciting essentially the same testimony as given by Wyatt Earp.

In cross-examination, Gryden forced Masterson to admit that he hadn't actually seen the defendant at the mayor's house. Masterson further admitted, albeit reluctantly, that someone other than Kennedy could have fired the shots. Gryden then went to the matter of identification.

"Tell the court," he said. "When the horseman fired at you, what did you do?"

"Why, I ducked," Masterson said. "Happened real fast and took me by surprise. Course, quick as anything, I fired back."

"Let me understand, Deputy. Someone fired at you and, quite naturally, you ducked. And as we all know, the lamplight at the corner of Second Avenue isn't all that bright. In fact, in the direction of the railroad tracks, it's mostly shadows, isn't it?"

"Yeah, there's some shadow past the corner."

"And that's where the horseman was," Gryden went on. "You'll remember, I was only thirty yards or so behind you, and I was ducking, too. In the heat of the moment, with bullets flying and in poor light, all those shadows—you just assumed the horseman was James Kennedy, didn't you?"

"Looked like him to me."

"But you're not absolutely certain, are you? On a horse, in the shadows, it could have been someone who resembled Kennedy. In the bad light, that's possible, isn't it?"

"Well . . ." Masterson hesitated, rubbed his jaw. "Yeah, I suppose it's possible."

"Thank you, Deputy."

On redirect, Sutton tried to correct the damage. But Masterson appeared confused and Sutton finally let it go. City Marshal Charlie Bassett then testified as to what he'd seen at the mayor's house, and Gryden declined cross-examination. Deputy Nat Haywood testified next and Gryden again offered no questions. Sutton called Sheriff Bat Masterson.

In a straightforward manner, Masterson related the capture. His hunch, he told the court, was that Kennedy would ford the Cimarron at the Western Trail. Masterson led his posse overland and arrived at the river crossing the afternoon of October 5. They found no fresh tracks and settled in to wait near an abandoned sod house. Late that afternoon, a horseman approached and, upon spotting them, halted some distance away. Masterson recognized the horseman as Kennedy and yelled for him to surrender. Kennedy reined his horse about and fled.

"Go on," Sutton prompted. "What happened then?"

"We opened fire with rifles," Masterson said. "Killed his horse and wounded him in the shoulder. He didn't give us any trouble after that."

"Did he say anything when you took him into custody?"

"Cursed us to blue blazes when we bound up his shoulder."

"And as to the murder of Dora Hand?"

"Why, naturally, he claimed we'd got the wrong man. I told him to tell it to a jury."

"Excellent work, Sheriff." Sutton turned away with a smug look. "Your witness, Mr. Gryden."

Gryden rose from his chair. "How far away was Mr. Kennedy when he stopped his horse?"

"Hundred yards," Masterson said. "Maybe a little more."

"I'm amazed you recognized him at that distance, Sheriff. Certainly he couldn't make out your faces or see your badges. How did he know you were law officers?"

"I yelled loud enough for him to hear me."

"Even so," Gryden said in a musing voice. "You could have been robbers posing as lawmen. Small wonder he fled for his life. Did you and your deputies all fire on him?"

"Yessir, we did," Masterson said proudly. "Three slugs in his horse and one in him. Pretty nice shooting."

"And I assume you unloaded his pistols when you took him captive?"

"Unloaded both pistols and his rifle."

"Had his pistols been fired? A man of your experience would know right away. Was there the smell of burnt powder?"

Masterson squinted querulously. "That doesn't mean anything, counselor. He could've cleaned them after he left town."

"Of course," Gryden said. "In which case you would have smelled gun oil. Is that it?"

"No, he could've wiped them down."

"Sheriff, you didn't smell burnt powder and you didn't smell gun oil. I put it to you that James Kennedy's pistols had not recently been fired. On the evidence, you arrested the wrong man, didn't you?"

"Maybe he traded guns before we caught him."

"Yes, and bird dogs fly, too, don't they?"

The remark brought snickers from jurors and spectators alike. Sutton tried to undo the damage on redirect, but the jury wasn't buying it. Finally, eliciting a positive response on the defendant's attempt at flight, he dismissed Masterson from the stand. Sutton then rested the case for the state.

"Mr. Gryden," Judge Strang said, "you may proceed with the defense."

"Your Honor, we call James Kennedy."

Kennedy was young, his hair freshly barbered, his mustache neatly trimmed. He took the stand, careful not to jostle his left arm, and swore on the Bible to tell the truth. Gryden moved forward.

"James Kennedy," he said forcefully, "as God is your witness, did you kill Dora Hand?"

"No, I did not," Kennedy said with a look of genuine shock. "I never harmed a woman in my life."

"Did you attempt to assassinate Mayor James Kelley?"

"No, sir, I sure didn't. I got drunk once and Kelley whipped me good. But I'm not one to hold a grudge."

"Where were you on the night Dora Hand was murdered?"

"Well, I was in one of the houses—"

"A house of prostitution?"

"Yessir."

"Which one?"

"I don't rightly recollect," Kennedy said sheepishly. "I was pretty drunk at the time."

"And afterward?" Gryden asked. "Where did you go then?"

"I rode on across the bridge. Trailin' season was about over and I was headed home. Back to Texas."

"And the next day, when you reached the Cimarron crossing, why did you attempt to flee from the sheriff's posse?"

"I didn't know they were lawmen. They were yellin' and waving guns and I took off like a scalded cat. I thought they were fixin' to rob me."

"Look at the jury." Gryden waited until Kennedy

turned to the jury box. "Were you in any way involved in the death of Dora Hand?"

Kennedy ruefully shook his head. "God strike me dead if I'm not tellin' the truth. I never shot nobody, especially a woman."

"Your witness, Mr. Sutton."

"God may well strike you dead," Sutton announced, moving forward. "Two law officers saw you hardly a minute after the murder. How do you explain that?"

"Can't explain it," Kennedy said. "I was down on Maple Street, or already across the bridge. It wasn't me."

"Then why did you fire a gun at them?"

"I didn't fire a gun at anybody. They've got me confused with somebody else."

"You testified that Mayor Kelley—to use your words—whipped you good. And on the night of October 4, you fired into his house, attempted to exact revenge, and killed Miss Dora Hand. That is the real truth, isn't it?"

Kennedy gave him a choirboy look. "Mr. Sutton, I'm likely a sinner in the eyes of the Lord. But I was raised to respect women and respect the law. I didn't shoot nobody."

"Indeed?" Sutton said with heavy sarcasm. "At the Cimarron crossing, Sheriff Masterson ordered you to halt. And please, don't ask this jury to believe you didn't recognize a party of lawmen. Furthermore, you have professed your innocence before God and mankind. So why did you attempt to elude arrest? Why did you run?"

"They were a hundred yards or more off. It'd take eagle eyes to make somebody out that far. I figured them for robbers and I skedaddled. Anybody would've."

"I return to the central issue. You were identified moments after the brutal murder of a gracious young woman. Are we to believe the officers who identified you are liars?"

"No, sir," Kennedy said with wide-eyed sincerity. "They just mistook me for somebody else. I wasn't there."

"Yes, Mr. Kennedy, you *were* there. And everyone in this courtroom knows it."

Sutton stalked off with the last word. Kennedy returned to his chair and Gryden rested the case for the defense. In closing argument, Sutton underscored Kennedy's grudge against Mayor Kelley, his identification moments after the shooting, and his clear intent to escape arrest and prosecution. Finally, in a voice crackling with emotion, Sutton spoke to the vile murder of a woman in the flower of her youth. He demanded the death penalty.

Gryden's closing argument was delivered with a calm appeal to logic. He stressed the fact that the prosecution's key witnesses, Wyatt Earp and Jim Masterson, could not place James Kennedy at the scene of the murder. He elaborated on how Masterson himself had repudiated his own identification of the defendant. Then, with flawless reason, he laid bare the circumstantial nature of the prosecution's case. He reminded the jury that a single reasonable doubt was sufficient to acquit, and then, one-by-one, reviewed a list of reasonable doubts. He urged the jurors to find his client innocent.

The jury was out for almost three hours. When they returned to the courtroom, many of them seemed disgruntled and some looked almost ashamed. The jury foreman felt obliged to comment on the legal theory of reasonable doubt before he announced a verdict of not guilty. Judge Strang polled the jurors and several with open reluctance confirmed their vote for acquittal. Sutton was furious, the crowd appeared dumbfounded, and Judge Strang could barely control his disgust. He ordered the defendant released from custody.

Gryden refused to shake hands with James Kennedy and ignored the congratulations of Miflin Kennedy. He stuffed papers into his briefcase and walked out of the courtroom, avoiding baleful stares from those in the crowd. The verdict affirmed what he'd suspected during jailhouse interviews over the past week. Spike Kennedy was an engaging liar.

On the street, Gryden hurried toward his office. He told himself that he was a criminal attorney, that he had fulfilled his duty to the client and the court. Yet it was a pyrrhic victory and he felt somehow soiled. A part of something coarse and vulgar.

Dora Hand, murdered in her sleep, would never know justice.

TWENTY-THREE

Gryden was still sleeping on the sofa. The suite was a place of frigid silence, aggravated by the outcome of the trial. Belle was morose and angry and maddeningly silent.

Three days after the trial, Gryden decided he'd had enough. He hadn't yet resolved his own sense of guilt, and he felt oppressed by the silence. Either they worked it out, he told himself, or it was time to move on. He wouldn't spend another night on the sofa.

Belle looked particularly lovely, if somewhat aloof. She was still in her peignoir, seated in a chair by the window, breakfasting on toast and coffee from room service. Gryden was dressed for work, ready to leave for the office, and not at all certain how to broach the subject. He decided to take the direct approach.

"We have to talk," he said. "We're not getting anywhere this way."

She took a sip of coffee. "What would you like me to say?"

"Tell me to go to hell, or tell me I'm out of the doghouse. It's bad enough that everybody else treats me like I have leprosy."

"They should," she sniffed. "You only took the case to humiliate Sutton."

"You know that's not true," Gryden said. "Kennedy was entitled to a defense and I couldn't let personal feelings stand in the way. It had nothing to do with Sutton."

"You and your ethics! Everyone loved Dora and now they blame you for getting her murderer off. I blame you, too, Harry."

"So we're all in agreement. I'm a damn fool and I let everybody down. Most of all myself."

"Yourself?"

"Of course," Gryden said. "Do you think I don't regret Kennedy going free? I'd like to see him burn in hell."

"Maybe someone will shoot him and do us all a favor. Do you really regret taking the case?"

"What I regret most is that it's come between us. I don't want to lose you."

She looked at him for a long moment. Her eyes suddenly puddled with tears and she scrambled from her chair. "You won't lose me, sugar," she said, touching his cheek. "I may take forever to forgive you, but I'm still your girl. Nothing will change that."

Gryden took her in his arms. "We'll work through it somehow. A good start would be letting me back in your bed."

"I missed you, too," she said warmly. "How about right now?"

"God, I wish I'd asked sooner. I'm due in court."

"Not another murder!"

"No, it's a divorce case."

"Well, we could always skip supper. Who needs food, anyway?"

"Not me," Gryden said with a loopy grin. "I'll be here with bells on."

She kissed him softly. "I won't have anything on."

"You're a little hussy."

"I'd rather be wicked than good."

"I like wicked myself."

"Then you get your wish."

Gryden was tempted to forget the divorce case. He kissed her and hurried off before he could change his mind. Outside the hotel, he turned uptown and walked briskly toward the office. His talk with Belle had left him in high spirits, as though a burden had been lifted from his shoulders. Yet he was reminded that he had a long way to go to restore his reputation.

The resentment generated by the trial had been profound. Dog Kelley was no longer speaking to him, and every lawman in town treated him with thinly veiled contempt. The *Dodge City Times* had vilified him in an article, and he expected the sporting crowd to start throwing stones at any moment. Even his Democratic cohorts were offended, for they thought he'd let the party down. He was almost certain to lose the election.

"Good morning, counselor."

Doc Holliday was walking toward the hotel. He wore a cape over his gray suit, and his hat was tilted to block the sunshine. His features were haggard and he appeared on the verge of exhaustion. He reeked of cigar smoke and whiskey.

Gryden nodded amiably. "Late night, Doc?"

"Very late indeed," Holliday said. "I have just come from a poker game that began yesterday evening. I am, as you can see, on my last legs."

"Hope it was worth it."

"Oh, I won handsomely, thank you. And how are you faring, if I may ask?"

"Not too bad," Gryden said. "Some people still speak to me."

Holliday coughed a phlegmy chuckle. "We pariahs have to stick together. The opinion of others is as ephemeral as fog."

"I'll try to keep that in mind."

"Well, in any event, if ever I am arrested, I want you as my advocate. You are as much magician as lawyer."

"Doc, call on me anytime."

"I shall, and now, good day to you, Harry. I am in desperate need of sleep."

Holliday ambled off toward the hotel. Gryden was encouraged by the conversation, for it seemed he still had one friend among the sporting crowd. Perhaps, he told himself, the situation was not as dire as it appeared. He'd made peace with Belle, and the brief encounter with Holliday indicated he might yet have friends in town. All in all, not a bad way to start the day.

Velma looked up as he entered the office. "I was beginning to worry," she said. "You're due in court at nine."

"I'll make it with time to spare. Did you put the Sawyer papers together for me?"

"Everything's on your desk."

Thomas Jones followed him into his office. As Gryden began placing documents in his briefcase, Jones dropped a copy of the *Ford County Globe* on the desk. He pointed to a headline on the front page.

"Hot off the press," he said. "The army finally caught the Cheyennes."

"About time," Gryden said. "When was this?"

"Just yesterday, somewhere in Nebraska."

Gryden quickly scanned the newspaper article. On October 24, the 7th Cavalry Regiment had surrounded the encampment of Northern Cheyennes on Chadron Creek. Little Wolf and Dull Knife, the warrior chiefs, surrendered rather than lead their people into a suicidal battle against overwhelming forces. The band was escorted to Fort Robinson, in northwest Nebraska.

The odyssey of the Northern Cheyennes, which began on September 9, had ended in humbling defeat. The Indians had fought countless engagements, pushing ever northward on a trek of a thousand miles, in an effort to reach their sacred homelands in Dakota Territory. In six weeks almost a hundred soldiers and civilians had been killed, but army commanders voiced grudging admiration for the military prowess of the Northern Cheyennes. There was little to equal it in the annals of plains warfare.

"You have to hand it to them," Gryden said. "They almost made it to Dakota."

Jones frowned. "You sound somewhat sympathetic. Aren't you forgetting the people they killed?"

"I just suspect historians will commend their courage. A band of three hundred against the entire U.S. Army? That's quite a feat."

"Even so, they left a string of graves in their wake. I hardly find that commendable."

"Tom, I tend to side with the underdogs these days. The Kennedy trial gave me a whole new insight into being ostracized."

"You brought it on yourself," Jones grumped. "I

warned you about taking that case."

"So you did," Gryden said. "Some Greek philosopher once observed that we spend our lives backing into the future. Today, I've decided to go straight at it. Full bore."

"I must say, you never cease to amaze me, Harry. What brought this on?"

"Something William Blackstone wrote in his *Commentaries on the Law.* 'When the pursuit of justice is linked with politics, the search for truth is reduced to a quest for power.' I woke up this morning with no great taste for power."

"You're saying damn the election, aren't you?"

"I'm saying I wasn't cut out to be a politician. I lack the ability to dupe people."

"Yes, I suppose you do," Jones said. "To paraphrase Blackstone, politics is the antithesis of truth. Or justice, for that matter."

"Speaking of which, I'm due in court in ten minutes."

Gryden walked into the courtroom at three minutes before nine. His client was Mary Sawyer, a heavyset woman of thirty-one with button eyes and an upturned nose. She had three children, two boys and a girl, and her marriage of ten years had eroded into periodic beatings by her husband. Her suit for divorce was on the grounds of extreme cruelty.

Fred Colborn was representing the husband, Nathan Sawyer. Although Sawyer had not contested the divorce, he'd filed countercharges of adultery, claiming his wife had carnal knowledge of a neighbor, Larry Farwell. Based on the adultery charge, Sawyer further contended his wife was unfit to be a mother and petitioned for custody of the children. His sole asset, according to a brief submitted to the court, was his house.

Gryden called Mary Sawyer to the stand. She testified that her husband physically beat her when he was drunk, at least once a week. Sarah Farwell, a neighbor and the wife of the accused adulterer, was a witness for the plaintiff. Sarah testified that she'd often seen Mary with a black eye or a cut lip and that Nathan Sawyer was drunk more often than not. She went on to say that her husband was a faithful man and a good father to their children. She denounced the adultery charge as "pure rubbish."

Nathan Sawyer was employed as a locomotive engineer with the Santa Fe. His job required frequent travel, and he contended that in his absence his wife entertained Larry Farwell after the children were put to bed. He further stated that his wife, in a moment of spite, had taunted him with the lurid details. In rebuttal, Gryden called Larry Farwell to the stand.

"Tell the court," Gryden said. "Have you ever had illicit relations with Mary Sawyer?"

"Never!" Farwell protested. "My wife would kill me."

"You wife is a small woman, rather dainty in fact. I take it that 'kill me' is just a figure of speech?"

"Oh, sure, I didn't mean she'd hurt me or nothing."

"So there has to be some other reason, correct?"

"Yeah," Farwell said hesitantly. "Mary's a good woman and all, you understand. But she's a little too . . ."

"Plump?" Gryden provided. "Are you saying you're not attracted to stout women?"

"Well, you know, I like 'em on the small side."

"Not plump, or heavyset? Petite."

Farwell offered a dopey smile. "Like they always say, the closer the bone, the sweeter the meat."

Fred Colborn attempted to impeach the testimony. But there was no way to offset the image of Farwell's rather visual metaphor. Everyone in the courtroom believed it.

"To conclude, Your Honor," Gryden said, approaching the bench. "I believe the defendant filed a brief as to his net worth."

"Yes, he did," Judge Strang said. "His assets consist of a house on Fourth Avenue."

"I submit to the court a notarized statement from the First National Bank. Your Honor will note that Nathan Sawyer has on account the sum of two thousand, four hundred dollars and eighty-one cents."

Judge Strang studied the statement at length. He finally looked up and nodded. "So entered into the record, Mr. Gryden."

"Thank you, Your Honor," Gryden said. "I ask the court to find for the plaintiff on every count. I might add that, until this very moment, Mrs. Sawyer had no knowledge of her husband's thrifty nature. She was never aware he had a bank account."

Mary Sawyer was awarded a divorce, with custody of the children. She was further awarded the house, half the bank account, and thirty dollars a month in alimony. Gryden thought of it as justice with a frontier twist.

The closer the bone, the sweeter the meat, had won the case.

October 31 marked the official end to trailing season. Winter would soon be upon the land, the graze dried by frost and snow squalls howling out of the north. Longhorn herds were blocked from the plains of Kansas by nature's immutable barrier.

The South Side, almost overnight, drifted toward winter's downturn. The throngs of cowhands vanished from the streets, leaving the year-round trade of soldiers, railroad crews, and workingmen. Some gamblers, along with many girls in the red-light district, moved on for the winter season to western mining camps. Like locusts and prairie flowers, they would return in the spring.

The sporting crowd treated October 31 somewhat as a rite of passage. The date was marked as a time of interlude until the Texans and their longhorns again trailed north. To celebrate, the annual Dodge City Shooting Bee was held at a river embankment on the south edge of town. The contestants paid an entry fee of fifty dollars and the pot was sweetened with a thousand dollars donated by saloonkeepers, variety hall impresarios, and whorehouse madams. The contest was winner-take-all and nothing to the losers.

Everyone on the South Side turned out for the occasion. Saloons and gaming dens closed after the noon hour rush, and the soiled doves on Maple Street treated it as a holiday. The matches were scheduled to start at one o'clock, and by quarter of one the flats behind the embankment were mobbed with spectators. A festive atmosphere prevailed, for the sporting crowd admired men who were proficient with firearms. The prize purse was a lure, but the bragging rights were far more important. Any man with a gun coveted the title of the best shot in Dodge.

Luke Short and Ham Bell were the unofficial bookmakers. Short planned to compete for the title, but no one objected to him taking wagers. There were forty-eight men entered, and the prize purse had swelled to over three thousand dollars. The favorites in the betting were Ben Thompson, Bat Masterson, and Wyatt Earp, with Luke Short a distant fourth. Doc Holliday, although a renowned shootist and mankiller, was something of an unknown; no one in Dodge City had ever seen him fire a shot. Last year, Thompson had won the title, with Masterson a close second. The odds on them were even money.

The competition was limited to pistols. The weapon of choice for most men was a Colt Peacemaker, but many carried a Remington New Model Army or a Smith & Wesson Schofield. Stout wooden frames had been erected in front of the embankment, set twenty-five paces from the shooting line. The targets were playing cards, the ace of spades, tacked in the center of the wooden frames. Every contestant was required to fire five shots, the number of rounds routinely loaded in a six-gun; for safety purposes, the hammer was always lowered on an empty chamber. The score was a matter of who put the most rounds in the diameter of the ace of spades.

Gryden and Belle found a spot beneath a cottonwood near the firing line. They were accompanied by Lloyd Franklin and several bartenders and chorus girls from the Comique. The town lawmen, still smarting over the Dora Hand trial, treated Gryden with cool indifference. But his reconciliation with Belle had brought the sporting crowd around, and they again welcomed him as one of their own. The matches were about to begin, and the talk centered on who represented the best wager. Ham Bell wandered by taking bets.

Belle looked perplexed. "I can't decide between Masterson and Thompson. They're both so good."

"Yep, it's a toss of the dice," Bell said. "Thompson took it last time by a hair."

"Oh, all right, ten dollars on Thompson."

Bell made a notation in his ledger. "How about you, Harry?"

Gryden considered a moment. "What are the odds on Doc Holliday?"

"Three to one."

"That's better than I'd hoped for. Put me down for a hundred."

"Hundred!" Bell squinted at him. "You know something I don't?"

"Get a hunch, bet a bunch, Ham. I've got a feeling about Holliday."

Holliday walked past with his mistress, Kate Elder. She was just shy of homely, with a large honker of a nose and beady, deep-set eyes. By contrast, Holliday's eyes glittered with liquor, and he appeared to be in unusually good health. He overheard Gryden's remark and smiled as he went by.

"A hunch indeed, Harry," he said. "How can you win wagering on an invalid?"

Gryden laughed. "You look pretty spry to me, Doc."

"Yes, I could waltz the night away and never miss a step. The question is, can I shoot?"

Holliday moved off into the crowd. A moment later, Ab Webster, owner of the Alamo Saloon, began the contest. A major contributor and a man noted for his honesty, he'd been appointed referee by the sporting crowd. Two men at a time were called to the firing line, the parings having been determined by random draw. They each faced a target frame, their guns in hand, and they were allowed two minutes to get off five shots. Webster timed it with his gold pocket watch.

Few of the men took the allotted two minutes. They stood in a target shooter's stance, right arm extended and sideways to the target, cocking and firing their pistols. For the most part, the matches were easily decided, with rounds punched through the playing cards but few centered on the ace spot. The winners were cheered by the crowd as they holstered their pistols and moved to the rear. There they awaited their next turn as men were eliminated from the competition. Their numbers dropped from forty-eight to twenty-four to twelve in rapid order. No one disputed Ab Webster's call on a match.

By four o'clock, there were only four men left in the competition. The luck of the draw pitted last year's finalists, Masterson and Thompson, in the first match. Masterson placed four holes in the ace spot and squeaked past when Thompson only managed three. Holliday, his arm steadied by several nips from a flask, easily dispatched Earp by a score of five to three. The crowd roared their approval, for they saw the final match as Holliday for the South Side and Masterson for the law. The betting, now heavily partisan, favored Holliday.

"What do you think, sugar?" Belle said as the men walked to the firing line. "Will Holliday win it?"

"I think he might," Gryden said. "He's shooting well today."

"Too bad it wasn't Holliday and Thompson. I'd hate to see Masterson take the title."

"I've still got a hunch about Doc."

Holliday and Masterson squared themselves facing the

targets. They were both using Colts with 43 ¾" barrels, and on Webster's command they began firing. Holliday was quicker, hardly pausing between shots, and his five rounds completely punched out the ace spot. Masterson was more deliberate, drawing a careful bead, and shot out the black spade. The spectators were hushed as Webster walked to the target frames. He closely inspected the cards.

"It's a draw," he declared. "They both shot out the ace. We'll have another go-round."

A murmur swept through the crowd as Webster tacked fresh cards into place. Once he was back at the firing line, Holliday and Masterson assumed the marksman's stance. On Webster's command they opened fire, Holliday rapidly placing his shots and Masterson taking deliberate aim. Everyone held their breath as Webster again went forward to the targets. He removed the cards, shaking his head, and returned to the firing line. The ace spot was punched out on both cards.

"Too close to call," Webster said. "Way you gents are shootin', we're liable to be here come dark."

"We may well be," Holliday agreed. "I suggest we switch to moving targets."

Webster cocked an eyebrow. "What kind of moving targets?"

"Empty bottles," Holliday replied, gesturing toward the river. "Floating downstream."

"How about it, Bat?" Webster asked. "You go along with the idea?"

"Why not?" Masterson said confidently. "I'm game for anything."

One of the onlookers was dispatched to Webster's sa-

loon. He returned ten minutes later toting a gunnysack of
quart whiskey bottles; the bottles were empty and stop-
pered with corks. Webster huddled with Holliday and
Masterson, who agreed the bottles could be fired on until
they floated out of sight. He then flipped a coin to decide
who would shoot first. Masterson won the toss.

The man with the gunnysack walked thirty yards upstream. On the signal from Webster, he tossed five bottles,
one at a time, into the river. The bottles bobbed along in
the current, floating swiftly past the firing line. Masterson
fired twice, spraying geysers of water inches behind the
first two bottles. He steadied himself, catching the bottles
more fully in his sights, and aimed slightly ahead. He
broke the last three bottles.

Upstream, the man lobbed five more bottles into the
river. Holliday leveled his Colt and the first bottle erupted
in shards of glass. He thumbed the hammer, eyes sighted
along the barrel, and the second bottle exploded. He
swung the Colt in an arc and locked onto the third bottle
and blasted it from the water. Then the next bottle disappeared and finally the last as the current swept it past the
firing line. He'd taken less than five seconds to shatter all
five bottles.

The crowd seemed stunned by the performance. Then,
laughing and shouting, they suddenly roared their approval. "We've got a winner," Webster yelled over the din.
"I declare Doc Holliday the cham-peen shootist of Dodge
City!"

Holliday toasted the crowd with a long nip from his
flask. He accepted the prize purse from Webster and
stuffed the wad of bills into his coat pocket. Masterson
and Earp shook his hand, and Thompson swatted him

across the back. With Kate Elder on his arm, he turned
from the river and started along the flats. The jubilant
spectators parted to let them through.

Gryden and Belle stood with the group from the
Comique. Holliday paused, patting Kate on the hand, and
nodded to Gryden. "Well, Harry," he said in a jestful tone.
"Your hunch proved to be a good one."

"Wonderful shooting, Doc," Gryden said. "I doubt
anyone here has ever seen anything like it. You left Masterson with his mouth hanging open."

"Bat was at a handicap," Holliday said. "As a tender
youth, my father taught me to hunt ducks. You soon learn
to lead the target."

"So you snookered him into shooting at bottles."

"Why, of course, old sport. In a contest of arms, always look for the edge. How else have I survived this
long?"

Holliday walked off with a wry smile. Kate Elder
laughed, as though he'd just told an uproarious joke. Belle
watched them with a curious expression.

"Was he talking about shooting bottles or shooting
men?"

"Men," Gryden said without hesitation. "The bottles
were just amusement."

Belle looked quizzical. "Amusement?"

"Don't you see, today he got to show his stuff. No one
in Dodge really knew how good he is."

"And now they do?"

Gryden chuckled. "Let's just say Doc won't die from
gunfire. His lungs will do him in."

Belle thought she would much prefer a bullet to the

ravages of consumption. But then, of course, her name wasn't Doc Holliday. Nor was she proficient with a gun.

Perhaps, in the end, that was the difference. The will to live a little longer and the gun. So quick and accurate.

A means to survive bottles and men.

TWENTY-FOUR

The hotel dining room was almost empty. Once the trailing season ended, the hotel was dependent on regular patrons and transient guests. The diners this morning were an assortment of drummers and townspeople.

Gryden was seated at a table by a window. Before him was a platter loaded with sunny-side eggs, a rasher of bacon, fried potatoes, and buttermilk biscuits. He was scheduled in court for a murder trial and he'd left Belle to sleep late. His breakfast, larger than normal, was to stoke him for the day ahead.

On the table beside his plate were copies of the *Dodge City Times* and the *Ford County Globe*. The date was November 12, a week after an election that had been a sobering lesson in humility. The *Times* was still crowing victory and the *Globe* was relatively silent in defeat. Politics, in the end, had little to do with issues.

The election had been a landside for the Republicans. Gryden had held his ground with the sporting crowd, even though there were lingering hard feelings over his defense of Spike Kennedy. But the voters as a whole clearly rejected the notion of a county attorney who had won acquittal for the murderer of Dora Hand. Mike Sutton had claimed a large plurality throughout Ford County.

Gryden, though somewhat humbled, came to terms with his defeat. Against his better judgment, he had allowed the Democrats to draft him for a job he'd never wanted in the first place. Nor was he about to apologize to anyone, in public or in private, for what he considered an ethical decision to represent James Kennedy. The decision had cost him the election, but he wasn't all that disappointed, for he had never coveted political power. He was just sorry that he'd lost to Mike Sutton.

Breakfast finished, Gryden paid his bill and walked through the lobby. As he emerged from the hotel, the overnight train from Topeka pulled into the station with a squeal of breaks. He turned uptown as shops and stores along the plaza began opening for business. At the corner of First Avenue, he waved to Dan Frost through the window of the *Globe*. Frost hurried out the door.

"Harry!" he called. "How about a quote before the trial starts?"

"Are you trying to jinx me?" Gyden said amiably. "Predictions have a way of coming back to haunt you. I'm as superstitious as the next lawyer."

"C'mon, you don't have to make any predictions. Just something a little racy to get attention."

The trial centered on a love triangle involving a rancher, a gambler, and a woman of easy virtue. Even before the first witness was called, there were all the elements of a sensational and titillating news story. Readers liked nothing better than a tale of lechery and lust.

"Try this, Dan," Gryden said. " 'Defense attorney

charges prosecutor with using lowbrow smut to advance his case.' It's factual and salacious."

"Fantastic!" Frost whooped. "Sutton will get his bowels in an uproar."

"I couldn't think of anyone more deserving."

Gryden walked off with a wave. By now, his friends and supporters no longer alluded to the overwhelming defeat at the polls. A week of wallowing in self-pity and humiliation was apparently all the angst they could endure. Nor were they determined to hold a grudge that the Dora Hand affair had cost him the election. They seemed resigned to another two years of Republican rule in Ford County.

Gryden entered the office shortly before eight o'clock. Velma looked up with a wary expression. "Mr. Driskill is waiting to see you." She lowered her voice to a whisper. "And he's not the least bit happy."

"Not happy about what?"

"I'm sure I have no idea."

Gryden found Jack Driskill seated in his office. "Good morning," he said, taking the chair behind his desk. "Did we have an appointment?"

"No," Driskill said flatly. "With what the Association pays you, I don't need an appointment."

"Well, now that we have that cleared up—what can I do for you?"

"Take yourself off the Gill case."

"Pardon me?"

"Get the beeswax outta your ears, counselor. I won't have you defendin' John Gill."

Driskill was accustomed to giving commands. As the largest rancher in Ford County and head of the Western

Kansas Stockgrowers Association, he seldom had to repeat himself. His attitude was that of a man who expected to be obeyed.

"Even if that were a request," Gryden said, "it's too late now. The trial starts in less than an hour."

"I've talked with Mike Sutton," Driskill said. "He's agreed to ask the judge for a continuance of a week. That'll give Gill time to find another lawyer."

"How is it you've shown up at the last minute?"

"Not that it's any of your business, but me and the missus spend a month in Chicago after fall roundup. Got in last night and heard Henry Heck had been murdered."

Henry Heck was a rancher and a member of the Stockgrowers Association. Three weeks ago, in a dispute over a woman, he'd been killed by a gambler, John Gill. The state had charged Gill with first-degree murder.

"I can't say I'm surprised," Gryden remarked. "Sutton would prefer not to go up against me in a courtroom. Was this his idea or yours?"

"All mine," Driskill said. "You work for the Association and Heck was on our board of directors. You're not gonna defend his killer."

"I have good reason to believe it was justifiable homicide. Gill was only protecting himself."

"I'm not here to argue the thing one way or another. I've done told you to take yourself off the goddamn case. That's how it's gonna be."

"No, you're wrong," Gryden said curtly. "I choose my own clients, Mr. Driskill. You have nothing to say about it."

Driskill glowered at him. "You'll take orders or you're through as the Association's attorney. I mean right here and now."

"You're forgetting we have a contract."

"You'll play hell enforcin' it. I won't pay you another nickel."

"Perhaps I'll sue you."

"Do any damn thing you please."

"On the other hand—" Gryden abruptly changed his mind. "We were never birds of a feather anyway. Consider the contract voided."

"Done!"

Driskill rose, his features knotted in anger, and started out of the office. Gryden waited until he was at the door.

"Mr. Driskill."

"Yeah?"

"You'll recall our contract prohibited me from defending horse thieves and cattle rustlers."

"So?"

"So my door is now open to anyone and everyone who steals livestock."

"Go to hell."

"Good day to you, too."

Driskill stalked through the anteroom and slammed the street door. Gryden came out of his office and Velma gave him a questioning look. He shook his head and smiled.

"Velma, I think I just lost a client."

"Good riddance," she said. "He has the manners of an alley cat."

"Or more like it, a polecat."

Gryden crossed the room to his partner's office. "Good morning, Tom," he said. "I have excellent news to report."

"Oh?" Jones said. "I heard Driskill yelling. What happened?"

"We no longer represent the Stockgrowers Association."

Gryden went on to explain Driskill's demands and the resulting confrontation. "There was nothing for it," he concluded. "We parted ways with a few choice words."

"You did the right thing," Jones said. "Although I'll miss their monthly retainer check. It was like found money."

"Yes, but I'm back in business with horse thieves and cattle rustlers. I feel like I've been liberated."

"Criminals were always your forte anyway. I suspect you were bored with honest cattlemen."

"After today, I wouldn't categorize Driskill as 'honest.' What he tried amounted to extortion."

Jones nodded thoughtfully. "Do you think Sutton had a hand in it?"

"I wouldn't put it past him," Gryden said. "Sutton's not above stacking the deck in legal matters. He probably wanted me off the Gill case."

"Well, he didn't get his wish, did he?"

"Tom, I'm going to belt him six ways to Sunday. He won't know what hit him."

Gryden hurried off to court. Jones watched him rush out the door, freshly energized and spoiling for a fight. He thought his partner had few regrets about losing the election. Things were back to normal.

Don Quixote and Harry Gryden were on the march again.

Townspeople as well as members of the sporting crowd were drawn to the trial. The defendant was a gambler, the deceased was a rancher, and the girl was the cause of it all. The spectators turned out for what promised to be a courtroom melodrama.

There was the added attraction of legal adversaries who were personal enemies. The election was only a week past, and after months of acrimony and mudslinging Sutton had humiliated Gryden at the polls. The antagonism between the two men mirrored their politics, and it was nothing less than incendiary. Everyone expected fireworks.

All day yesterday had been devoted to jury selection. Sutton, to no one's surprise, attempted to pack the jury with cattlemen and farmers. The victim was a rancher, and Sutton was intent on securing the death penalty. Gryden was no less intent on picking jurors from the sporting crowd, for the defendant was known and respected on the South Side. The jury in the end was almost evenly balanced.

Judge Jeremiah Strang presided in the case of *The State of Kansas versus John Gill.* Sutton's opening argument painted a picture of foul murder committed by a notorious gambler and a man of low moral character. Gryden followed with an opening argument that wove a tapestry of passion run amok and brute violence fueled by jealousy. The tenor of the trial set, Judge Strang turned the stage over to the prosecution. Sutton called Dr. Thadius McCabe as his first witness.

The Ford County coroner related that the deceased, Henry Heck, died of a gunshot wound to the throat. Dr. McCabe's professional opinion was that the victim, shot in the carotid artery, had expired within three or four minutes. Gryden stipulated that the defense would accept Dr. McCabe's verdict as to cause of death. The next witness was Frank Tuttle, a faro dealer at the Lone Star saloon. Sutton first determined that Tuttle was a resident of the

Western Hotel, located on First Avenue south of the railroad tracks. He then went to the night of October 22.

"Where were you on the night in question at approximately four in the morning?"

"I was asleep," Tuttle said. "In my room at the hotel."

"And is your room directly across the hall from the room of the defendant, John Gill?"

"Yessir, it is."

Sutton stood at the end of the jury box. "Tell us what transpired when you were awakened in the middle of the night?"

"Well, first, I heard a loud crash," Tuttle said. "Then I heard a gunshot, and right after that, a woman started screaming."

"What did you do next?"

"I went and opened my door."

"Describe for the jury what you saw."

"Gill's door was open," Tuttle said. "There's lamps in the hall and I saw a man halfway through the door, sprawled out down on the floor. He was bleedin' like a stuck pig."

"Shot in the throat," Sutton added. "And where was John Gill?"

"Standing back by his bed with a gun."

"Was he alone?"

"No, him and his girl, Callie Moore, live together. She was the one doing the screaming."

"Very well," Sutton said. "And who is Callie Moore?"

"Nobody," Tuttle said, then caught himself. "I mean she doesn't work anywhere I know of. She's just Gill's girlfriend."

"How long has she lived with the defendant?"

"Oh, no more than a month or so."

"And what is the defendant's occupation?"

"Why, he's a gamblin' man. Plays poker, mostly."

"And the man lying on the floor bleeding to death? Did you know Henry Heck?"

"Not to speak to," Tuttle said. "I heard he was Callie's fellow before she took up with Gill. I saw her arguing with him on the street a couple times."

"Henry Heck, you mean," Sutton clarified. "What were they arguing about?"

"Well, way it sounded, he was trying to get her to come back. She'd lived with him out at his ranch."

"So we might infer Miss Moore is a woman of loose morals. Is that a fair statement?"

"Objection," Gryden said. "Leading the witness."

Judge Strang nodded. "Sustained."

"Nothing more," Sutton said, turning away. "Your witness."

Gryden moved forward. "When you came into the hall, you said, 'Gill's door was open.' Would you elaborate?"

"Door was busted in," Tuttle replied. "Hanging off on one hinge."

"As if it had been kicked in, or rammed with someone's shoulder. Is that it?"

"Yeah, I remember thinkin' that's what'd woke me up. The door being busted open."

"And this was immediately before the gunshot, correct?"

"That's right."

"You were there almost instantly," Gryden said. "You saw the splintered door and the body on the floor. Was it your impression that Henry Heck forcibly broke into the room of John Gill?"

"Sure was," Tuttle said. "Couldn't have happened any other way."

"How were John Gill and Callie Moore dressed?"

"Gill was in his long johns and Callie had on a night-gown."

"So they were awakened when Heck kicked in the door?"

"Looked that way to me."

"Was Heck armed?"

"There was a pistol in his holster."

"Let's be clear," Gryden said. "An armed man broke into John Gill's room in the middle of the night. Is that your testimony?"

"Yessir," Tuttle acknowledged. "That's what I saw."

"No further questions, Your Honor."

Sutton called Assistant City Marshal Wyatt Earp to the stand. After being sworn, Earp recounted that he and Deputy Marshal Jim Masterson had been summoned by the desk clerk of the Western Hotel. Earp placed the time at approximately four fifteen a.m. the night of October 22.

"Upon arriving at the hotel," Sutton went on, "tell us what you found at the scene of the murder."

"Objection!" Gryden yelled. "Prosecutor is attempting to prejudice the jury with his reference to 'murder.' All he's proved so far is that Mr. Gill acted in self-defense."

"Your Honor, that's absurd," Sutton retorted. "Counsel for the defense is deceptively making his own case to the jury. I ask the court to admonish Mr. Gryden from such tactics."

Gryden jumped to his feet. "Your Honor, it's Mr. Sutton who is being deceptive. He's trying to plant thoughts in the minds of the jurors."

"That's enough," Judge Strang said firmly. "I caution you gentlemen to behave yourselves in my courtroom. Objection is sustained and jurors are instructed to disregard the prosecutor's last question. Continue, Mr. Sutton."

"Marshal Earp," Sutton said with exaggerated patience, "what did you discover at the hotel?"

"Henry Heck was dead," Earp said. "Callie Moore had herself wrapped in a blanket over by the far wall. Gill was sitting on the bed, still holdin' his gun."

"Did Gill make any statement?"

"Yes, he said he'd killed Henry Heck. Claimed he didn't know it was Heck that busted in the door."

"Did your investigation lead you to conclude otherwise?"

"Yessir, it did," Earp said. "Deputy Masterson and myself found out Heck and Gill had exchanged words the night before in Peacock's saloon. Heck told him he wanted his girl back."

"That would be Callie Moore," Sutton said. "What was her relationship to Henry Heck?"

"She'd lived with him at his ranch for almost two years. Most folks figured that made her his common-law wife."

"How did that relationship change?"

"Why, John Gill stole her away about a month ago. She's been livin' with him at the hotel ever since."

"Let's return to the conversation between Heck and Gill in Peacock's saloon. Did Gill threaten Heck in any manner?"

"Yeah, I'd call it a threat," Earp said. "Gill warned him

to stay away from Callie. Told him if he didn't, he'd kill him."

"I see," Sutton said. "And were there witnesses to this threat?"

"Woodrow Tucker, one of the bartenders at Peacock's saloon. He told me and Deputy Masterson he'd heard the whole thing."

"Did you question Gill about this threat?"

"After we found out," Earp said. "Marshal Bassett and Sheriff Masterson talked to him in the jail the next day. He claimed he'd never made any such threat. Said he'd just told Heck to stay away from Callie."

"To be clear," Sutton said, "Henry Heck did not draw his gun upon entering the room. When he was killed, his gun was still in the holster. Isn't that a fact?"

"Yessir, we found his gun in the holster."

"Marshal Earp, you regularly patrol the South Side. What is John Gill's reputation among the so-called sporting crowd?"

"Objection," Gryden said. "Immaterial and irrelevant."

"On the contrary," Sutton snapped. "It goes to the character of the defendant and his propensity for violence."

"Objection overruled," Judge Strang said. "You may answer the question, Marshal."

"Gill's a hothead," Earp said. "Couple times I remember, he got in fistfights over poker games. Other players called him a card cheat."

"A card cheat," Sutton repeated with a knowing look at the jury. "No further questions, Your Honor."

Gryden rose from his chair. "When a professional gambler is called a card cheat, doesn't it usually lead to a gunfight?"

"On occasion," Earp hedged. "Not all the time."

"How long have you known John Gill?"

"I suppose it's three or four years now."

"Has he ever resorted to the use of a gun in that time?"

"Not that I recollect."

"So he's a fistfighter," Gryden declared, "not a gunfighter. Correct?"

Earp shrugged. "I guess you could say that."

"Lawmen sometimes have to kick down doors to arrest people. How many doors have you kicked down?"

"Never had any reason to keep count. I'd say maybe a half dozen."

"And of those six times, where was your gun? In your hand or in your holster?"

"Well . . ." Earp fidgeted, sensing the trap. "Most times it was in my holster."

"Why not in your hand?"

"Kickin' down doors, you might lose your balance. You don't want to do that holding a gun."

"In other words," Gryden said, "you draw your gun after breaking through the door. Isn't that so?"

"Yeah," Earp admitted. "That's the safest way."

"Which explains why Henry Heck's pistol was in his holster. He hadn't yet had time to draw it."

"Objection," Sutton said. "Counsel is drawing conclusions not in evidence."

"I have nothing further, Your Honor."

Deputy Jim Masterson was called to the stand. His testimony was much the same as Earp's, and Gryden offered only a perfunctory cross-examination. The next witness was Woodrow Tucker, the bartender at Peacock's saloon.

To prove premeditation and establish a motive for murder, Sutton elicited testimony about the barroom argument over the affections of Callie Moore. As Tucker was the prosecution's last witness, the purpose was to leave the most damning testimony fresh in the jurors' minds. Tucker swore he'd heard Gill threaten the life of Henry Heck.

On cross-examination, Gryden tired every trick in the lawyer's handbook. He addressed the matter of distance, and Tucker said he was within five feet of Gill and Heck and they were arguing loudly. Gryden then turned to the noise in a saloon, drunken laughter and a piano playing, and Tucker insisted the noise hadn't affected his hearing. In the end, despite a heated interrogation, Tucker wouldn't budge and Gryden returned to his chair. Sutton rose, pausing for effect, and offered the jurors another knowing smile. He rested the case for the state.

Gryden called Callie Moore for the defense. She was an attractive woman, in her early twenties, with china blue eyes and a svelte figure. She readily admitted she had lived with Henry Heck on his ranch west of Dodge City. Under Gryden's coaching, she said she regretted hurting Heck and felt miserable every time he accosted her on the street. Gryden then brought her to the night of October 22.

"What happened when Henry Heck kicked in the door?"

"I leaped straight out of bed," she said, batting her eyes. "I was never so terrified in my life."

"Did you know it was Heck when he came through the door?"

"No. The light from the hallway was behind him. All I saw was a big shadow of a man. And Lord, it all happened so fast!"

"Too fast to think," Gryden said. "Were you surprised when Mr. Gill fired his gun?"

"I felt so thankful," she said in a small voice. "I just knew someone was about to murder us, or do some horrible thing. John saved our lives."

"When was the last time you saw Henry Heck alive?"

"The afternoon before he broke into the room. He stopped me on the street outside Zimmerman's Mercantile."

"What did he say to you?"

"Well, he was more upset than I've ever seen him before. He told me he couldn't live without me, and he said if he couldn't have me, no one would. He was very . . . scary."

"Scary indeed," Gryden observed. "When he said if he couldn't have you, no one would—did you interpret that as a threat?"

"I didn't know what to think." She paused, dabbing at a tear with a lace hankie. "Henry frightened me, and I just wanted to get away. He was so overwrought."

"So overwrought that he broke into your room that night?"

"Yes."

"So determined no one else would have you that he went mad?"

"Yes, he did."

"So crazed with jealousy that he came there to kill John Gill!"

Gryden turned away before Sutton could object. On

cross-examination, Sutton bombarded Callie Moore with a rapid-fire interrogation. He was trying to rattle her and rarely allowed her to answer before he jumped to the next question. Throughout the grilling, she remained composed and never erred in her look of little-girl-lost in a world of suffering and pain. Gryden could have objected any number of times, but he sensed the jury was sympathetic to her ordeal. Sutton finally sat down with a head-wagging show of disgust.

"Your Honor," Gryden said confidently, "the defense calls John Gill."

Gill was a man of striking looks, with wavy dark hair and a trim mustache. He was sworn in, then seated himself, adjusting the drape of his suit coat. Gryden walked forward.

"Mr. Gill, on the night of October 22, did you threaten the life of Henry Heck?"

"No, I did not," Gill said. "He braced me at the bar in Peacock's and warned me there'd be trouble unless I ended it with Callie. I told him if he messed with me, he'd get the short end of the stick."

"What did you mean by that?" Gryden asked. " 'The short end of the stick'?"

"I figured he was threatening me with fisticuffs. I meant I'd whip him, if it came to a fight."

"Woodrow Tucker, the bartender at Peacock's, testified he heard you threaten to kill Heck. How do you explain that?"

"Woodrow's got it wrong." Gill fixed the jurors with a steady gaze. "He must've thought 'the short end of the stick' meant more than a fistfight. I never even hinted I'd kill Heck."

"Later that night, did Heck announce himself when he kicked in the door of your hotel room?"

"No, he never said a word. Just busted through the door."

"And what did you think?" Gryden asked. "When you were startled awake, what was your first reaction?"

"I thought it was a robber," Gill said. "I'd won at poker that night, and I had over a thousand in cash in the room. Lots of people knew I'd won big."

"So in a very real sense, you feared for your life?"

"My life and Callie's, too."

"And you fired to protect yourself and Miss Moore?"

"Anybody would've if a man busted into his room in the middle of the night. I figured we were about to be killed."

"When you saw it was Henry Heck . . ." Gryden turned to the jury, paused to emphasize the question. "Why did you surrender peacefully to the law officers? Why didn't you try to escape?"

"Because I'd done nothing wrong," Gill said earnestly. "I thought I'd shot a man that was a robber, fixing to kill me. Happened too fast to think otherwise."

"And every man has the right to self-defense." Gryden nodded, allowing the jury a moment to consider the statement, then walked away. "Your witness, Mr. Sutton."

Sutton stood, moved forward at a measured pace. "At Peacock's saloon, you goaded Henry Heck into an irrational act. You set in motion an insidious plan to murder him, Mr. Gill. Isn't that a fact?"

"No, sir, it's not," Gill said. "He's the one that came looking for me. I tried to warn him off."

"Yet you were heard to say, clearly and without equivocation, that you would kill him. Are you calling Woodrow Tucker a liar?"

"I wouldn't never call Woodrow a liar. He just mistook what I said to be something else."

"Oh, did he?" Sutton said with open skepticism. "The difference between 'short end of the stick' and 'I'll kill you' beggars belief. And that very night, you killed him, didn't you?"

"Not the way you mean," Gill said. "I shot a man who broke into my room. I didn't know it was Heck."

"Yes, we've heard your fairy tale about a robber. But you were waiting in that room with a gun and you knew it was Henry Heck. That is the truth, isn't it, Mr. Gill?"

"No, sir, I told you just the way it happened."

"You stole his woman in some nefarious manner. Are we to believe you would hesitate to steal his life?"

"Callie came to me of her own free will. I didn't steal *nothing*."

"You are a man of glib words and a fast gun, Mr. Gill. We'll let the facts speak for themselves."

In closing argument, Sutton belabored the theme of premeditated murder. He spoke of motive and how a man inflamed by passion might be manipulated to break down doors. Sutton labeled it a trap—a skillfully planned murder trap—one that resulted in a respected cattleman bleeding to death in a cheap hotel. Finally, in a voice ringing with certainty, he reviewed the testimony that put the words "I'll kill you" into the killer's mouth. The sole rebuttal, he noted, was from a tinhorn gambler of low morals and with every reason to lie. He asked the jury for a sentence of death.

Gryden's closing argument went to the heart of the evidence. The deceased, he pointed out, had confronted his client, not the other way around. Moreover, Gryden went on, Henry Heck had further raised the level of violence by kicking open a door in the middle of the night. John Gill, fearful for his life, had fired in a darkened room at what he could only assume was an intruder bent on robbery. Every man, Gryden contended, was entitled to the right of self-defense and no less to the defense of loved ones. He told the jury the evidence cried out for a verdict of not guilty.

Judge Strang instructed the jury that there were three possible verdicts. Guilty, with an automatic death sentence; guilty of manslaughter by not acting prudently; or not guilty by reason of justifiable homicide.

The jurors were out for an hour and ten minutes, and when they returned to the courtroom several of them glanced toward the defense table. Judge Strang asked for a decision and the jury foreman informed him that the panel, by unanimous vote, had delivered a verdict of justifiable homicide. The sporting crowd whooped and cheered, and Sutton stormed out of the courtroom. John Gill was released from custody.

Callie Moore threw her arms around Gryden's neck. "Oh, thank you, thank you!" she gushed, her eyes brimming with tears. "I could just love you to death!"

"Thank yourself," Gryden said, shrugging out of her embrace. "Your performance was what turned the trick. Quite convincing."

She fluttered her eyelashes. "Do you really think so?"

"Well, let's just say the jury bought it. You'll never do better than that."

Gryden left her peppering John Gill with kisses. On his way out of the courthouse, it occurred to him that Shakespeare had it right with that line about "all the world's a stage." The Ninth District court was no exception.

Callie Moore had transformed it into a theater.

TWENTY-FIVE

The Long Branch was unusually quiet. Thanksgiving had come and gone just yesterday, and business was all but at a standstill. There were three men at the bar, and only one player was seated at the faro layouts. The bartender busied himself polishing glasses.

Luke Short was dealing draw poker. Business was so slow that he'd left the other houseman, Frank Loving, to handle the faro layouts. The men seated around the poker table were Gryden, Doc Holliday, and Chalk Beeson, Short's partner in the Long Branch. They were reduced to playing a four-handed game.

"Everybody ante," Short said. "Open on whatever tickles your fancy."

The ante was five dollars, and bets were limited to ten dollars. The men were killing time, forced to play among themselves, and they kept the stakes low. For no apparent reason, the saloon trade was always slow on the night after Thanksgiving. Still, for professional gamblers, any game was better than no game at all. Gryden was the only layman at the table.

Holliday, seated to the left of the dealer, opened for five dollars. Gryden studied his cards a moment, then folded, and Beeson raised ten dollars. Short and Holliday just called the raise, and both of them tossed three cards into the deadwood. Beeson took only two cards on the draw, and when Holliday checked to the raiser he bet ten dollars. Short folded and Holliday slowly spread the cards in his hand. He shrugged.

"Against my better judgment"—he dropped ten dollars into the pot—"I'm forced to keep you honest, Chalk."

"Got lucky." Beeson flopped his cards. "Three little deuces."

"Quite enough to beat a pair of kings."

Holliday poured himself a drink from a bottle of bourbon on the table. He tossed off the shot, grimacing slightly, and knuckled his mustache with a forefinger. His gaze drifted around the table.

"Aren't we the bunch," he said derisively. "Playing penny-ante poker and not a high roller in sight."

"Tell me about it," Short said. "Only one player at faro tonight, and he's no high roller. Damn slow."

Beeson nodded. "Things drop off the closer we come to winter. Have to depend on railroad men and soldiers."

"Perhaps I'll travel to Denver," Holliday said. "Not that I don't enjoy you gentlemen's company, but low stakes aren't my style. Certainly not for the entire winter."

"Lots of action in Denver," Short said. "Course, I don't care much for winter in the mountains. Too much snow to suit me."

The deal passed to Holliday. As he began shuffling, Gryden poured himself a drink. The talk of Denver reminded him that Dodge City seemed almost somnolent without the Texans carousing through the South Side. Yesterday he and Belle had taken Thanksgiving dinner with Dan Frost and his family, and there would be other festive occasions over the course of the winter. All the same, with the next trailing season six months away, the saving grace for Gryden was his work. The Ninth District court was never idle.

One thought triggered another. Early last week Sutton had sworn out arrest warrants for the Indian chieftans Little Wolf and Dull Knife. Sutton cited the murders of over forty people in Ford County and demanded extradition of the Northern Cheyenne leaders back to Kansas. The army might well grant jurisdiction to civil courts, and with a jury of white men there was small doubt that the red men would face the gallows. The matter of retribution provided strong incentive to convict.

Gryden wondered if he should volunteer his services as defense counsel. In his opinion, the army would shift jurisdiction to civil courts in the certain knowledge that Little Wolf and Dull Knife would hang. The generals would consider that preferable to conviction by a military tribunal and execution of Indian leaders who had humiliated them on the battlefield. Ever sensitive to criticism, the generals would not want to be seen as taking vengeance on warriors who had outfought them across a thousand miles. Gryden thought it might make an interesting case.

"Five card stud," Holliday announced after the ante. "Bet the limit on an open pair or the last card."

In five card stud, the players each received one card in the hole and one faceup. After an initial bet on the two cards, they received three more cards, all faceup, with a bet on each card. By standard rules, a player could bet the limit if any player's hand showed a pair faceup. The limit could also be bet on the fifth card, and stud often built a larger pot than draw poker. Holliday dealt the first two cards.

Gryden peeked at his hole card, an ace, and found that it matched his up card. A pair of aces, with one hidden, was the top hand, and he tried to keep a straight face. "Ace bets five."

"Raise five."

Beeson, who had a jack showing, tossed ten dollars into the pot. Short had a three on the board and he quickly folded. Holliday, with a queen up, looked at Beeson. He wagged his head.

"Chalk, I do believe you're trying to run us out. Raise it five more."

Gryden could scarcely believe his luck. He was holding a pair of aces and Beeson and Holliday were raising. He considered taking the last raise, then decided to lay back until the opportune moment. He called both raises and Beeson, after a moment's hesitation, called the raise. Holliday began dealing the third card.

"Watch yourselves, gents," Short said abruptly. "Trouble just walked in the door."

The men followed his gaze across the room. Levi Richardson, a gambler of small repute, stood at the door with a pistol in hand. A leaden silence settled over the saloon as customers at the bar and the lone player at the faro layout scattered for cover. Richardson was known to have a running feud with Frank Loving. He advanced a step into the room.

"Defend yourself, Loving! I mean to kill you."

Loving, who was behind the faro layout, rose and moved around the table. He halted beside a potbellied stove as Richardson raised his pistol, fanning the hammer with the heel of his left hand. The reports blended together, slugs thunking into the stove and spraying fiery sparks onto the floor. Richardson fanned off five shots before Loving was able to draw his gun. Untouched, Loving coolly sighted and fired three spaced shots.

The slugs pocked red splotches along the front of Richardson's jacket and shirt. He reeled backward under the impact, dropping his empty pistol, and bounced off the wall beside the door. The light went out in his eyes and he slumped to a bloody heap on the floor. There was a moment of prolonged silence as the crowd looked from the body to Loving, who slowly lowered his pistol. All five of Richardson's shots had plowed through the potbellied stove.

Holliday broke the silence with polite applause. His manner was that of someone who had just witnessed the virtuoso performance of an artist. He nodded to the men at the poker table. "A lesson for us all," he said. "Speed is fine, but accuracy is final."

The men looked at the riddled stove. The lesson was apparent, for Loving was hardly a foot from the stove and Richardson's fancy gunwork had failed by that narrow margin. The faro dealer, under fire but not unnerved, had placed his shots with deliberation. He would live to tell the tale.

Loving crossed the room to the poker table. He extended his pistol to Gryden. "Harry, I'll likely need a lawyer," he said. "Will you represent me?"

Gryden accepted the pistol. "I'd be honored, Frank. Although I doubt you'll be arrested. It was clearly self-defense."

The door flew open. City Marshal Bassett and Deputy Nat Haywood, guns in hand, burst into the saloon. They stopped, their attention drawn to the body, and Haywood stooped down to check for a pulse. He looked at Bassett and shook his head.

"All right," Bassett said, glancing at the men around the room. "What happened here?"

Gryden walked forward with Loving at his side. He quickly explained the situation, pointing from the dead man to the stove, and handed over Loving's pistol. Everyone in the saloon verified Gryden's version of the shooting, and Bassett agreed there was no reason to arrest Loving. Nonetheless, there would be a coroner's inquest, and he ordered Gryden to be there with his client. Haywood was dispatched to fetch the undertaker.

The poker game was called off. Even Holliday thought it unseemly to continue while a body was being removed from the saloon. Gryden regretted not winning on his pair of aces, but the shootout rather than poker was the topic of conversation. Frank Loving was the man of the hour, and Beeson offered a round of drinks on the house to celebrate his good fortune. Holliday, ever the wit, toasted Levi Richardson for killing a stove.

The inquest was held the following morning in City Court. Dr. Thadius McCabe presided over the inquest, and City Attorney Fred Colborn conducted the hearing. There was no question as to who had shot Levi Richardson, and that left only the matter of whether charges were warranted. Luke Short, Chalk Beeson, and the Long Branch bartender were called as witnesses and testified as to the circumstances of the shooting. Frank Loving was the last to take the stand.

Colborn, the inquisitor, seemed displeased with the testimony thus far. He approached the stand with a look of skepticism. "Mr. Loving, what was the cause of your antagonism with Levi Richardson?"

"Guess you'd say it was personal," Loving replied. "I wouldn't allow him to play at my faro table."

"Why not?"

"Richardson was a cheat, and a bad one. He'd pull dumb tricks and try to move his bets on the layout. I barred him from my table."

"In other words," Colborn said, "you labeled him a dishonest gambler?"

"Well, yeah," Loving said. "That's what he was."

"So you besmirched his reputation and humiliated him in public. In effect, you goaded him into a gunfight. Isn't that true?"

"Let's not be ridiculous," Gryden interrupted loudly. "Richardson came with gun in hand and he fired first. My client was simply defending himself."

"Your *client*," Colborn said snidely, "provoked the altercation. He is responsible for a man's death."

"And you are sadly misinformed," Gryden countered. "Old English common law holds that a man has no obligation to retreat in the face of a threat of death or bodily harm. Our laws are based on that very principle, and the principle has stood for over a thousand years. Mr. Loving was completely within his rights."

Colborn flushed angrily. "Don't presume to lecture—"

"Gentlemen. . . ." Dr. McCabe paused until he had their attention. "Mr. Colborn, you are out of line and Mr. Gryden is correct. We are interested in who started the fight, not who ended it."

"Hardly," Colborn said in a testy voice. "A man must be held accountable for provoking violence."

Dr. McCabe stared at him. "I rule the death of Levi Richardson to be justifiable homicide. This inquest stands adjourned."

Colborn opened his mouth, but no words came out. He sat down heavily, as if he'd just swallowed his tongue. Frank Loving grinned like a horse with a mouthful of briars. He wrung Gryden's hand.

"Harry, you just saved my ass!"

Gryden smiled. "You saved yourself, Frank."

"How's that?"

"Who shot Levi Richardson?"

"Why, hell, Harry, I did."

"Case closed."

Overcast skies threatened a snowstorm before nightfall. The date was December 16, and a line of people braved the frigid weather for a seat in the courtroom. The most sensational murder trial in the history of Ford County was about to start.

John Hardesty, a rancher, and one of his cowhands were charged with first-degree murder. The *Dodge City Times,* with underplayed decorum, wrote that the dead man had "dishonored" Hardesty's wife. The *Ford County Globe* informed its readers that the deceased had been "shot to ribbons."

The voir dire process of selecting a jury had consumed all of yesterday. This morning, Gryden was seated at the defense table as the courtroom filled to overflowing. Sheriff Bat Masterson brought in the prisoners, John Hardesty and Thomas Brown, who worked on Hardesty's

ranch. Masterson removed their manacles, and they took
chairs beside Gryden. A deputy was posted near the defense table.

Hardesty was one of the largest cattlemen in Ford
County. His ranch was on the Arkansas River, near the
Colorado border, over a hundred miles west of Dodge
City. He ran five thousand head of shorthorn cattle on a
spread that encompassed over thirty thousand acres. He
was a man of wealth and power who had forged a cattle
empire in a land distant from the law. On November 16,
the day after he'd been arrested, he had retained Gryden
as defense counsel.

The bailiff called the court to order as Judge Jeremiah
Strang took his seat on the bench. The jury was brought in
and the judge ordered opposing counsel to proceed with
their opening arguments. Sutton wove a lurid tale of a
vengeful rancher who had summarily executed a loyal
cowboy for a transgression yet to be proved. Gryden told
the jurors of a woman ravished by a brutish fiend and a
husband driven to restore her honor. Everyone in the
courtroom craned for a look at Mrs. Edith Hardesty, who
was seated in the front row.

The prosecution's first witness was Ezra Roden. With
Sutton's prompting, Roden testified that he was the undertaker in Syracuse, a small settlement near Hardesty's
ranch. He then related that on the morning of November
14 Hardesty had brought the body of Barney Elliott to his
funeral parlor in Syracuse. The body had been transported thrown over a horse, and Hardesty was accompanied by two of his cowhands, Tom Brown and Joe Davis.
Hardesty had paid Roden to arrange burial in the town
cemetery.

"Barney Elliott, the dead man?" Sutton said. "How had he met his death?"

"Shot to pieces," Roden observed. "I counted eleven bullet wounds altogether. Ones that killed him was in the head and heart."

"Where else was he wounded?"

"Chest and arms, and one in the leg."

"Did John Hardesty tell you how these wounds had occurred?"

"No, sir, he didn't say nothing and I didn't ask. He dropped the body off and paid me fifty dollars cash money. Then him and his boys rode out of town."

"All very businesslike," Sutton said. "What did you do next, Mr. Roden?"

"Well, it was a mite suspicious," Roden said. "No explanation or nothing, and a man shot full of holes. I went and got the town constable, Bob Tyler."

"And upon viewing the body, what did Constable Tyler say?"

"Why, he said just what I was scared to say in front of Hardesty. He said it looked like murder."

"No further questions, Your Honor."

Gryden rose from his chair. "I have only one question. Did it appear to you that Joe Davis was there of his own volition? Did it seem he'd been forced to accompany Mr. Hardesty?"

"Nooo," Roden said slowly. "Didn't look like anybody'd twisted his arm. He was there just like the others."

"Thank you, Mr. Roden."

Sutton called Town Constable Robert Tyler to the stand. Tyler testified that the condition of the body, particularly the excessive number of wounds, led him to believe Barney Elliott had been murdered. He wired Sheriff Masterson, and the following day the sheriff arrived in Syracuse by train. That same evening, Tyler said, he and the sheriff arrested Hardesty, Brown, and Davis. The next morning, Masterson transported the prisoners by train to Dodge City.

"Nothing further," Sutton said. "Your witness, Mr. Gryden."

Gryden stood. "I have no questions of this witness, Your Honor."

Sheriff Bat Masterson was called and took the oath. "Tell us, Sheriff," Sutton asked. "Did you view the body of the deceased?"

"Yessir, I did," Masterson said. "The weather was cold enough that they could hold over the burial. Constable Tyler took me by the funeral parlor."

"And can you verify the number of gunshot wounds?"

"Mr. Roden had him laid out in the back room and I counted eleven wounds. Looked like he'd been shot by a firing squad."

"Indeed," Sutton said. "Did Hardesty admit to killing Barney Elliott?"

"No, he didn't," Masterson responded. "But one of his cowhands, Joe Davis, told me Hardesty and Tom Brown had executed Elliott. He said he saw it happen."

"Where and when did this take place?"

"The afternoon of November 13, twenty miles south of Hardesty's ranch."

"And Davis used the word 'executed' with regard to the death of Barney Elliott?"

"Yessir, he said they shot him down like a dog."

"No further questions."

Gryden moved forward. "Let's be quite clear on this, Sheriff. Did Davis make his statement before or after you arrested him?"

"I don't . . ." Masterson hesitated, then shrugged. "I guess it was after."

"After you brought him here and locked him in the county jail. Why did he wait so long?"

"I couldn't say."

"Was Davis offered immunity from prosecution if he agreed to testify against Hardesty and Brown?"

"You'd have to ask the county attorney."

"No, I'll ask you directly and to the point. Did Davis take part in the killing of Barney Elliott?"

Masterson again shrugged. "I couldn't say."

"You mean, you *won't* say. Lying by omission might be construed as perjury, Sheriff. Are you familiar with the penalty for perjury?"

"Objection!" Sutton said. "Argumentative."

Gryden turned away. "I'm through with this witness."

The prosecution next called Joseph Davis. Sutton directed his attention to the morning of November 13, the morning John Hardesty returned from an overnight trip inspecting the ranch's line camps. He testified that Hardesty first went to the main house and then came to the bunkhouse in a rage, looking for Barney Elliott. Davis went on to say Elliott had disappeared during the night.

"So Elliott was gone," Sutton said. "Why was Hardesty looking for him?"

Davis squirmed, ducking his head. "Way he told it, Mrs. Hardesty said Elliott—well, you know—took liberties with her. Claimed he'd snuck into her bed the night before."

"She accused Elliott of assaulting her, of carnal knowledge. Is that it?"

"Yeah, that's what Hardesty said."

"What happened then?"

"Hardesty was plumb set on takin' out after Elliott. The rest of the crew was off in winter line camps, and me and Tom Brown was the only ones in the bunkhouse. Hardesty ordered us to come along."

"Did you in fact locate Barney Elliott?"

"Yessir, just before sundown. Hardesty figgered he was most likely headed for Indian Territory. We tracked him to a crossing on the Cimarron."

"When you caught him," Sutton prompted, "describe what took place."

"Elliott begged like a baby," Davis said. "Told Hardesty he was sorry and got down on his knees, askin' to be spared. Hardesty wouldn't listen, and him and Brown shot him to pieces. Executed him right there on the riverbank."

"Let us be perfectly clear. Barney Elliott was killed in cold blood, murdered even as he pleaded for his life. Is that your testimony?"

"Saw it with my own eyes."

"One last question, Mr. Davis. Did you fire your gun at Barney Elliott? Were you involved in his execution?"

"No, sir, I shorely wasn't," Davis said vehemently. "Never once figgered Hardesty meant to kill him cold as ice. I wouldn't be a party to no such thing."

Sutton turned away. "No further questions, Your Honor."

"Tell us, Mr. Davis," Gryden said, moving forward.

"Isn't it true County Attorney Sutton offered you a deal? Immunity from prosecution in return for your testimony?"

"Guess that's what it was," Davis said. "Course I didn't do nothin' to be prosecuted for."

"Then why did you wait until you were in jail to make a deal? Why not profess your innocence when you were arrested by Sheriff Masterson?"

Davis averted his gaze, unable to frame an answer, and Gryden went on. "I submit that you fired one or more shots into Barney Elliott. I submit you were indeed a party to the killing and that you are nothing less than a liar. Isn't that the truth of the matter?"

"No, it ain't," Davis said, fidgeting in his chair. "I never did no such thing."

"Why should this jury believe you?"

"'Cause I didn't have nothin' against Elliott. Didn't matter to me that he'd crawled in bed with Mrs. Hardesty. Wasn't none of my business."

"You weren't concerned that a woman had been *violated*? A woman you know and respect?"

"Don't go puttin' words in my mouth. Nobody ever treated me better'n Mrs. Hardesty. Nothin' snooty or highfalutin about her. She's good folks."

"Then you *were* concerned that she'd been violated. Do you consider Mrs. Hardesty a religious woman, a decent woman?"

"Course I do," Davis said. "She's a regular churchgoer and a mighty fine Christian lady. Always got a kind word."

"Not a woman to be abused by a sneaking, no-account thug. Is that it?"

"Barney shouldn't never have done that. He's gonna roast in Hades till doomsday."

"I believe everyone in the courtroom would agree with you, Mr. Davis. Nothing more at this time, Your Honor."

Sutton was only too aware that Gryden had deftly extracted sympathetic testimony from the state's star witness. On redirect Sutton once again turned Davis to the Cimarron, to a man begging for his life, and to a merciless execution. He left the jurors with a vivid image of Barney Elliott on his knees amid the roar of gunfire. Then he rested the case for the state.

Judge Strang nodded. "Defense may proceed with its case."

"If it please the court," Gryden said, "the defense calls John Hardesty."

Hardesty was in his late thirties, a rawboned man with salt-and-pepper hair and features weathered by the sun. He wore a dark suit, with a crisp white shirt and a somber tie, and the high-topped boots of a cattleman. The bailiff administered the oath.

"Mr. Hardesty," Gryden said almost casually. "Is what you're wearing today your normal attire?"

"No, I'm cleaned up," Hardesty said. "I generally wear range duds and smell of cows. It comes with workin' livestock."

"A smell associated with all men who work cattle and horses. Has anyone ever commented on the physical resemblance between you and Barney Elliott?"

"Lots of folks have. Didn't look alike in daylight, but we were of a size so far as height and build goes. He could've worn my clothes."

"Or vice versa?"

"Yeah, we joked about it a few times."

"So there was a striking resemblance?"

"Fairly much," Hardesty said. "Elliott was a little more bowlegged than me. Not a whole lot, though."

"I see," Gryden said. "And how did Elliott compare to you in age?"

"We were just a year apart. Thirty-eight to thirty-seven."

"So you were quite similar in appearance. You were of the same age, the same build, and you could have worn the same clothes. Is that correct?"

"Yeah, that's right."

"And of course you both smelled of horses and cows."

"That, too."

Gryden walked away. "Your witness, Mr. Sutton."

Judge Strang peered down at Gryden with a strange expression. Sutton seemed momentarily at a loss, his features creased in an owlish frown. He got to his feet, darting a suspicious glance at Gryden, and went around the prosecution table. He moved forward.

"Tell this jury," he said pointedly. "Did you or did you not kill Barney Elliott?"

"Objection," Gryden said. "Prosecution's cross-examination cannot exceed the scope of direct examination."

"That's preposterous!" Sutton retorted. "The state has every right to explore details of the killing."

"No, sir, you do not," Gryden said. "The Kansas criminal code is quite clear on the matter. You are limited to the scope of direct examination."

Judge Strang sighed heavily. "Mr. Gryden is correct, Mr. Sutton. Objection sustained."

"Your Honor, I protest," Sutton said, waving his arms.

"Counsel for the defense is resorting to trickery to prevent the defendant from testifying. This is outrageous!"

"Defendant has testified," Gryden said. "You are free to question him within the legal parameters."

"You are subverting justice!" Sutton shouted. "The jury has no interest in his clothing, or how he smells."

Gryden smiled. "I believe the jury will be very interested, Mr. Sutton."

"That will do," Judge Strang said sternly. "The court has ruled, Mr. Sutton, and the objection is sustained. Do you have further questions of this witness?"

Sutton glared at the judge. His face was mottled with anger and his jaws clenched as he gritted his teeth. He flung out his arm in a dismissive gesture and marched back to his chair.

Judge Strang nodded impassively. "You may call your next witness, Mr. Gryden."

"Thank you, Your Honor," Gryden said. "The defense calls Mrs. Edith Hardesty."

A low murmur of surprise swept through the courtroom. Edith Hardesty came forward, her features taut and her head held high. She was somewhat plump, with an oval face and a rounded figure. She seated herself in the witness chair after being sworn. Gryden positioned himself by the jury box.

"Mrs. Hardesty," he said gently. "I know you've been through an ordeal any woman would prefer not to talk about. We appreciate your willingness to testify here today."

"I want to testify," she said. "I'm the only one who knows the truth."

"Then allow me to ask you as delicately as possible. Did Barney Elliott assault you on the night of November 12?"

"Yes, he did."

"In your own words, and please stop if it becomes too much—would you describe the assault?"

Edith Hardesty gathered herself. "John, my husband, was away on business. Sometime during the night, I woke up and a man was in bed with me. I was still drowsy and I thought John had returned early from his trip. And then . . ."

"I know it's difficult for you, Mrs. Hardesty. Do you wish to continue?"

"And then . . ." Her voice cracked. "The man started to have his way with me. At first, I thought it was my husband and I was happy. But then . . ." She took a shuddering breath. "I realized it wasn't John."

Gryden had never been fully satisfied with her version of the seduction. But he needed the jury to believe it. "Your husband and Barney Elliott were of similar height and build, and it was dark. How did you suddenly realize it was Elliott?"

"John doesn't chew tobacco," she said. "I smelled it on his breath."

"What about the rest of the men in the bunkhouse? Don't they chew tobacco?"

"No, only Elliott did. I just didn't know it was him until . . . until it was too late."

"What happened then?"

"I screamed and cursed him by name, and he ran. He grabbed his clothes and boots and ran. I can still hear the jingle-bobs on his spurs."

"What did you do when he was gone?"

Tears spilled down her cheeks. "I thought about killing myself. I'd been violated and ruined and I wasn't sure John could still love me." She raised her head, blinked through the tears. "Thank God, he understood."

"You're a brave women to share such a tragic time with the jurors and the court. I have no further questions."

Gryden returned to his chair. Sutton approached the stand like a pianist with broken fingers. He had no choice but to play, even though he sensed it would be painful. To convict the husband, he had to impeach the wife. He knew she was lying.

"I'm frankly at a loss," he said in a skeptical tone. "The night the incident occurred, why didn't you report it to the men in the bunkhouse? Why didn't you seek their help?"

"You know nothing of women," she said. "I would never have told them. I was too ashamed."

"So you waited for your husband to return. How did he react when you told him of the . . . incident?"

"My husband is a good man, a decent man. He consoled me."

"And he was angry, in a terrible rage. Isn't that true?"

"Yes, he was angry."

"What did he say he intended to do to Barney Elliott?"

"He didn't say."

"Come now, Mrs. Hardesty," Sutton demanded. "Are you asking us to believe he said nothing?"

"I was hysterical," she said softly. "John stayed with me for the longest time, and then he went out. He didn't say where he was going."

"Your husband was gone for a day and a night.

Weren't you worried that he left you alone so long after your ordeal?"

"I can take care of myself, Mr. Sutton. There was no reason to be worried."

"And when he returned home on November 14? What did he say he'd done to Barney Elliott?"

"There was nothing said," she replied. "The first I knew of anything was when he was arrested."

"How very convenient," Sutton said with open scorn. "Are you protecting yourself or your husband?"

"What do you mean?"

"Something went awry, didn't it? You were having a liaison with a hired hand and your husband somehow found out. That's why he killed Barney Elliott, isn't it?"

"No, it isn't!" she cried. "I would never be unfaithful to my husband!"

"Do you expect us to believe that?" Sutton said, mocking her. "Never a flirtation, never a stolen kiss? Nothing?"

Gryden started to object. But then, glancing at the jury, he saw that they were disturbed by the accusation. Disturbed and sympathetic to Edith Hardesty. He let it pass.

"Barney Elliott was murdered," Sutton said. "On his knees, begging for his life, he was shot eleven times. Do you have any regrets for his death? Just an iota of remorse?"

"I was raped," she said woodenly. "Everyone has avoided using the word. How polite that it's called an assault, or a violation, or an *incident*. I was raped and the courts sentence men to death for rape." She stared Sutton in the eye. "So no, I have no regrets for the death of Barney Elliott. No regrets at all."

Sutton knew then that he'd lost the case. He had attempted to trap her into further implicating her husband, and she'd trapped him with the word almost never spoken in open court. A woman raped was a woman who inspired vengeance in all men. And most of all, her husband.

The jury took only seven minutes to acquit John Hardesty and Tom Brown. Judge Strang ordered them released from custody, and Edith Hardesty rushed forward and hurled herself into her husband's arms. The crowd grinned and nodded approval, confident that justice had been served. Any man there wanted to believe he would have done as much for his wife.

Gryden was particularly pleased with the outcome. He crossed the aisle and stopped before Sutton. "Just to satisfy my curiosity," he said. "Suppose Barney Elliott had been charged with rape. Would you have asked for the death penalty?"

"Yes, I imagine so," Sutton said. "Now, perhaps you can satisfy my curiosity on something. Was Mrs. Hardesty telling the truth?"

"About the alleged liaison?"

"Alleged or otherwise."

"Well, like the fly walking across the mirror said: It all depends on how you look at it."

"What the devil does that mean?"

"Why, it's always in the eye of the beholder."

"Beholder?" Sutton said. "What beholder?"

Gryden smiled. "A jury of twelve good men."

TWENTY-SIX

A steady snowfall dusted the land on Christmas Eve. The plaza was a field of silvery white under the luminous glow of muzzy starlight. Street lamps flickered in a swirl of snowflakes all along Front Street.

Gryden stood staring out the window across the plaza. A cheery blaze crackled in the fireplace and a Christmas tree occupied one corner of the sitting room. Belle had decorated the tree with cranberries and popcorn strung together on thread and gaily colored ribbon bows. Her most treasured ornaments, ordered from Chicago, were white satin angels with gossamer wings and shiny glass balls. The tree was crowned with a silver papier-mâché star.

Tonight Gryden and Belle would celebrate Christmas at the Third Annual Masquerade Ball. By now a traditional affair, the ball was hosted by the Dodge City Social Club and held in the dining room of the Dodge House. Membership in the social club was comprised mainly of the uptown crowd, merchants, businessmen, professionals, and their ladies. The ball was always held on Christmas Eve, and everyone was required to attend in costume. It was the social event of the year.

In the reflection of the window Gryden smiled at himself. He was disguised as Abe Lincoln, attired in a swallowtail coat, a creamy white shirt, and somber tie. One of the comics at the Comique had loaned him a fake beard and side-whiskers, now plastered to his face with spirit gum. Though hardly as gaunt as Lincoln, he thought he looked the character to a passable degree. He inwardly reveled that a die-hard Democrat was masquerading as the quintessential Republican. The irony of it amused him.

"Lah-da!"

Belle came through the door of the bedroom. She struck a pose, one hand on her hip, vamping him with a coquettish look. Gryden extended a leg and bowed at the waist.

"Madame Pompadour," he said in a sonorous voice. "You are absolutely stunning."

"Why, thank you, Mr. Lincoln," she said gaily. "You're quite a sight yourself."

"M'lady, I am but a moth drawn to your flame."

"Well, sugar, you sound more like a courtier than a president. We do make a pair!"

Belle was costumed as the Marquise de Pompadour, the mistress of Louis XV. She wore a period gown with daring décolletage, made by a local seamstress especially for the ball. Her hair was hidden beneath a white beehive of a wig, ordered from a theatrical costumer in New York, and an imitation diamond pendant hung suspended between her breasts. Her face was powdered and her cheeks were bright with rouge. She looked like a courtesan in search of a king.

"No pun intended," Gryden said, "but you will be the belle of the ball. All the ladies will turn green with envy."

"I certainly hope so," she said with a dazzling smile. "I didn't go to all this trouble for nothing."

"Trust me, I'll have to fight the men off."

"No, sweetheart, you'll only have to fight the Republicans. Wait till they see you tricked out as Abe Lincoln."

"Serves them right." Gryden crooked an elbow. "Shall we make our grand entrance?"

"I'm with you, Abe," she quipped, taking his arm. "As we say in the theater, on with the show."

The hotel dining room had been cleared of furniture. The floor was waxed to a sheen, and a small orchestra, formed from the Dodge City Brass Band, was seated on a platform along the north wall. A refreshment table, with a punch bowl for the ladies and whiskey for the men, was positioned opposite the door. The ball was already under way, with the orchestra playing a sedate waltz. Several couples swirled around the dance floor.

Gryden and Belle came through the door. All the men paused, darting hidden glances at Belle, and their wives stared openly. She was easily the most attractive woman in the room, and her costume was by far the most revealing. The men associated with Gryden began gravitating toward the door, bemused and delighted that he'd chosen to come as Abe Lincoln. Thomas Jones was attired in the uniform of a Confederate general, a full white beard covering his jawline and a sheathed sword at his side. His wife wore the gown of a genteel Southern lady.

"Good evening, Mr. Lincoln," Jones said formally. "I trust you've been advised of my surrender at Appomattox."

"Yes, of course, General Lee," Gryden replied. "I must say, you look no worse for the experience."

"Old soldiers often live too much in memory. I chose to prosper in the land of the Yankees."

"General, I endorse the sentiment. As some philosopher once remarked, living well is the best revenge."

"No question of it," Jones agreed. "Although seeing you in the guise of Abe Lincoln has much the same effect. Sutton and his cronies will correctly deduce you're mocking them."

The Republican contingent was standing across the room. Sutton wore the varicolored uniform of Napoléon Bonaparte, and Florence, his wife, was dressed as Empress Josephine. Robert Wright was a riverboat gambler, with a broadcloth coat and ruffled shirt, and a diamond stickpin in his cravat. Fred Colborn, also in uniform, posed as a somewhat dwarfish George Washington. His wife played the role of Martha.

On the fringe of the group, Bat Masterson imitated his idol, Wild Bill Hickok, with a frock coat, a gaudy sash, and a brace of pistols with ivory grips. Dog Kelley was dressed as a clown, with baggy pants and a bulbous red nose, his face caked with white makeup and a frayed hole in his derby hat. Nick Klaine vaguely resembled Saint Nicholas, attired in a flowing robe, with a peaked cap and a scraggly beard. The entire contingent stared across the room at Gryden.

"No love for Abe tonight," Gryden said, returning their stares. "If looks could kill, I'd be a dead man."

Belle laughed. "Wasn't that the whole idea, sugar? You *wanted* to rub their noses in it."

"Nothing succeeds like success," Jones said. "You've got them hopping mad, Harry."

"Well, why not?" Gryden said humorously. "I'm here to spread the Yuletide spirit."

Dan Frost swung his wife off the dance floor and moved forward. He was adorned as Harlequin, with spangled diamond-pattern tights, a bright mask, and a slouch hat. Melodie, his wife, was costumed as Columbine, the mythic sweetheart of Harlequin the buffoon. Frost did a toe-stepping dance shuffle and cocked his hat.

"How now, Great Emancipator," he said with a jester's grin. "Do I hear the 'Battle Hymm of the Republic' somewhere in the distance?"

"No, actually it's 'Dixie,' " Gryden said. "Where'd you get that outfit?"

"Ordered it from a costume house in Saint Louis. How do you like it?"

"You're a brave man to appear in public in tights. I wouldn't have the brass."

"Yes, but you're a lawyer and I'm a lowly newspaper editor. Besides, every party needs a comic."

"Oh, good!" Belle exclaimed, clapping her hands. "Tell us a joke, Sir Harlequin."

Frost swept his wife onto the dance floor. "Watch close," he called over his shoulder. "When I dance, everybody thinks it's a joke."

They laughed as he went stomping about in his tights, dragging Melodie around the dance floor. Deacon Cox appeared from the crowd, the very incarnation of Daniel Boone. He was wearing buckskins and a coonskin cap and carried a Kentucky flintlock rifle inlaid with brass. He stopped before them, the rifle dangling from his arm.

"Evenin', folks," he drawled. "You know what I always say afore I go b'ar huntin'?"

"No," Gryden said, playing the straight man. "What do you say before you go bear hunting?"

"'O Lord, help me kill that b'ar, and iffen you don't help me, O Lord—please don't help the b'ar'."

Jones guffawed and the others shook their heads in amusement. Chalk Beeson walked by and stopped to join in the merriment. He was dressed as a Tortuga pirate, complete with a black eye patch and a cutlass thrust through his belt. He jerked a thumb at Cox.

"Don't believe this old reprobate," Beeson said. "Way I heard it, Daniel Boone was the worst liar that ever crossed the Alleghenies."

"Listen to him talk," Cox retorted. "What's a pirate know about the Alleghenies?"

"Well, Dan'l, I'd say a mite more'n you know about hunting bear."

"That's rich, coming from a man that never stepped aboard a sloop. Or did they call them galleons?"

"Tell you the truth, I always get 'em confused myself."

Frost and Melodie glided to a halt before the group. "I thought of a joke," Frost said. "You remember the editorials I wrote about Sutton? When I called him Little Caesar?"

"Of course," Jones said. "Is that the joke?"

"Take a gander at his outfit," Frost said. "I'd say he's shown his true colors tonight. From now on, he's the Napoléon of Ford County."

"Fitting enough," Gryden observed. "Too bad we can't exile him to Saint Helena."

"Never heard of it," Beeson said. "What's Saint Helena?"

"Some pirate!" Cox gibed. "It's the island where they sent Napoléon. After he was defeated at Waterloo."

"Yeah?" Beeson said with a puzzled frown. "What's Waterloo?"

Everyone broke out laughing. Cox proceeded to lecture Beeson on the Battle of Waterloo and Napoléon's defeat by the Duke of Wellington. Jones and Frost gathered their wives and moved onto the dance floor. Gryden took Belle's arm.

"Care for a glass of punch?" he said. "I could use a little refreshment."

"Careful, sugar," she said. "Sutton and his crowd have the punch bowl staked out. You're venturing into enemy territory."

"I'll be the soul of discretion."

"You've never been discreet in your life."

"Well, the least we could do is exchange Christmas greetings."

"I can't wait to see it."

Gryden led her across the room. Sutton and his friends were standing near the refreshment table and pretended to look the other way. Gryden dipped glasses of punch for himself and Belle and turned to face Sutton. He lifted his glass in a toast.

"Merry Christmas," he said cheerfully. "Peace on earth and goodwill toward all."

Florence Sutton shot Belle a glance, then averted her gaze with a sniff. Colborn and Masterson and the others ignored the toast and began conversing among themselves. Sutton inspected Gryden's costume with a hard stare.

"Was your intent to insult Abraham Lincoln?"

"I rather admire Honest Abe," Gryden said. "I've never held it against him that he was a Republican."

"Always the wiseacre," Sutton said crossly. "I wish I'd heard the last of you."

"You'll be rid of me soon enough."

"What does that mean?"

"Why, it means I'm fighting a delaying action. You'll kill off the cattle trade and turn Dodge into a farmers' town. That's not for me."

"Tell me something," Sutton said. "If you know it's going to happen, why do you fight it?"

"To hold on a while longer," Gryden observed. "The frontier's disappearing fast enough on its own. One day we'll look back and say these were the good old days— the best of times."

"You sound as though you prefer anarchy to progress."

"There's something to be said for a little anarchy. Wild and woolly suits me just fine."

"You're fighting a lost cause. The Texans and their longhorns will soon be a thing of the past."

"And more's the pity for it," Gryden said. "Anyway, in the spirit of the season—Merry Christmas."

"Yes, of course," Sutton said stiffly. "Merry Christmas to you, too."

Gryden strolled away with Belle on his arm after depositing their glasses on the refreshment table. Her expression was subdued, quietly thoughtful, as they circled the dance floor. She finally glanced at him.

"Well, lover, I have to say you surprised me. You all but told him you're bowing out."

"Do-gooders always win in the end," Gryden said. "Who knows, perhaps God is on their side."

"I don't believe it," she breathed. "Are you really calling it quits?"

"Not anytime soon. We've got another cattle season, maybe two or three, before it's over. Sutton hasn't seen the last of me in a courtroom."

"And when it's over . . . what then?"

Gryden chuckled. "For one thing, you'll be out of a job. Farmers are the worst prudes in the world. They won't came anywhere near the Comique."

"Who cares?" she said, suddenly animated. "The nightlife will never die out in the big cities. There's always Denver or San Francisco."

"And where there's nightlife, there's the sporting crowd."

"And where there's the sporting crowd, there's criminals."

"And a demand for criminal lawyers."

"Sugar, you'll get filthy rich in San Francisco. I'll bet they never saw a lawyer like you in California."

"I'll bet they never saw anyone like you on a stage, either. You'll have your name in lights."

"I feel like hopping a train tonight."

"You know," Gryden said with a wide grin. "The future's looking brighter all the time. Talk about a Christmas present!"

Belle thought he didn't know the half of it. She had a Christmas present for him that was far different from anything he expected. She'd already made up her mind that before the New Year, one way or another, he was going to propose. He just didn't know it yet.

Gryden took her in his arms and they joined the couples on the dance floor. She nestled her head on his shoulder, and as he looked around at the other couples it occurred to him that the Masquerade Ball was symbolic of all he'd spoken about earlier. Civilization had overtaken Dodge City and he somehow hadn't noticed it. The old days were already gone.

"Sugar," she said in a dreamy voice. "I was just thinking."

"Oh?"

"You know you were talking about the frontier dying out . . ."

"What about it?"

"Why wait?" she said softly. "We could be in San Francisco for New Year's Eve."

"Are you serious?"

"Try me and see."

Gryden wondered if all he'd heard was true. The tales about the City by the Bay, and the Golden Gate, and the Barbary Coast. The place where lovers stayed young forever.

He thought they would find out together.

America's Authentic Voice of the Western Frontier

Matt Braun
Bestselling author of *Bloody Hand*

HICKOK & CODY

In the wind-swept campsite of the Fifth Cavalry Regiment, along Red Willow Creek, Russia's Grand Duke Alexis has arrived to experience the thrill of the buffalo hunt. His guides are: Wild Bill Hickok and Buffalo Bill Cody—two heroic dead-shots with a natural flair for showmanship, a hunger for adventure, and the fervent desire to keep the myths of the Old West alive. But what approached from the East was a journey that crossed the line into dangerous territory. It would offer Alexis a front row seat to history, and would set Hickok and Cody on a path to glory.

HC 8/02

READ THESE MASTERFUL WESTERNS BY MATT BRAUN

"Matt Braun is a master storyteller of frontier history."
—Elmer Kelton

THE KINCAIDS

Golden Spur Award-winner THE KINCAIDS tells the classic saga of America at its most adventurous through the eyes of three generations who made laws, broke laws, and became legends in their time.

GENTLEMAN ROGUE

Hell's Half Acre is Fort Worth's violent ghetto of whorehouses, gaming dives and whisky wells. And for shootist and gambler Luke Short, it's a place to make a stand. But he'll have to stake his claim from behind the barrel of a loaded gun . . .

RIO GRANDE

Tom Stuart, a hard-drinking, fast-talking steamboat captain, has a dream of building a shipping empire that will span the Gulf of Mexico to New Orleans. Now, Stuart is plunged into the fight of a lifetime—and to the winner will go the mighty Rio Grande . . .

THE BRANNOCKS

The three Brannock brothers were reunited in a boomtown called Denver. And on a frontier brimming with opportunity and exploding with danger, vicious enemies would test their courage—and three beautiful women would claim their love . . .

IN 1889, Bill Tilghman joined the historic land rush that transformed a raw frontier into Oklahoma Territory. A lawman by trade, he set aside his badge to make his fortune in the boomtowns. Yet Tilghman was called into service once more, on a bold, relentless journey that would make his name a legend for all time—in an epic confrontation with outlaw Bill Doolin.

OUTLAW KINGDOM

MATT BRAUN

AVAILABLE WHEREVER BOOKS ARE SOLD
FROM ST. MARTIN'S PAPERBACKS